WILD DARK SHORE

Also by Charlotte McConaghy

Migrations

Once There Were Wolves

WILD

DARK

SHORE

Charlotte McConaghy

FLATIRON
BOOKS
NEW YORK

WILD DARK SHORE. Copyright © 2025 by Charlotte
McConaghy. All rights reserved. Printed in the United States
of America. For information, address Flatiron Books,
120 Broadway, New York, NY 10271.

Designed by Donna Sinisgalli Noetzel

www.flatironbooks.com

Library of Congress Cataloging-in-Publication Data

Names: McConaghy, Charlotte, author.
Title: Wild dark shore / Charlotte McConaghy.
Description: First edition. | New York : Flatiron Books,
    2025.
Identifiers: LCCN 2024018128 | ISBN 9781250827951
    (hardcover) | ISBN 9781250827999 (ebook)
Subjects: LCGFT: Novels.
Classification: LCC PR9619.4.M3798 W55 2025 |
    DDC 823/.92—dc23/eng/20240423
LC record available at https://lccn.loc.gov/2024018128

Our books may be purchased in bulk for promotional,
educational, or business use. Please contact your local
bookseller or the Macmillan Corporate and Premium Sales
Department at 1-800-221-7945, extension 5442, or by email
at MacmillanSpecialMarkets@macmillan.com.

First Edition: 2025

10 9 8 7 6 5 4 3 2 1

For my children, Finn and Hazel

There is a land of the living and a land of the dead

and the bridge is love,

the only survival, the only meaning.

—THORNTON WILDER, *THE BRIDGE OF SAN LUIS REY*

WILD DARK SHORE

Rowan

I have hated my mother for most of my life but it is her face I see as I drown.

The face I see when I wake from drowning is different. It is rough and wind-bitten and scratchy. It is what I'm looking at when the sudden arrival of pain overcomes me, and I know the image of him will forever be as one with this pain. Whenever I see this face I will remember the burning sting of being dragged upon rocks and flayed open, left raw, I will feel the bursting pressure in my chest; the sensation will be so vivid it will be like it's happening all over again. His face, a return. A drowning.

Fen

She washes in with the storm, draped upon a tangle of driftwood. The girl sees her from among the seals. She picks her way through their fat sleeping bodies and moves to the surging waterline. Rough waves carry the lump closer, in with the tide. A shape of milky white lit by the moon. A shoulder, she thinks. And seaweed for hair. A hand draped delicately over wood.

The girl wades into the black roar. She dives under and swims out. Reaches for this bulbous thing to help steer it free. When her feet hit sand she rises, dragging the driftwood behind her. Swell slaps at her thighs and hips but she knows how to move with the water so as not to be tumbled. Preparing all the while for something terrible. Something altering. But a last wave sends the tangle onto the beach and the girl parts the curtain of snarled kelp to reveal a face, and it is not swollen or blue or nibbled; it is breathing.

The girl's name is Fen and she lives here now, on this exposed patch of coastline with the petrels and the shearwaters and the penguins and the seals. She hasn't been up the hill in a while, to where her family dwells in the lighthouse. She doesn't like to leave the sea. But tonight the storm, the woman. Lightning on the horizon and rain she can hear approaching fast. She thinks quickly, and then, rather than trying to pull the body free, she drags the entire driftwood barge up the black sand as far as she can. She allows herself another look at this face, at this creature carried in from a sea too vast to make sense of. A gift for them or something rejected? And then Fen runs.

·

This is a place of storms, but *this* storm, this one will be the worst they've endured since coming here. She knows it as soon as she reaches the crest of the hill and collides with the wind. It takes her off her feet. In the distance she can see the lights of the building. A white shape flies end over end through the air: a bedsheet from the clothesline. They all know not to hang things overnight; someone will be in trouble for that lost sheet. Behind it one of the tool trolleys careens through the grass, is lifted up off its wheels and dumped again, spilling its guts, and this—these precious items being left out—is even worse than the sheet.

In the end she doesn't have to struggle all the way to the house. Her dad's been watching and the second he sees her cresting the rise he is running. They meet in the dark, on the trail to the shore. Even his considerable size is nothing against this wind, and he's stooped almost double as he gathers her toward home.

"Stop!" she shouts. "Dad! We need Raff."

"I'm here," says her brother, materializing to take her other side in arms almost as big as their father's, both of them hurrying her on.

"Wait!" Fen says, knowing that time now will be divided into before and after. "There's a woman."

Dominic

You are not meant to have favorites, but my youngest is that. If only by a hair, and with a gun to my head. If I really, really had to answer. And not because we are most alike: that is my oldest and me. Not because we are least alike: that is my daughter and me. Maybe it is because he is curious and kind and so smart it can make your eyes water. Maybe it's because he whispers to the wind and hears its voice in return. Most likely I don't know why. But it may also be because, for one brief moment long ago, I wished him dead.

⁓

I leave my youngest safe and warm in bed; he is too little to be taken out into a storm, though he'd rather not be left behind. The rain has come, as I follow my two eldest to the beach. The seals have retreated below the waves. The penguins are huddled in their nests. Raff and I lift the woman between us and inch our way back up the long winding trail. No trees to give cover; there are none on the island, only mounds of silvery tussock grass and a passage that grows slower with each step into the wind. It screams in our ears. In this kind of storm there is a danger we could be tumbled off our feet and back down the hill.

"Keep going, mate," I say, and ahead of me Raff does, dogged.

My daughter is saying the woman was breathing. That somehow, she was breathing, and I know Fen is silently urging her to keep on, she is willing this body to cling to life. I have less hope, but I also suspect that to have made it so far, to have survived in an ocean so wild, she must be strong, this woman.

I've seen a body taken by the sea, and the state of it will rid a man of any hubris. We are soberingly weak under its hammer. This woman, delivered by such a sea—one more powerful than most—is clinging on with a bewildering defiance. She has been opened on one side, all down the left of her, and I can't imagine how there's not water on her lungs, but my first concern is the hypothermia; her breathing and her heart rate both seem very slow.

Back at the house, my three children and I carefully remove the woman's clothes, what's left of them. I set Orly to the shoes and socks and allow Raff and Fen to help me with the rest, leaving only the undies untouched. Fen takes her own clothes off too—"You don't have to," I say—and without a word she climbs into the bed to press her warmth around this stranger. The only way, truly, to warm her up. My boys and I pile blankets over them and monitor the woman's temperature. It rises slowly. Hours pass as we hover, watching and waiting, and I wonder what it is my daughter thinks about as she uses her body like this, to save another.

Later, when the woman seems warm enough and I don't think we can delay it any longer, Fen gets dressed. There is blood on the sheets, and on her skin. She pretends not to notice. We turn our minds to treating the wounds, using tweezers to painstakingly pluck out fragments of cloth. The woman's limbs are lean and strong, her head shaved. The face, which I have barely looked at, is clenched and angular. Her strong jaw works against her teeth. Once she is free of material and debris, I stitch the worst of the wounds, my fingers too big to be anything other than clumsy. We slather the scrapes with disinfectant and then as much gauze as we have before bandaging her body. There is fever now: she is scalding to the touch. She makes sounds that frighten all of us and I come to my senses and send my nine-year-old from the room. He makes a fuss, he wants to help, and I know he is more frightened of the storm than he is of this woman's noises. I relent, let him stay. This feels like a night to be together.

We sit with her and bear witness to the throws. Outside the storm is rabid. When the windows shake, Orly whimpers but the old stones hold together. Inside the sea is still fighting for her, it retains its hold. I think, deep in the darkest hours, that even if she survives this night that ocean will have her back one day.

Dominic

I brought my children to Shearwater Island eight years ago. I was not expecting the island to feel so haunted, but for hundreds of years the lighthouse we live in was a beacon to men who built their lives upon the blood of the world's creatures. The refuse of those sealers and whalers remains to this day, discarded along the lonely stretches of black coast and in the silver shimmering hills. The first time Orly admitted he could hear the voices, all the whispers of the animals killed on this ground—including, for good measure, an entire *species* of seal bashed on the head and wiped out entirely—I thought seriously about taking my children away from here. But it was my ghost who told me they might be a gift, these voices. A way to remember, that surely *someone* ought to remember. I don't know if that burden should fall to a child, but here we are, we have stayed, and I think that actually my wife was right, I think the beasts bring my boy comfort.

Mostly it is quiet here. A life of simple tasks, of day-to-day routines, of grass and hills and sea and sky. A life of wind and rain and fog and of smiles huddled around a heater and of books read each evening. Of hands clasping a hot cup of chocolate or the bend of a head against the weather, of wet clothes flung off at the door and trying to pick out the difference between a giant petrel and an albatross at distance. Of frozen food and sometimes downloaded movies and schoolwork and training and music. Of the gurgling roar of an elephant seal or the banana pose of a fur, of the flamboyant orange eyebrows of the last royal penguin colony in the world. Of seeds. Of parenting. Of grappling constantly with what to tell them about the world we left behind.

Ships come every so often to bring supplies and scientists. Despite its wonders, Shearwater is not a tourist island: it's too remote, too difficult to reach. Mostly no one comes here but a handful of researchers studying the wildlife, the weather, the tides. Certainly people don't wash in from the sea. I am having trouble making sense of how she's alive—the ocean around us is perilous and so cold, and there is no land for many thousands of kilometers. She must have come off a boat, but it doesn't make sense that there should be a boat close enough to our shores. The supply ship isn't due for weeks and the only ships that pass by are way out at sea, following the passage south to Antarctica, and to come off one of those would mean certain death. Unless of course this boat of hers was coming here, to Shearwater.

In the morning Raff and I assess the damage. Gutters are down and water has come under the doors, but our lighthouse has held strong even in the face of such a battering. The power sources can't say the same. My son and I walk up the hill to see that both wind turbines have come clean off their shafts. One of them is face down hundreds of meters away—it has flown—while the other is protruding up out of the ground in a salute to its own demise. The solar cells are scratched, and the roof of the shed has been lifted up and off, leaving the batteries within to take an absolute beating. I'll need to replace that roof but for now we set up a tarp to try to protect the remaining batteries—too complex to move and rewire all the cabling. Half of them are dead, anyway. The other half have some power stored in them, and this will have to stretch a long way.

Surviving in remote places is all about setting up contingencies. If one thing goes, there's another option to take its place. It's never occurred to me that all the solar cells, half the batteries, and both the wind turbines could go at the same time.

"We've still got the diesel," Raff says as we walk home. I can't hear any fear in him, just a focused kind of concern.

One thing we can't do without is heating. I don't know if we'd survive the kind of cold it will be without heating. Normally we'd be straight on the radio to the mainland, calling for help. Repairmen, new parts, more gas, more diesel. Alas.

Raff and I walk home along the headland. There is no real reason to do this, but I am letting him guide the way and his feet often lead him here. Shearwater is long and skinny and divided into two parts, its northern side mountainous and mostly unexplored, its southern side smaller, more inviting. This is where the various buildings have been placed, including our lighthouse, the field huts, the communications station, and the seed vault. There is a finger of land that joins the two sides, an isthmus, narrow in shape and low in altitude. We call it the pinch, and it's where the research base sits. The base is several long white shipping containers made of aluminum so as not to rust in the salty air, as well as several wooden cabins. A hodgepodge of seventeen little buildings built over many decades. A dining hall and kitchen. The labs. A hospital. The storage unit. Sleeping quarters. Until recently a buzzing community of people, the pinch now holds a collection of empty buildings. And just as well because there is water lapping at walls and doors. The research base looks like it's floating on a pond.

"Bloody hell," Raff says.

High tide has never been this high before.

I am shaken but I'm not about to let him know that.

We still have some gas for cooking and manually heating water, and diesel for the generator to keep the freezer running so our remaining food stores don't spoil, but everything else is getting turned off. No more lights, no computers or phone chargers or stereo, no washing machine or vacuum cleaner, no power tools. The kids don't complain when I tell them; keeping this place running is a never-ending exercise in problem solving, and they understand that. What I am concerned about is the power to the seed vault down at South Beach, and whether it's gone too. I get Raff started on repairing the damaged gutters and pack myself an overnight bag. It's a ten-kilometer hike south to the vault so I'll stay the night in one of the field research huts down there.

First I look in on the woman. Orly is perched on the end of her bed, reading to her from a book on botanicals that his astounding mind has no doubt memorized. He has barely left her side since she arrived.

"How's she doing?" I sink into the chair by the window.

He shrugs. "Seems okay? She's breathing."

"You don't have to stay in here."

"I know." He fiddles with a corner of a page, dog-earing it and then smoothing it out. "Just seems like someone should be here when she wakes up."

I consider how much to tell him about my fears for the vault. In the end I just say, "I'm headed south for the night."

"Can I come?"

"Not on this one, mate."

The woman mutters something under her breath and even though she is not dead, there is something unnatural about it. A corpse reanimated. Her hand, the long fingers of it, clench once into a fist, then relax.

"Don't get too tied up in it," I tell Orly.

"In what?"

"In her surviving. She might not. Do you understand?"

"Yeah." He studies her face, I study his. "It's just . . . why isn't she waking up?"

"I don't know, mate. She swam a long way. She might still be swimming."

The Shearwater Global Seed Vault was built to withstand anything the world could throw at it; it was meant to outlast humanity, to live on into the future in the event that people should one day need to regrow from scratch the food supply that sustains us. Specks, most of them. Tiny little black dots. That's all they are. These treasures we keep buried in boxes below ground, down here in the arse-end of the world. The last hope of their kinds, but also of our kind.

The idea is a big one: to save humankind. But in all honesty that's not why we came here. I needed a job, and I needed it to be far away.

The purpose of it came later; in truth it came when my youngest recognized its magnitude.

While the seed vault is owned by the United Nations, the management of it has been allocated to the Tasmanian Parks and Wildlife Service, which also manages the nature reserve on the island as well as the research station—Shearwater Island belonging to Australia by virtue of its location. I was hired as caretaker of every building on this island, including the enormous frozen vault at its far south, and so in the beginning, when we first arrived, I was making the trip across island often. Because he was so little, I had no option but to take Orly with me, and I resented these regular hikes, when I could have been attending to the maintenance of the research base or the lighthouse. But as Orly got older, he would explore as we walked, touching and smelling and picking, and as he learned to talk he spoke the names of the plants we saw, and then the seeds we were there to visit, and I began to see, through his eyes, that in fact this job was *important*. I started imagining the use of these seeds, I imagined the world that would require them. I felt better about being here, on the island that was protecting this last floundering hope, rather than back on a mainland that would need rescuing. And with every danger that came upon Shearwater, every struggle, I would think, at least we're not back there, dealing with fires and floods and food scarcity and all the rest of it.

At least we are here, in a place that seems hostile until you look more closely. Until you begin to see its beauty and its tenderness. Until you see the hidden abundance of it.

I never loved a place before we came here.

And now it's over. The seed vault is closing. It was meant to last forever, and now we are sorting and packing the seeds for transport, and in just under two months we, too, will be leaving, with all the lucky little specks important enough to be chosen for relocation.

The tunnel is dry, always. It must be: it's part of the design. Except that today, when I step into the mouth of the long descent, my boots splash.

I stop and peer into the darkness. The wrongness of it stands the hairs on my arms. The impossibility of it.

I splash down into the earth, to the underground chamber, to its vacuum-sealed door. Like the door of a fridge. If the water has gone beneath it, we will be in real trouble, but it hasn't, and I remember to breathe. Just the tunnel then, that's alright. It will be alright. Within the vault it's still dry. But as I check the temperature gauge my fears are confirmed. The lights are working but the cooling system has shorted out. It's already a degree warmer than it should be in here.

It has been made very clear to us that keeping the seeds safe is more important than keeping ourselves safe. Quietly, down in the corners of me, I consider whether I could let thousands of species go extinct in order to save the lives of my three children. If I were to reroute the energy we use for heating the lighthouse I might buy the seeds a little extra time. But the answer is easy, and I don't think they should have sent a man out here who has kids. That man would never make the choice they want him to.

I set up a pump in the tunnel, uncoiling the long dark tube until it snakes out the opening into daylight. If the water level reaches a certain height, the pump will turn on automatically. Next I walk each of the thirty aisles of the vault. They are dry, so I don't hang around. Despite it all, despite the importance of this place and these specks, I don't enjoy being down here. I'm not sure why, really, it's a mystery even to myself. Something, maybe, about the pre-life-ness of it, which in a way is death, though Orly would tell me I'm mad, that this place is the opposite of death. Maybe it's the stasis of it then, the way that life is being kept dormant. Maybe it has nothing to do with the seeds at all, and is simply the underground of it, or the deep, deep cold. Whatever the reason, the place unnerves me, so I let my boots splash their way back up to the surface.

I climb to the crest of the hill, where the shrubs give way to the long tussock grass, and I turn and look out at the horizon. It is like gazing off the edge of the world. Way down there sits Antarctica but mostly what lies before me is a boundless ocean and this edge is sharp. If I take one step in the wrong direction I will fall, and I am never, for a single moment, able to forget it.

The field huts sit among mossy hills on the shoreline, accessible only via a crooked set of metal steps built into the rocks. It takes me the rest of the day to reach them. I will sleep here tonight; we don't travel after dark and usually we don't travel at all unless in pairs. I am breaking a rule, but I can't bring my children to see what's waiting. The huts are pods, delivered here fully furnished on the back of a freight ship many years ago. The blue hut (so named because of its blue door) is closest, while the red hut is a little farther along and closer to the water. Once there were four scientists living within them. Now the huts sit empty. Once there was a third, its door green.

The blue hut is the last place I want to set foot inside. The unconscious woman isn't going anywhere fast, but if she wakes she could eventually find her way down here, which means I can't put this off any longer. I push inside. It takes my eyes a moment to adjust to the dark. The smell is a shuddering kind of bad.

There are two single bedrooms, and I move past them to the kitchen.

It's not as grim as I remember it, but it is pretty grim.

In the backpack I've brought a scrubbing brush, cloths and towels, and bleach. I get to my hands and knees and start cleaning up the blood.

Fen

It's about calm. She has learned this over years spent in the water, and it's something she's good at, a skill she has cultivated. It started because she didn't want to leave the seals beneath the surface—she wanted her body to be capable of more, to be like theirs, so she worked at it. She learned about making her exhales longer than her inhales to decrease her heart rate. She learned about reducing her oxygen consumption. She learned about enduring the pressure that turns to pain, she understands that there is nothing to fear from pain. She is very good at calm.

Except, of course, where her dad is concerned.

He is stubborn and strict and unbendable. He refuses to talk about anything. He frustrates her. And maybe that's normal for a seventeen-year-old, but Fen's willing to bet most seventeen-year-olds don't have to deal with their dads talking to their dead mothers and refusing to admit there's a problem with that.

Fen loves her dad. And she loves Shearwater, maybe more than any of them do, but she can see that, little by little, the island is killing them.

She doesn't sleep much; it's hard to sleep without walls or curtains over windows, and there aren't many hours of true darkness on Shearwater at this time of year. She rises and swims with the males and the females who aren't soon to give birth, she stretches her lungs and her muscles, she kicks and arches and follows the paths of their flippers as they move with so much more power and grace than she will ever have. King Brown, as Alex named him, does a showy loop and finishes by brushing his whiskers against her cheek, as if to say *beat that*, and she laughs beneath the surface. Silver, a young female, circles her once, twice, then trails her hind flippers through Fen's hair, daring her. She kicks after the sleek pale seal, trying her best to keep up—they want to race her but she will never win, she is all too human and has to break for the surface. Silver's face pops up beside her and Fen can almost imagine a grin there, it's in her eyes, the amusement, the triumph. "You win then," Fen says. "For the millionth time."

She means to go and check on the woman in the lighthouse; she can't stop thinking of her, of this body washed in that is somehow still alive. But on the beach she can hear a kerfuffle and she knows what it means.

She swims to shore and picks her way among the colony, trying to find the female who is first. She's in one of the larger harems—this is King Brown's group—so there are lots of females clustered around. It's Freckles, Fen sees, named for the smattering of dark spots on her face. She is flapping and moving awkwardly, tilting her head back and forth, and a couple of other females keep trying to duck their faces to her bottom, to where there is a dark little shape emerging.

Fen stays back, giving them space, but she will be ready in case she needs to help. When she sees the placenta break and the head push out, she is worried because the pups are usually born flippers first—this baby's eyes and mouth are shut and it doesn't look to be breathing. But Freckles flaps and moves, she pushes. She turns her head back and reaches her snout down to the motionless pup, licking its face. She turns in circles to try to work it free, she pushes and pushes. Fen grows more worried by the second—the pup is showing no signs of life and the birth is taking too long. She isn't sure if she should try to help but something makes her wait.

And soon the dark little body comes free, it tumbles onto the sand and it moves, it lifts its head. Smiling, Fen watches the mother seal nuzzle and lick this wet furry creature. The other babies will come now, all the females will start to give birth and the beach will be covered in bleating seal pups. It is Fen's favorite time of year. It's what she will miss most when they leave. She has always come down to the beach for pup season. Even before this inhospitable stretch of coast became her home. Her escape. Even before she learned that there is a different kind of fear from the one you feel when you hold your breath.

———

The air of Shearwater is thick with the spirits of the dead. Fen knows this and isn't bothered by it. Raff doesn't believe her, but in the hours of true night she has seen them. The specters, flickering green lights out at sea or in the mountains above her, and even once quite close on the beach. She wonders if this means she is marked for a different kind of life, if it is yet another oddity that will ensure she doesn't fit in back on the mainland. But she isn't frightened of the dead. It is only the living who have the power to harm.

Orly

Let's start with the greatest traveler among them, shall we?

In aisle E, row 34, sits the *Taraxacum officinale*. Otherwise known as the common dandelion. The dandelion is found all over the world in pretty much any habitat. It's a survivor. It can grow in lawns or fields, in rocky hillsides or woodlands. It might be the first to sprout up in a new ecosystem, or the longest standing in an old one.

The story of this particular dandelion is a good one: you will want to pay attention.

It starts its life in an apple orchard in North America, let's say Wisconsin. It nearly gets trodden on so many times, but luck is on its side. Because it bursts to life early in spring, much earlier than most flowers, it's an important source of food to a whole bunch of insects and birds. Its pollen is rubbed onto the underside of a leaf-cutting bee, then carried to a female dandelion. The bee goes on to pollinate lots of other wild plants and flowers in his travels, but let's stay with the dandelion for now. Its nectar is feasted on by the earliest butterflies and moths to emerge from their cocoons. Today this nectar also happens to feed a hummingbird and a woodpecker. As it ages, the dandelion's head turns from its bright-yellow petals to become a seed head, or, as I like to call it, a blowball. The blowballs have a whole lot of single seeds with tiny hairs on top. These seeds fly in a way we humans had never seen before we saw the dandelion fly. On a balmy afternoon, the seeds of the blowball are lifted by a gust of wind. Some of them land not too far away and are gobbled up by sparrows and goldfinches. Some travel a different way to be eaten by a quail, a wild turkey, and a grouse. One is eaten by a field mouse, one by a chipmunk.

But there's one seed that strikes out farther than the rest. It really flies. Across state lines into Minnesota. Floating and dancing. It travels a hundred kilometers. One hundred! That is a mind-boggling distance for a tiny seed, carried only by wind. Can you imagine? The farthest a seed has ever traveled by air.

But it's not finished, what is left of this dandelion. It has more to do.

When it lands in Minnesota, it's right in the path of a hungry white-tailed deer. The seed of the dandelion feeds the deer until it walks into the path of another creature. A gray wolf. She's been looking for food for a long time. She devours the deer, taking enough meat to survive for weeks and sharing the rest of it with her mate and pups. It keeps her going a little longer in a difficult, hungry life. The wolves keep hunting together, keep the deer on the move, and allow the plants and trees of this land to grow. They keep rivers and soil healthy, they attract insects and mammals and birds to the ecosystem. They make it healthy enough for more dandelions to seed and sprout and start the whole cycle again.

But the dandelion—this single flower that has given nourishment to countless other living creatures—is considered a weed.

Rowan

I think, in this darkness, that I have seen a man's face. The sense of him lingers inside the crashing seas of my body, so that it begins to feel like he's the one pummeling at my edges.

At some point, it could be seconds or a million years later, the pain changes. No longer an ocean but a sting. The sting becomes a flame becomes a fire. I know this fire. I thought I had escaped it.

But. Here is the strangest part. The fire is not alone. There is something else here. Something battling it, trying to hold it back.

A voice.

Let's start with the greatest traveler among them, shall we?

Curious.

It is light and high, and from within these flames I cling to it.

It's not finished, what's left of this dandelion. It has more to do.

There are sounds in the room and I realize they are from me, I am weeping in pain. Something touches me. I'm not sure where. I drag my eyelids open and am shocked at the brightness. I blink and blink until I can see: a small hand has taken mine, is holding mine, and perhaps I have died after all. The voice, that sweet little voice is saying *I'm here, I won't leave you*, and I start crying for a different reason.

He seems to be here on his own. I come to this conclusion only when I have enough brainpower to come to conclusions, and this is only after he's given me painkillers. He is small, I'm not good with children's ages, but he is a child, and he is striking in the light spilling through the window. Pale blue eyes and almost-white hair, perhaps he is Nordic—he has the look of a Viking in miniature, there are even slender plaits in his long straight hair. And he has been speaking to me of seeds. It's how I know I am in the right place.

"Is this the research base?" I ask him.

"No. This is the lighthouse."

I frown, trying to make sense of that. "Where are your parents?"

"Dad's across island."

"Why?"

"The storm that brought you. It's taken most of our power. He's gotta check things."

The storm that brought me. I am back in it. My body thrown up into the ceiling of the cabin, then slammed back to the floor. I can hear his shouts from the deck, faint among the roar. I'm not sure what he's trying to tell me. Is he saying to stay below? Or to get free? I have no intention of going down with this boat, so I surge up the last steps and without even a chance to take a breath I am lifted, carried, dumped into the sea. A tiny thing in the mouth of a beast. I will never forget the weakness of my body. This body I have always taken pleasure in making strong. I will never make sense of the powerlessness or how it is that I'm still here.

"Is there an adult I can talk to?" I ask.

"No."

I rub my aching eyes, trying to wrap my head around what's going on and why I seem to be alone in a lighthouse with a child.

"What's your name?" the boy asks me.

For a brief moment I can't recall it. What a thing.

"Rowan," I tell him.

"I'm Orly Salt. And you're on an island in the middle of the Southern Ocean, fifteen hundred kilometers from any other landmass. Closest is Antarctica. So my question for you is: How did you get here, Rowan?"

I look at him. "We can have this chat when your dad gets back."

"He won't be back until tomorrow."

"Do you know if he radioed for help?" I ask. "A coast guard?"

Orly shrugs.

"Can you get me something to drink? Anything strong and straight."

"I'm not allowed to touch the alcohol."

"I won't tell anyone."

He considers me, then shrugs and jumps up. "Guess these are mitigating circumstances, huh?"

"Guess they are."

"I'll say you manipulated me, if Dad asks."

"You do that."

He trots out.

I take a look around the cramped and crooked room. Low ceilings with heavy wooden beams. Stone walls and floor. A thick wool rug, wardrobe and bookcase both full to bursting. The window is small, the sky too glary for me to see anything and after a glance I don't want to, it makes my head pound.

The kid returns with vodka and I get drunk. It helps with the pain, not with the memories. He's also brought me a Vegemite-and-cheese sandwich on bread that isn't entirely defrosted and a cup of tea with long-life milk and about sixteen sugars, by the taste of it. It's all very unpleasant.

When I've finished I lie still, so little energy in my body I can do nothing but watch the shadows move on the walls. Orly carries on chatting about seeds. It takes a long time for night to fall. I wish the minutes away.

"How long have I been in this bed?" I ask the boy at some point.

"We found you last night. You've kinda been coming in and out of consciousness. You don't remember?"

I shake my head. Just a man's face in the dark. "What's actually . . . what's happened to me?" There is flickering candlelight and I need a break from the seeds, I need to understand what's going on under these bandages. I am afraid to look, afraid not to.

"You mean . . . ?" He gestures to my body. "You had hypothermia, that was the main thing. It was crazy, you were hardly breathing. And you got scraped up pretty bad. There's a bunch of rocks offshore, the waves dragged you over them to the beach. You're lucky, though. If the Drift current had got you, you'd be dead, no questions asked, dead."

"No questions asked, huh."

"The Drift is merciless. Instead you got Fen."

"What's Fen?"

He grins. "My sister. She swam out and got you, pulled you to shore. She's the best swimmer you'll ever meet. Born for the water, Dad says."

"Was there . . ." I stop. Best not to ask too many questions. If they'd found a boat, the boy would have told me. "You should get some sleep, kid."

"Yeah," he agrees, and then he curls up at the foot of my bed like a dog and nods straight off. I stare at him in disbelief and then I finish the vodka and roll over. The room is spinning and I think getting drunk was a bad idea because it feels like the rocking sea and the boat, it feels like his voice calling out to me only I can't find him and I know he's gone now, the Drift must have got him, and it was my desire, my arrogance, the stupidity of this quest that drowned him.

＿＿＿

His name is Yen. He is the only one brave enough or mad enough to take me, I'm told. Don't even bother asking anyone else. He used to be a whaler. He doesn't ask me questions about why I want to be taken to a mostly uninhabited island so far away, he just asks me how much money I have, and when I tell him he nods once and says we will be fine if the weather holds. I ask him what will happen if it doesn't and he says the sea will decide, which is an irritatingly sailor thing to say.

He doesn't talk to me much on the four-day journey, but I will remember his voice. I will remember the sound of it calling my name and the way that name was swallowed by wind and waves.

＿＿＿

I wake in the deep night with an aching need to do a wee. I don't know how long it's been since I went, but as I've been lying here for a couple of days now it's a fair assumption that some poor person has had to clean up after me. It hurts to sit upright. The pain feels both deep and also right at my surface. I don't make a sound, terrified of waking the boy and having to talk to him again.

My head spins and I'm not sure my wobbly legs will carry me. The house is dark. And odd. I flick light switches but they don't work, the power's been shut off. The staircase has a wooden banister to cling to. The walls seem to be curved and there are a lot of stairs. I don't have the time or the desire to poke my head through every door I pass, looking for a bathroom, so I go to the ground floor and stagger out what looks to be the front door (there are coats and boots beside it, I pull both of these on) and into the night.

I gasp. Blinded by the sky.

The stars are electric and so dazzling I sink to the ground, unable to catch my breath. The cold is a blanket, wrapping around me and sinking within, and these pajamas aren't mine, they are too small, and even with a coat they are nothing against the bite of the air. I need to move but I can't. It is too beautiful.

When finally I get to my feet I see the building behind me, the lighthouse without a light, and before me is a hillside of long silver grass swaying in the starlight. Bits of me are going numb so I drop my pajama pants, but since there is no way my trembling thighs will lower me into a squat, all I can do is spread my legs wide and hope.

"What are you doing?"

I look over my shoulder. The kid is standing in the doorway, watching me.

"What does it look like I'm doing?"

"A wee?"

"Bingo."

"Why are you doing it out here?"

"To make sure I wouldn't be bothered."

"Oh."

He stays.

I finish my wee, then pull my undies (mine, thank god) and pants back on. The effort causes me to tilt sideways and then, almost slowly, I am back on the ground.

"Are you okay?" the kid asks.

I blink through my spotty vision and wait for my head to stop spinning. He pulls on his gumboots and coat and bounds out onto the grass. I don't have the energy to move again and, since I guess he doesn't know what else to do, he just sits down beside me. Together we gaze at the windswept hills before us.

"So this is Shearwater, huh?" I say.

"Sure is. One hundred and twenty kilometers squared. We're a tundra climate with mostly mosses and lichens, and over forty-five vascular plant species, and we have over eighty thousand seals on the island, as well as the last colony of royal penguins in the world, and over three million breeding seabirds. And we're a UNESCO World Heritage Site because we're the only place in the world where the earth's mantle is pushing up and being exposed."

I can't help smiling. "You get all that from Wikipedia?"

He shrugs. Which I guess means yes.

Orly points toward the ocean. "That's where Raff and Fen are, down on the beach." Before I can question what his brother and sister are doing on a beach in the middle of the night, he points what I assume is south. "Down that way is the seed vault. Where Dad is."

"What's the seed vault?" I ask, already knowing the answer but curious about what he'll say.

"It's where the world sends its seeds to be stored in case we ever need to rebuild a population of something."

"Why's it all the way down here?"

"To protect it. The permafrost keeps the seeds cold and it's too far away for any people to reach." He looks at me. "Seed banks aren't a new thing, you know."

"Okay."

"It's just that this is one of the last. And it has the largest collection of seeds from all over the world. A whole lot that don't exist anywhere else—rare and endangered and even extinct in the wild. And it doesn't just have agricultural seeds either, it has everything."

"How old are you?"

"Nine."

"Is that old enough to know what's good for you?"

"What do you mean?"

"Should we go inside? It's pretty fucking cold."

He giggles, possibly at the swearing. "I'm used to it, but you're not." He starts for the door but I don't yet follow him. I am trying to figure out how to return to my feet, how I could possibly climb those stairs again. Big mistake, coming down here; I should have just wet the bed.

The boy, Orly, returns. He seems to understand, because he pulls one of my arms until I am more upright, then he offers me his shoulder to push off. A sound leaves my mouth as I drag myself up his body and steady myself upon it. His feet stagger under my weight, but we both manage to remain standing. Together we do an awkward drunken stumble back to the lighthouse. The mere sight of the stairs causes my insides to heave and instead I swing sideways into a living room, collapse onto an old velvet couch. My skull is trying to crack open and the rocks are feeding on me. Orly drapes a blanket over me. I am dismayed to see him lie down on the floor at my side. "Don't you have a bed?"

He nods. Closes his eyes.

I try to close mine too but I can feel him there, shivering. "I thought you said you were used to it."

"I . . . am." He can barely get the words out between the chattering of his teeth.

Irritated, I hold the blanket open for him. "Come on. Hurry up."

He wriggles up next to me, there is barely room but we warm each other. I end up with my cheek pressed against his back, listening to the pat pat of his heartbeat. That little beat feels immensely small and vulnerable under the expanse of that sky, and I think of the stone walls of this building and the empty rooms and his dad off on the other side of an island. I think of him alone here, with only me, who is basically no one.

The question forms inside me along with a warning not to ask it.

"Where's your mum, Orly?"

His voice when it comes is muffled beneath the blankets. "She's dead."

I sigh. Listen to the pat pat. After a while I say, "Mine too," and feel him drift off to sleep.

Dominic

In the dark she tells me not to open my eyes. That if I try to look she will go. I already know this and am squeezing my lids shut so tight I'm getting a headache, but for her anything.

I'm here, she says, and it's like she is, I can feel her breath on my cheek, against my lips. I am not so far gone that I don't know it's a lie. Even as I hear her words I hear my own telling me to stop this, for god's sake stop it. But she is so soft and in the end I am a coward. I let my wife hold me and I keep my eyes shut in the dark.

Sunny moments here on Shearwater are brief. This morning the sky is pale gray and there is a mist of rain on my face as I head out from the field hut. I carry on around the rocks at low tide, careful to keep my footing.

Mostly this trip south was to establish the situation with the vault and to deal with the mess in the field hut, but I've also been looking for a boat.

There is only one place I did not pass on my way down here, a craggy bay difficult to access on foot. I round the rocks of a curved headland and start descending the steep, crumbly cliffside until the angle opens up and reveals a dark pocket of water below. The fierce current we call the Drift comes to rest here upon a bed of jagged rocks. And wedged within these teeth, its pieces smashed into new shapes, is the small craft that delivered a stranger to our shores. I know without any doubt that whoever else was on that boat is dead.

My two eldest aren't up in the lighthouse, they're on the beach of the pinch. I make my way toward them, skirting around lumpy elephant seal bodies. Most of them ignore me, but I get a couple of warning gurgles to watch where I walk and one of them flicks sand over my boots.

Raff is sitting on the fine, silt-like black sand, saying something to Fen, who is standing before him, idly moving through leg stretches.

They look at me as I approach. Both share their mother's blue eyes and blond hair. All but twins, we used to say. Born ten months apart, and my god, what delirium their infancy was, a miracle our marriage survived it.

"Is she awake?" I ask.

"We haven't been up yet," Raff says, apologetic.

"The cows are birthing!" Fen announces.

I glance past them at the mass of fur seal bodies farther down the beach—they are certainly making more racket than they usually do.

"I don't like Orly up there alone with her," I say, looking at Raff.

He stands and brushes himself off. "Sorry."

"She was barely alive," Fen points out.

I look at my daughter. Her nose and cheeks are covered in freckles and sun marks; I worry often she'll wind up with skin cancer. There is no shade anywhere on this island, no cover from any of the elements. For this reason I suppose we are lucky the sky is mostly gray, but the gales can be just as damaging: Fen has the wind bites to show for it. I study her, drink her in, think how beautiful she is and how much I miss her, knowing too that she is far too trusting. "I need you both to keep your guards up, alright? We don't know her. We don't know anything about what she's doing here."

Raff nods but something slides across Fen's face, an expression of disappointment, even of pity, that this is an insane way to think of an injured woman in need of help, and maybe she's right but what the look tells me more than anything is that my daughter no longer trusts me. If I worried she was slipping away before, now I'm sure of it. She doesn't feel safe with me, or maybe it's that she has no expectation of me keeping her safe, of my ability to recognize danger, which is my only job as her father. I am filled with panic: I must keep hold of her, and I don't know how to.

"I need you up home with us," I say. The woman, when she wakes, will need help changing, washing, toileting. Best to have another female around for that.

Fen peers at her seals and I wait to see if she will argue with me, but she simply starts off toward the hill. Raff and I follow.

As we walk I take note of the beach and how it's changed under the rising tide—the ocean has taken great mouthfuls of the land. Many of the rocks are gone, washed away by the storm. This coastline looks nothing like it did when we arrived here eight years ago. We are all acutely aware of this fact, but we don't much talk about what rapidly rising sea levels mean: they mean losing the rocks and the beaches, losing the research base and all its buildings, losing the boathouse and its Zodiacs, losing a way to safely board a ship out of here.

What rising sea levels mean is the loss of our home.

Raff asks, "How was the vault?"

"Power's down."

His footsteps falter and he stares at me. I shoot him a quick, grim look over my shoulder, but carry on.

"How long can it stay cold without power?" Fen asks.

I shake my head slowly. "Supposed to be at least several weeks."

We don't say it, how close that will come. The naval ship RSV *Nuyina* is due to collect us, and the seeds, in about seven weeks.

"I found the boat," I tell them, to change the subject.

"It wrecked?" Raff asks.

I nod.

"Where?" Fen is quick, she adds, "Did the Drift take it?"

Another nod.

"Then we won't get to it," Raff says.

"Probably not."

"But the people," Fen says. *The bodies*, is what she means.

"They'll have to wait until the ship comes."

She looks horrified. "They'll be . . ." Shakes her head. "I can make it."

That may well be true. She is a very strong swimmer. But she still wouldn't fare any better than the splintered boat. Besides which, I'm not about to let my seventeen-year-old daughter dive for drowned bodies.

"They should be buried, Dad," she says. "We can't just leave them out there."

"We can. It's only their bodies."

This quiets them. I see them both turning it over in their minds, pondering its meaning, its truth. I can see it makes sense to Raff but it won't be enough for Fen, who grows more convinced by the day of the unquiet spirits on this island.

In the end they're still kids, though, and by the time we reach the bottom of the slope the gloomy mood has already lifted off them and they share a grin before bursting into a sprint. They rarely miss an opportunity to race each other to the top. I laugh, and Christ, their energy, their *youth*, I feel ancient.

But something occurs to Raff and he pauses, losing his lead. "Dad. Don't tell Orly about the vault, okay? He won't cope."

I'd had the same thought, but murmur, "You ever manage to keep anything from that boy, you tell me your secret."

Rowan

The baby in my belly is so hot it has begun to burn my whole body. I curl myself over it, holding my stomach and trying to soothe it through the walls of my skin. I breathe all the cold air I have, hoping to cool it, and see that it is no longer inside me, no longer a baby at all but the blowball of a dandelion, and with one breath it erupts, it flies, it disintegrates—

Rain falls hard on my face.

Not rain. A shower. I am lying in a bathtub with a shower battering me, and the fever has returned, I am so hot. There is a person crouched beside the tub but it isn't the boy. It is a girl, I think. She strokes my burning forehead and tells me the water will help cool me. I think I fall back to sleep because the next time I open my eyes I am being lifted, naked, out of the tub, by warm strong hands, at least six of them, and then my body is dried gently, tenderly, and it's just the girl again, she is carefully toweling me down and then wrapping me once more in bandages. I still don't know what's beneath them. She helps me step into underwear and clothes, moving my limbs like they are a child's, guiding me through leg and arm holes. My eyelids are so heavy it is difficult to keep them open. I ask her name as I lean on her.

Fen, she says. The girl who swam out to save me. She helps me back to the bed and makes me swallow painkillers before she lets me sleep.

Some time later I wake enough in the dark to listen to the voices. I can't see them, and I don't turn my head to look.

"Do you have enough layers? Take a few more blankets down." A man, voice deep and scratchy.

"I have enough." The girl, Fen.

"You don't sleep on the beach, alright, you sleep in the boathouse."

"I know, Dad."

"Easier if you just stay here the night."

I hear a movement, and then Fen's voice telling him firmly, "I'm going, Dad. I have to."

There is a silence, and then the man says, "You're safe here."

"I know," she says too quickly, and I hear her leave.

I keep my eyes closed, aware there is a man in this room with me, one I can't see and don't know. I consider speaking to him—there are things I need to know—but I'm so tired.

The next time I wake it is morning and the fever has broken. I am sweaty and need the bathroom again. It is less difficult to stand and walk this time, and when I reach the hallway there is a near collision with a small darting figure.

"You're up!" Orly declares.

"Can you show me to the bathroom?"

"No way, you're supposed to stay in bed."

"And how am I meant to go to the toilet?"

"I didn't ask and I don't want to know," he says, then bounds off down the stairs. I limp my way down and around, considering that each step will be one I must climb back up. The bathroom, I discover, is on the ground floor.

I try a tap and find that the plumbing works. But the light doesn't and there is no window in this bathroom, so it's only a shadow woman who stares from the mirror, and she looks mad. She looks frightening. Hollow eyed and thin cheeked. The space is so small I can barely turn without knocking an elbow, but I painstakingly remove the pajamas that aren't mine. The mirror woman becomes an Egyptian mummy wrapped in bandages. I am scared of what lies beneath but I have to get them off.

I go slowly at first, unwinding and rolling, but it's taking too long and my heart is leaping forward, the thrumming is building in my chest, I start pulling at the bandages, and I'm not even really finished with one before I'm pulling at another and everything is getting tangled, and this is how he finds me.

With no warning at all there is a man in the tiny bathroom with me. We stare at each other, shocked by the other's presence. I have seen this man before, I think I have dreamed of him.

As he takes in the state of me his expression changes. There are no clothes but the undies. There are bandages, but these are half unraveled. One breast is covered, the other hangs out. He is not looking, he is turning to go. "Sorry."

"Can you help me." I am dismayed at the break in my voice.

Slowly he turns back. His large hands unroll the remaining bandages until I am revealed. It's both worse and better to see what's beneath. Strangely, the damage has been contained to my left side. Some of the wounds are deep chunks of flesh either gone or sewn back onto me with clumsy black stitches. Others are shallow grazes. There are dark, sickly bruises blooming in a few places. It is frightening to see so much damage.

I sink onto the closed toilet seat and rest my head in my hands.

"It's just a body. They either hold on or they don't."

I look at him.

"Yours did," he clarifies.

"It doesn't feel like it has."

"And yet here you are, though you should be dead."

This man, whoever he is, is looking at me, at my body in pieces. He has seen me come apart, tried to put me back together again.

"Who are you?" I ask.

He looks surprised to be asked the question probably hovering on his own tongue. He is very tall and his chest and shoulders are wide, but he is quite lean, his strength sinewy. He looks nothing like his son, who is fair; this man has dark, short hair, a short beard, and dark eyes. There are deep lines around these eyes and wind marks on his cheeks. "Dominic," he says, his voice rough as though he doesn't much use it. "Dom. Who are you?"

"Rowan." I watch for any sign the name rings a bell.

"Where'd you come from?"

Where did you come from. Meaning, what are you doing here.

I tell him I don't know.

∼

I eat a little, take more painkillers, and then sleep again, but this time it is different, it's unburdened by fever or dreams, and when I wake I know the worst of the illness has passed. The wounds will take longer to heal but the pain of them feels less overwhelming. Mostly it is a deep muscle ache, a sense that my body has taken a battering and needs to move slowly for a while. I borrow some clothes from the wardrobe, pulling pants and a jumper carefully over the bandages that will need changing again soon. I need to find the kitchen—I'm famished.

Downstairs I take in the lighthouse with clearer eyes. The cozy lounge I slept in but did not really see sits in the main circular area of the building and has the dark-green velvet couch, bookshelves, a thick furry rug. There is a fireplace all boarded up in favor of an electric heater. Everything looks very old, as if nothing has been replaced in a long time. I step into the adjoining kitchen to be met by a wall of light. Above the sink is a long, wide window. It faces the sea, though this is really only a smudge of gray in the distance, down beneath the fall of the hill we sit atop. The sight of it sets my insides rolling and I think I will be sick.

I feel for the chair behind me and sink into it, breathing through the nausea.

"Sea legs."

"*Jesus Christ.*" I spin around, clutching my chest in fright. There is a boy, another one. He's sitting at the long timber dining table.

"Sorry," he says.

He is tall like his dad, blond like his little brother. I'd pictured all three kids around Orly's age, but this boy is a teenager, and so was Fen. He has a couple of textbooks open in front of him, and a giant bowl of cereal he's working his way through.

"You lot are all the same," I accuse. "Lurking around."

He has a spoonful.

"You're Raff then?"

A nod. "Takes a while for your body to forget being on the boat."

"When did I get here?"

"Week ago."

One week. I've lost days, somehow, lying in bed, mostly unconscious. Many things have likely happened during this week, but still there has been no mention of a boat, or of Yen, and I guess I know what that means. The pit in my stomach opens again.

"Can you point me to a bowl of that?" I ask, of his cereal.

Raff unfolds himself from the chair—he is much taller than I realized, his head automatically ducking for lights and doorways. He returns with a big jar of muesli and a carton of long-life milk, then passes me a bowl and spoon to make my own. I wolf it down, I can't get it into me fast enough, it is the best thing I have ever eaten. The boy watches me. "Feeling better then."

I finish the bowl and make myself another.

Raff points at the coffeepot on the stove, and I nod, and he makes me a strong dark coffee that sets half the world right. As I sip he doesn't try to make conversation, just gets back to his textbooks. He is slow, meticulous. His finger moves beneath each line, lips silently mouthing the words as he goes. I notice him going over the same line half a dozen times before he moves on. I crane my neck to see what the subject is, and make out *Year 9 Standard English*. He looks a lot older than year nine.

"You're doing distance ed?" I ask him.

Raff nods. "Summer holidays now but I'm already behind."

"How long have you been out here?"

"Eight years."

I stare at him. "You're kidding."

He stares back. He is not kidding.

My eyes travel around the little room, the cluttered but very clean kitchen, and through the arched doorway to the old-fashioned lounge. It feels warm and lived in; there are home-drawn pictures stuck to walls and art and craft supplies scattered in one corner, half-finished projects in another. A Lego sculpture takes up half the living room. The normal detritus of children. But there is little modern tech—I can't see a television or a computer, no speakers for a sound system, no *phones*. Maybe I haven't looked closely enough, but from where I'm sitting now, the lighthouse could belong to another time. Another world entirely. I think of the fathomless sky above and the gaping black space around this little building, I think of the days it took me to get here, on an immense and lonely ocean. I think of eight years. Not unreasonable for an adult wanting solitude, wanting wildness. But for teenagers? I can't wrap my head around what the isolation might do to them.

At the whim of my curiosity now, I get up and poke my head into the storeroom. It is long and dark and cool. There are dozens of shelves holding containers of dry goods. Someone has labeled and measured everything: a container of flour has a line for every week marked across six months. Every container and jar is the same. Rationed. I think how spartan and disciplined a person must be to live here.

"Is this how often the supply ships come?" I ask Raff through the door. "Every six months?"

He nods.

"Bloody hell. What if you run out of something?"

"Then you run out of it."

"What about medical supplies?"

"There's a mini hospital down at the base, it's pretty well stocked. If you had a serious emergency, you could call for an evacuation." Under his breath he adds, "Might take a while."

"What's the base?"

"The research base?"

We study each other. In this look I realize he is quite shrewd. He is letting me reveal how much I know about this island and in doing so explain whether I meant to be here. I give him nothing. I wait.

"Down in the pinch," he explains. "There's a research base, usually full of scientists."

"Usually?"

"They're gone now."

"Gone where?"

"Home."

"All of them?"

He nods.

My pulse thuds, loud. "You mean there's not one other human being on this island, except you and your family? The four of you."

Raff nods. But he is looking at me and he can hear my disbelief. My confusion.

"Why?" I ask, forcing my voice calm.

"Shearwater's being closed down." He thinks better of that wording and tries again. "People can't live here anymore."

"Why?" I ask again.

"It's too dangerous. The island's disappearing."

"Then why are the four of you still here?"

"We're just the caretakers, we're finishing up. We leave at the end of this season."

"Which is when?"

"About six weeks."

No way. If there really is no one else on this island, then I will not be staying for six more weeks. "Can you show me to your communications? I need to radio for an evacuation."

He doesn't say anything.

"Or did your dad already do that?"

Again, no reply. Raff just eats his cereal and I don't like it one bit.

"Raff, has anyone been notified that I'm here? That there's a boat missing? They'll need to send search and rescue for Yen."

"We have your boat," a voice says, and I turn to see Dom in the doorway. Watching me. The hairs on my neck stand on end; there is something nerve-racking in their caginess. In their vagueness.

"Where is it? Is the captain . . . ?"

"We've found no body," Dom says. "But he's dead."

God, the flat way he says it.

"Where is the boat?" I ask.

"It's in pieces at the end of the Drift."

The Drift. Orly mentioned that, didn't he? A current. A boat in pieces. I'd known, of course.

Dominic comes into the room and guides me to a chair, helps me sit. I shrug his hands off me.

"You said there was one man on board? The captain?"

I nod faintly. "Yen."

"And you."

Another nod.

"Were you coming here, Rowan? To Shearwater?"

I lift my head to look him in the face. His eyes, which I thought were dark brown, are actually a greenish gray; I can see them in the light from the window.

A sense of danger prickles my skin. All my life I have had more than a healthy dose of fear working at my edges, but I am also good at reading people, and there are things this father and son are not saying, something they are bristling with, a tension I have not imagined.

"No," I say, and with it I feel some of that tension seep away and know I am right to be wary.

"Then what on earth were you doing down here?" Dom asks, sounding genuinely confused.

I ignore the question and ask my own. "Who have you contacted?"

"No one."

I shift uneasily on the seat. "Okay. I'll go with you. We can go now."

It triggers a kind of shutdown in him. He looks done with the conversation, and with me. Dom leaves the kitchen without another look, only a quick directive: "Get some rest." I have been dismissed, and with that I am in no doubt that he doesn't plan to radio anyone.

Dominic

She's lying to me. I don't know why or about what, but I've seen shifty enough to recognize it. My granddad lived with us when I was a kid, just me, him, and Dad, and he'd always be up to some scheme or other, coming home in the middle of the night after breaking into a worksite or getting into a scuffle with his old biker mates; any way a guy could think to get in trouble, my granddad had done it first. He was a piece of work, but I loved him, and what's more, he taught me not only how to box but how to sense when someone is lying.

Weird theories chase themselves around in my mind about who this woman is and what she could be doing here. I go a few rounds with the bag to try to clear my head, get some perspective about what her presence means for us—now that I know she's unlikely to be dying anytime soon. Possibly it means very little. She's another mouth to feed, but she should also be another set of hands to help out. Possibly it means we're in trouble; it will depend on what she's lying about.

I find Raff in the laundry, hand-scrubbing the sheets Rowan's been sleeping on, now stained with blood. He won't get those stains out by hand, even with the bleach, but he's putting a lot of elbow grease into the effort, I'll give him that.

"You get a read on her?" I ask.

He glances at me, then nods through the window. I cross to his side and peer out. On the grass a little way down the hill is my youngest, doing some kind of performance with wild arm movements for a baffled-looking Rowan, who is hunched on the ground uncomfortably.

"She's a bit rough around the edges, but anyone would be," Raff says. After a moment he adds, "I think he's acting out a movie," and we both smile.

I take the second sink and give the sheets another round of scrubbing. Intermittently we watch the stranger; I watch the way she watches my son, wondering what she's thinking.

"She was worried," Raff says abruptly. "When I told her the researchers had left the island."

My gaze travels over her shaved head. I wonder why she's cut her hair so short. I wonder a lot of things. She is dwarfed in one of my windbreakers, but I see movement in the lines of her shoulders that tells me she's laughing. "An abandoned island is less hospitable than a populated one," I suggest.

"Yeah," Raff says. "But it seemed different from that. Like it wasn't what she was expecting."

The words confirm something and cause a skittishness beneath my skin. I don't like wild cards.

The wind picks up, making it too unpleasant for Orly and Rowan to be outside. I watch them hurry back toward us, then run my hand quickly over Raff's short blond hair. "Thanks, mate," I say, with a nod to the sheets, and head out.

Six weeks. We only have to hold it together for six more weeks, a limp to the end of this disastrous season.

Lie down.

It is late and as dark as it gets on this island. I have worked hard all day, harder even than I usually do. My body is so tired it can barely function. Exhaustion, I have found, is useful not only for my son's rage but also for grief. Grief finds power in the strength of my limbs, and if I happen to make it to the end of a day without having completely shattered myself, grief will be fueled by whatever's left of my energy. It will overcome.

But tonight I am liquid.

Lie down, she says, and I do.

My children are asleep, two of them under this roof, the third in a boathouse down a hill. I sent Raff down earlier with dinner for Fen, as I do each night, unable to go myself, terrified of my inability to say the right thing. If I go down there I'll hurt her worse, so I stay away, I leave her be.

Close your eyes, my wife says, a figure beside me on the bed.

"What if she's come because she knows something?" I ask aloud.

What could she know?

I shake my head. "I don't know. The timing feels weird."

Shhh. It doesn't matter. Close your eyes.

I close my eyes. I imagine the curve of her hip, her waist, the shape of her breasts, I can feel them. Her warmth seems real, her breath on my lips. Her hand on my body, or is it my own hand, they are the same, it doesn't matter where I end and she begins.

But maybe I shouldn't be allowing Orly to spend so much time with the stranger, he has been sleeping on the end of her bed like a lost puppy.

She is warm, and new, and interesting, my wife explains.

I shouldn't let him get attached.

Why not?

She's a stranger.

Only until she's not.

I feel the full press of her, and my mind finally starts to clear.

That's enough now, no more thinking.

And so I stop thinking and give myself over to her, to the memory of her and yet it's more than that, isn't it? It feels like so much more than that, a possession, almost, her body upon mine, moving gently, overcoming me.

My last thought, though, before I fall asleep, is not of the woman beside me but of the other. Why is she here?

Rowan

When my mother found out she was dying, she did not book plane tickets to travel the world. She didn't plan retreats to day spas or buy concert tickets. She didn't sell her things with abandon and move to a remote location, nor did she contact past loves or old friends. She didn't write letters to her children. She watched television. I didn't know what else to do, so I watched it with her. We sat on her couch and we watched every show we could think of and hundreds of movies, and we didn't say much to each other, and months passed, and then she died.

I gave away my own TV after that. Said it was because I had watched more than any one human should watch in a lifetime, but really it was because I couldn't stomach it. I would switch it on and I'd be back there, sitting with my mother, sick inside from all the unsaid things and with the noise of it always in the background, even while I slept, even in my dreams. It was panic, that feeling. Panic at the nearness of death, at its thickness upon the air.

I fight that same panic now, in this lighthouse, among strangers. It is hard not to feel trapped. Hard not to let my mind flap at the edges of my body, trying to escape the sinking feeling that something isn't right. I do not know why he hasn't contacted anyone for help. And I'm not sure I believe there is no one else on this island and no way off it; I will have to discover the truth of this for myself.

I find a broom and use it to help me walk. I have done almost nothing but lie in bed for a week and now I am off to the pinch and the research base. I don't care if it's too soon, I can't lie still any longer. The girl in whose room I am staying is a little smaller than me, so all her clothes feel too tight, too short. In her boots, my little toes curl in and soon they are throbbing. But I have the vodka and I sip it as I limp my way across the grassy hill. The first bottle is long since finished but I convinced Orly to steal me another. He told me "There will be a reckoning for this," which was both amusing and terrifying from a nine-year-old. Each step pulls at my bad side, at the torn skin trying its hardest to knit back together, and by the time I have made it to the edge of the headland I can feel fresh blood trickling down my leg.

I lift my layers to reveal that the bandage around my hips has soaked through; the stiches in a particularly tender wound have come open. I straighten and consider my options. From here, I can see the pinch. Way down at the bottom of this mountainous rise. Down by the sea. There doesn't look to be any clear path to it, just a series of steep drops and mounds of thick tussock to traverse around. I could go back. Ask Dom to help fix the stitches. Ask him again why he hasn't sent out an SOS.

Instead I grit my teeth and keep going. Stubbornness, maybe, but also fear.

What the fuck was I thinking when I got on that boat.

The descent is painful; my knees and ankles don't like it. Soon I am panting with the effort, swigging the vodka, keeping on. When the wind hits I have to pause. The force of it is mind-blowing, it must be traveling at well over a hundred kilometers an hour. Moving against it is too difficult and very dangerous—several times I am nearly swept right off the hill—so I curl myself into the protected side of a mound to wait for it to slow. I watch the lumpy grasses dance, their edges flashing from silver to green and back again like a light show. The sound is a deep, hollow roar. Gulls of different sizes fly overhead, their wings catching the pockets. I can see dark shag-type birds and something smaller, more darting. I sit for a long time and I think I catch sight of an albatross wheeling past, its white wings much wider than those of the other birds, its flight a graceful glide without a single flap.

The wind eases and I continue on. I reach a natural slope that takes me down to the pinch, where the various buildings of the research base are scattered.

I am on flatter ground now, and there are foot-worn pathways snaking through the tall mounds. Snuffles and grunts come from either side of me, and I am astonished to see heads poking up from behind the grass: seals are lying hidden among it, close enough for me to touch if I wanted to. I am stunned at their size, and their colors, too, ranging from the grays I think of seals being to different shades of tan and mustard yellow. Their bodies are enormous and heavy; I have no idea how they flop themselves out of the sea and across this lumpy ground. Their eyes are liquid and bottomless and I stop to stare.

"Hello," I say to one of them, and it gives a deep, rumbling gurgle that makes me jump. I decide to give them as wide a berth as I can on the narrow paths.

I emerge from the tussock mounds and see that the last leg of the walk will take me across the beach.

A long expanse of black silty sand is strewn with what the sea has rejected. Bright red-orange kelp, tubular and alien looking. Bleached white bones and teeth, so big I know they must belong not only to the seals but to whales, too. The ocean is very rough and loud in my ears.

My eyes scan for any boats I might use to sail home, but even if I were to spot any it's foolish to think I could captain one over a tumultuous ocean. I am far from a sailor and what's more, I have been terrified of the sea since long before Yen's boat wrecked.

I turn away and take in the island instead. Tall green mountains, their tops shrouded in gray mist. Rocky cliffs. There is a prehistoric feel to it. An overwhelming sense of the ancient, of time, and of something chilling. It is the bones, I think, and the bloodiness of the kelp, the black sand, it's the colors and the isolation and the outlandishness of the animals, the mist, I feel overwhelmed by the place, and despite its beauty I am frightened.

I put my head down and hurry for the base, soon forced to wade through shin-deep water. I don't think it's high tide; the time is wrong. It's as Raff said: this island is no longer safe.

It's an immense relief to close the container door behind me and shut out the wind. I'm in the messroom. Tables are laid out in neat lines, chairs sitting upside down atop them. I put one on the floor and sit wearily, meaning to rest for only a moment but sitting in a daze for some long, unknowable amount of time. The room is homely, with photos all over the walls. I can almost see the researchers eating at these tables, can hear their voices chatting, the scrape of the chairs, the clang of the cutlery on plates, the general din of a makeshift family at mealtime. Without all of that the room feels like a hollow place. The kitchen is attached and has the look of any commercial kitchen, or maybe one on an army base. I drag myself upright to inspect the storeroom, which still contains a fair amount of dry food, but the big fridge has been cleared out and switched off. In fact there's no power at all. I follow an enclosed tunnel to another container, this one the hospital. Low camp beds line one wall. It's been left stocked, so I scrounge around for as many pain meds as I can identify, plus disinfectant, more bandages, and antibiotics for infections.

I sit on one of the beds and struggle out of my top layers. I'm freezing, but I have to do something about the wound on my hip. I unroll the bloodied bandage and peel off the plaster. The half-moon-shaped wound is oozing dark blood. I wipe it clean and use butterfly clips to press the edges back together, then apply a clean plaster and a new bandage to hold it all in place. I doubt that will be enough—it'll probably need proper stitches again—but it's the best I can do for now. I take the opportunity to change my other bandages for fresh ones and it helps me to feel less disgusting.

With my clothes back on, I move out into the wind, traversing a short stretch of muddy ground to a different set of containers. The first is a science lab. There are cupboards full of jars and bottles, all neatly labeled. Fridges that hang open, their contents presumably compromised by now. Sinks and workbenches and beakers and microscopes. It is so chaotic and crowded—like a lost and found—that I have no idea how they kept track of what was actually in here. Next I find the sleeping quarters. Inside there are beds but no personal items. There is water around my feet, splashing as I walk. The entire base feels like it could float away at any moment.

In a common area is a wall of photos. I cross to it and peer at the faces. Some of the photos are candid, group shots of smiling team members and staff, photos with the wildlife, a few in the mess hall celebrating Christmas, the New Year's party. But there are also headshots with names and roles. I read each one, recognizing some. Searching for one in particular. I find him at the end, where he ought to be.

Hank Jones, senior botanist of the Shearwater Island Global Seed Bank, terrestrial ecologist, and research base team leader. A man in his forties, with warm brown eyes, a slightly crooked nose, and a smiling mouth. I'm having a hard time imagining why the team leader of this base would leave before a project was wrapped up, but there is no getting around it: he isn't here. No one is here.

I pocket the photo and move on.

Night falls. I can't make that climb in the dark. (I'm not sure I can make it at all, I've got myself into a mess here.) Without a working heater in the base, I can feel the temperature dropping. I eat from the storeroom, cold tins of beans and spaghetti, and then I climb into one of the abandoned beds in the sleeping quarters, pulling blankets on top of me.

I don't sleep. I listen to the ocean lapping at the feet of the bed, imagine it rising up and over me, sliding down my throat and into my lungs. For a moment today I'd had thoughts of moving myself down here until someone from the mainland comes to get me, but now I realize the lighthouse is a fucking resort compared to this place. The sea has claimed the base and there's no taking it back.

He finds me in the morning. I am pulling on his daughter's boots when Dominic bursts into the mess hall. He spots me and looks relieved but doesn't say anything. Instead he goes to the kitchen and makes us both a bowl of oats in long-life milk. We sit in silence and eat it. My jaw starts to ache.

"You find what you came for?" he asks me when we are done.

"No."

"Thought we'd lied to you."

"No." Not exactly. "If everyone had to evacuate then what are you still doing here?"

"Did Orly tell you about the seeds?"

"I can't get him to stop telling me about the seeds."

Dom's mouth quirks. "Did he tell you about the *vault*?"

"A bit."

"I'm gonna guess he didn't mention it's being shut down. He's not happy about it. We're packing up the seeds. Some of them. When we go, they go too."

"Where?"

"Smaller seed bank on the mainland."

I study him. He seems guileless. "And you're doing this without any supervision?"

He sits back in his chair, his limbs altogether too long for it. "You don't reckon my kids and I are capable of packing a few boxes?"

"Orly said this is one of the world's last banks and it has numerous extinct species."

"Yep, and it's still just packing boxes."

I meet his eyes. "Dom. How are we gonna get me off this island?"

I climb onto the quad bike behind him, making sure to keep a gap between our bodies. The second we take off over the rough terrain I have instant regret: it is so rough it feels as though my body might simply bounce into pieces. After a while I concede that I wouldn't have made the climb on foot—the communications building is, understandably, at the top of a high peak. By the time we reach it, I am weak from the strain of keeping my seat and there are spots in my vision. Dom helps me inside and onto a chair, offering me water from his pack. "You barely ate for a week," he points out. "It'll take a bit for you to get your strength back."

"So who do we call?"

Dom lifts the radio receiver and presses what I'm assuming is the power button. Nothing happens. He fiddles with a few other instruments, but there are no lights, no sounds. It's all dead. He looks at me and waits.

My blood starts to rise. "Just tell me."

"The comms are all down."

"Meaning what."

"Every instrument we use on this island to contact the mainland is dead. The radio system. The satellite internet. It's all broken."

I stare at him. There is a prickling sensation on the back of my neck. "What the fuck are you talking about? How is that possible?"

He spells it out. "They've been broken."

"By who?"

"I don't know."

The strangest sensation touches the back of my neck and I look behind me in the small space, almost, for a second, expecting someone else to be in here with us. But we are alone, and all the hairs on my arms are standing on end.

"I only noticed it after the last ship left," Dom says, and I turn back to him, trying to slow my racing thoughts.

"Meaning it could have been anyone who left the island?"

He nods.

"What—they busted up all the equipment and then bailed? To do what—strand you here? Why?"

"I don't know."

"That doesn't make sense."

"I know it doesn't."

"You must have some idea of why someone would do that to you."

"No."

We stare at each other. I don't believe him. He knows more than he's saying. But I am suddenly overwhelmed by what this means. The sea is beneath my feet again, a woozy sway.

"Won't whoever you're in contact with notice that you're not answering and send help?"

"They won't be expecting to hear from us, not until it's time to be collected."

"Well . . . fuck. Can you fix it?" I ask feebly.

A shake of his head, then, "But you can see why it's strange to me, your timing."

"What timing?"

"You showing up here, on an unscheduled boat, right after all our comms are taken out."

I work that one through in my head. "I don't have anything to do with your radio, Dom. I wasn't coming here."

His head tilts a little. "Yeah, you said that."

We peer at each other. Wind creeps through a window. My heart still won't slow.

The thing that isn't making sense to me is that he should treat me with so much suspicion. As though *he* needs to be wary of *me*. But what exactly is it that he thinks I'm a threat to? What is he trying to protect? It seems clear that shit has gone down here. If somebody's busted up the comms, there's been trouble. And he is hiding it from me.

I can't get back on the quad bike so soon, opting instead to take a very slow walk down the hill to the lighthouse, assuming it will be easier to go downhill. It's not. My knees and my thighs and my bum, all my muscles, all my joints, all my wounds. There is a place that pain takes you. I haven't known this place before. That is a privilege, isn't it? But I know it well now. It is both vast and minuscule. It is as far as my mind can travel and as contained as the blades of grass under my feet. It is my body. It is hard to make sense of the fragility of it. *It's just a body*, he said, and I try to make that true, but as I walk I can't be anything else, I am all body, only body, at its mercy. It becomes everything and then it starts to fail. My steps grow wobbly, my knees weaken and then buckle.

He returns for me on the noisy rumbling bike with an expression that says he does not have time for this. For my frivolity. As he lifts me I am aware, more than anything, of the way he smells. It is . . . I can't name it, but it fills me. He pulls me onto the seat behind him and instead of space there is its opposite, my arms encircling his body. My face rests against his back. I don't mean for it to but I am so tired. I despise needing him but I have no choice, for a few minutes I will have to surrender to him, to the texture and scent of him, and as I do I feel a surprising gentleness and somehow these bodies, our two bodies, feel oddly the same, they feel like one body, and when we stop and get off we will be two and I am delirious, I think.

We reach the lighthouse and he kills the engine, but neither of us moves immediately, maybe gathering ourselves for the task of climbing off, attempting the stairs.

"Dom," I say, and he tilts his face back toward mine. "My boat had a radio."

He nods, has already thought of it. "I don't know how to get to it."

I've had a thought about that, too.

There is a girl, and her brother says she is born for the water.

Before I can go in search of her: bed, again. My body's glad of it. I have left the curtains open to the eerie nighttime sunlight. My fingers reach to my pocket. For the photo within. I draw it out and look at his face. The handsome lines of it, the light behind his eyes, these features I will never forget the look of, for the man in this photo, who is the team leader of Shearwater's research base, is also my husband.

Dominic

I check on Rowan—the trip to the base and the comms tower was too much for her. She felt very warm on the bike behind me and I'm worried she might have an infection. I come across Orly, hovering outside her door.

"You alright, mate?"

"I knocked, but she said not to go in."

"She's not feeling well."

"Still?" He is worried, touching the door absently.

It makes my chest ache to see how quickly he has curled into her space, to realize how much he must have been yearning for it. Just for a second I allow a childish thought: *I try so hard to be enough but I never will be*—and then I banish it, come to my senses. His grief, his loneliness, the absence in our lives, none of that is about me. It's only natural for a child to want his mum, it's just that this wanting is being thrown into stark relief for the first time.

"You go back to your room now," I tell Orly.

"Can't I stay?" he asks. "I'll just sneak in. She might get cold."

"She'll be right. You worry about yourself getting cold, okay, you sleep with Raff tonight." I might even hop in with them, as much fun as three lads kicking each other all night will be.

He casts a long look at the door. "Will she go? If you fix the radio?"

"I can't fix the radio. I've tried."

He nods, relieved, and gives me a kiss before climbing the stairs to the room he shares with Raff.

I knock on the door and when I don't hear a response I open it a crack, wanting to make sure she's okay. I don't want her here, or trust her, but I still have a duty of care. She is a lump under the covers. There is a candle burning beside her and a shaft of light from the window. I edge my way in and very gently feel her forehead for fever. She is warm but not burning hot. The touch causes her to roll in her sleep so her face is lit by the window.

Yen, she said his name was. I wonder if he was her partner. I wonder if it's grief that pulls her back under. The room has the heavy feel of it.

Something catches my eye. A thing lying on the bed beside her, glinting in the light. I stare at it, slowly making sense of what it is, and then my heart is juddering.

Dazed, I cross to the window and pull the curtain closed so she won't be woken too early. Moving, really, without thought. When I turn back, meaning to leave, it's to see that her eyes are open and she's watching me in the dark.

The single candle throws flickering shadows onto the walls.

Do I ask her about the photo or pretend I haven't seen it?

She speaks first. "Did you break the radio?"

"No," I say.

"Do you know who did?"

"No."

There is a nakedness in this room and within it she seems to take me at my word in a way she didn't earlier.

Something in her relaxes a fraction. "Then you don't mean to keep me here?"

"No," I say softly. "For all our sakes I wish you'd never come."

Rowan

The slab is down and I am hosing it carefully to make sure it doesn't crack while it sets. The sun is scorching on my face but there is a crispness to the autumn air that means you can be cold while your skin burns. I am peering around at this land, my land, so recently acquired, and pondering how overwhelmed I feel by it. I don't know what to do here. This is all I have ever wanted: land of my own, a place to build a home. But now that I stand here, I feel dwarfed by the enormity of the space around this cement slab. I know I want wildness, I want to grow things, but I don't know how, or where to start, and I feel young and foolish and very alone.

It's only by chance that I turn and look out over the valley. At the reason I chose this place, those snow gums. Their ghostly white trunks streaked through with blood red and ocher yellow, their gnarled and twisted forms contorted into eerie sculptures. They are unlike any other tree I have seen. There is a man among them.

I turn off the hose and jump down onto the grass. My stride is as quick as my pulse. He is trespassing.

"Hi," I call.

He turns and sees me approaching. The sun is at my back; he lifts a hand to shield his eyes, squints to make me out. He is neither big nor small in stature. Neat brown hair, handsome but forgettable face. Not particularly remarkable. He wears a backpack and carries a notepad and pen. I think about these things because I may need to describe him to the police.

"Hi there," he says, his accent American.

"Do you need help?" I ask.

"Not unless you can tell me why the *Phoracantha* are increasing their damage on the *pauciflora*."

I study him, already knowing him. "Let me rephrase. Why are you on my land without permission?"

"Trying to figure out why the *Phoracantha* are increasing their damage on the *pauciflora*."

I must look unimpressed because he laughs and that's when I see it: there is something remarkable after all. It's his smile and that laugh, the warmth of it.

"Can I explain over a coffee?"

"I don't have coffee. I don't have a kitchen."

He peers up the hill at the worksite. "Incredible spot you've got here. What do you plan on doing with it?"

"Just . . . you know—house, garden."

"Can I take a look at the aspect from up there?"

I don't answer, wondering how I will get rid of this guy.

"Purely for appreciation," he says. "I love it here. I'm from New York, I'm studying the decline in your snow gums. You're wondering why, of course: I like to travel, I try to take on projects all over the world. It's taken me fifteen years to get here to the *Eucalyptus pauciflora* and they don't disappoint." He is gazing around at the rainbow snow gums, happy, it seems, to chat away without much response from me. I guess he remembers his manners because he offers a hand and says, "Hank Jones, professor of biology at NYU, I'm leading a research project into adapting plants to climate change, specifically swapping genetic modules between cells to create more drought tolerance. But as I'm starting to see, drought is not the only problem here, there's a wood-boring beetle using the drought's dryness to dig more deeply into the gums. The trees are dealing with a double-pronged attack."

The hand is still outstretched, waiting for me. Reluctantly I shake it. I really just want to get back to watering my slab.

I turn and head up the hill, letting him follow me. "It's triple," I tell him over my shoulder.

"What's the third?"

"Fire."

"Ah. Of course."

At the top he steps up onto the cement and takes in the view. In every direction are sloping hills and valleys, some covered in thick bush, some rocky outcrops glistening in the sunlight, and on the higher mountains in the distance is snow. I can feel how moved he is by it in the quality of his silence. Some of my impatience eases. I feel proud, suddenly, of this place I'm to make my home.

Unlike the rest of our surroundings, the stretch of hill we stand on is bare of vegetation, but for three enormous eucalypts.

"You could do a wildflower meadow," he says suddenly. He's jumped down onto the grass and is walking across the hill. "It's perfect here." I don't even know if he's talking to me but he is rapt by this idea. "*Craspedias* and *Stylidiums*, *Gentianellas*, *Leucochrysum*, *Ranunculus*, *Brachyscome*, *Euphrasia*—these mountains were underwater," he says abruptly, glancing at me with astonishment as though I have told him this fact instead of him me. "Hundreds of millions of years ago. And during the Ice Age there were glaciers all over it, which means that geologically speaking it's very interesting, the rocks are incredibly old and there's evidence that the unusual variety of botanical families found here date all the way back to Gondwana, which is why you can find species here that resemble flora of the northern hemispheres. Do you know how lucky you are that this is yours? You could do *Prostanthera cuneata*, and *Grevillea*, and *Myrtus*, they would all thrive in each other's company and the light is perfect . . ." He has barely remembered to breathe, he is so excited, and as he smiles at me with the delight of this, with the plants he has imagined and brought to life around him, I start to see what he sees. Not the plants specifically—I have no idea what any of those names mean—but I see the hill we stand on covered in color. He has painted it for me.

I walk over to the caravan and flick on the kettle for a cuppa.

⁓

I try to keep this memory in the forefront of my mind. I try to recall in as much detail as I can those first days and weeks and months of discovering that we were both in love with the same place, the same mountains, the same small patch of land—and by extension each other. He could see how to turn the land I'd bought into a home. I would build the house and, improbably, this man from across the world would plant the garden, and together we would create a life.

To find him now, to figure out why he left Shearwater without telling me, to ask him what on earth is going on—and to make sure he's okay—I need a girl who can swim out to retrieve a radio. If Hank isn't here, then I have come for nothing, and I need to get off this drowning island.

Fen lives on the beach, they've told me. So I am making the trip down the hill for the second time when I hear a noise and turn to see a flash of pale hair among the tussocks.

"Could that be a rare golden shag I see hiding in the grass?"

Orly stands up with an eye roll. "No such thing as a golden shag."

"No shit. What are you doing?"

"Following you."

"Why?"

"Dad said I have to leave you alone."

"This isn't doing a very good job of that." I turn and keep walking, but every now and then I hear him behind me, and eventually I call, "Either walk with me or go home, this is annoying."

He hurries to my side, a little skip in his step. "You're a bit grumpy, huh?"

"Am I?"

"A bit. How come?"

I think about it. There are several current reasons that seem obvious enough, but I try to think back to before all of this and ponder whether I've always been grumpy. "I think I've been pissed off for a while," I admit, though pissed off is not the right way to describe the state of me over the last year.

"How come?"

All I can think to say is, "I built a house."

"What kind of house?"

"Just a house. My sisters helped a bit, but mostly I did it myself. It took a long time, a lot of years. It had a garden." I stop, because I don't know how to talk about this garden, or really this house either. My life.

"Where was it?" he asks, his eyes alight at the mention of a garden.

"In the Snowy Mountains."

"Were there snow gums?" he demands.

I smile. "Yeah, there were snow gums. There were a lot of things. It was more of a wildlife corridor than a garden, I guess. We did a lot of work, but there were parts where you just stood back and let nature do its thing. The plants and trees were so varied that it meant the patch of land was full of animals. There were emus and dingoes, those were the ones everyone used to get excited about, but I really loved the platypus in the stream, and the family of wombats that had dug their burrows just outside my bedroom window. They have square poos, did you know that?"

He laughs. "No way."

I nod but I am finding it hard to keep my voice steady and it occurs to me that maybe this isn't the best thing to tell a nine-year-old about.

"What happened?" he asks.

"A bushfire came through."

We are both quiet for a while, thinking through all that that means.

"Was there . . . much left?" he asks. "The house?"

"No."

If I look up into the sky now I will see the way the ash fell like snow in the night, swirling and delicate.

The crazy thing is that I'd engineered the house to be as fire resistant as possible, I'd thought I was being silly, and then a fire comes along that reminds you that you know absolutely nothing about what nature is capable of, the power of it is ludicrous, beyond your capacity to prepare for, and everything—*everything*—burns if it's hot enough.

"The animals?" Orly asks. "The snow gums?"

I don't reply because he already knows the answer, I can hear it in his voice. "It was hard to be cheerful after that," I tell him.

"Will you rebuild?"

"No. There's no point in rebuilding. It'll go again, another fire will come."

"Because of climate change," he says, working it through.

"That's right."

"Will we die of climate change?" Orly asks, sounding more curious than scared.

"I dunno."

"But if you had to guess."

He's pushing me. I'm not sure what answer he's hoping for. What are you meant to do with kids? Protect them or be honest? I shrug, tell him what I think is true. "One day soon enough, everything is either going to burn, drown, or starve, including us."

He stares at me.

I spread my hands. "You asked."

We walk in silence for a bit and I start to feel guilty. "I'm only joking," I say feebly, but I don't think he's listening.

Orly asks, "So what will you do? If you won't rebuild."

I think about having nothing and what that can do to you. How it can paralyze a person. I was paralyzed for a while. Deep in my cells I was inert, I was lost. Until I got on that boat to come here. And now it feels like if I stop moving, even for a second, I will perish.

"Did you get to know any of the scientists who lived here?" I ask Orly a little later.

He nods. "Raff's friend Alex. He came up to the lighthouse for dinner a lot."

"Oh yeah? What was his job?"

"He was studying the fur seals. Do you know sealers nearly wiped them out? Thousands and thousands of them. Back in the 1800s. But people like Alex have been bringing them back."

I think on this. Leaning against my walking stick. A whole population of animals, clubbed to death. I can see the beach now, stretching below us. I can picture the ship, anchored a little way out. Can see their dinghy rowed in, men climbing out onto the black sand. Surrounded by such astonishing creatures, and, what's more, by the miracle of their trust. Animals who had never learned to fear humans. I feel sick, actually, and the vividness of the vision feels beyond me, it feels outside my body, like something I am being shown. I have a sense, now, of why this place feels so . . . creepy. It hangs upon the air, the memory of this violence.

"Who else did you know?" I ask him. "The base leader?"

"No," Orly says. "Not really."

But he answers too quickly.

"You didn't have anything to do with him? Didn't ever cross paths?"

"I mean, a little."

"What was he like?"

"Hank?" Orly thinks. "He was nice. Everyone liked him."

"Mates with your dad?"

"Oh no, not Dad."

I look sideways at him. "Really? Why not?"

"I dunno."

"Did they not like each other?" I press.

"Dad said once that he could see through Hank." Orly looks at me. "What does that mean?"

"Just . . ." I try to work it out too. "I guess it means he thought Hank wasn't who he seemed to be."

"Oh. Why do you care, anyway?"

"I don't," I say robotically, but Orly has already darted forward, not interested in my response.

My too-small boots hit the black sand of the beach. We have been picking our way around the big fat seals on the pathways. Some of them look up at us as we pass, some snort and give a lazy gurgle, while others don't bother lifting their heads.

"Meet the wieners!" Orly says. "Elephant seal babies. The adults have gone out to sea already."

I can't even imagine the size of the adults if these giants are the infants.

There is a human shape in the distance. Out among the fur seal colony. We make our way past the clumps of bright seaweed, over the bones. Birds fill the sky. I don't know what kinds they are.

"Mind the gentoos," Orly says, skirting around little waddling penguins with bright-yellow feet and beaks.

"They are much cuter than they have any business being," I comment. It is hard to take in that they are just . . . here. Right beside me. Completely unbothered by the presence of people on their beach.

"I know. My favorites are the royals. They have those long orange eyebrows, you know? They let you get close, too, you can hang out with the royals and the kings, they're down on South Beach, but these gentoos are more shy so we have to be careful not to disturb them."

"Got it."

We give them a few meters' berth. I can see about a dozen of them awkwardly wandering over the rocks, sort of idly making their way toward the roaring sea. When they reach the water I see that awkwardness morph into a smooth, sleek dive through the waves.

As we draw nearer to the fur seals, the sound of them crests. Could there be hundreds of them? The honks and snorts from the adults are coupled with what sounds like the bleat of lambs. In my confusion I look for the source of this and realize there are little squidgy shapes in among the adults, sand-covered babies with little ears poking out of their heads, dozens and dozens of them making these tiny lamb cries.

"Oh my god," I say.

"I didn't know they'd given birth!" Orly exclaims. "Let's not get too close."

As he says this a huge male starts flopping over to us with an aggressive bark. I am alarmed but Orly raises his hands above his head and says, "Shoo! Go away!" And the seal kind of considers him, gives a huffy sniff, and then flaps back to the colony. I can't help laughing.

"That was King Brown," Orly tells me, as though this explains the interaction.

"You guys name them?"

"Alex and Fen did."

A sleek, light-gray mother seal starts shouting, panicked, and as we watch, the girl, the human shape among this astonishing mound of furry bodies, picks her way over to the crying mother and without any hesitation she shoves an enormous male in the side, making him start with surprise and shuffle his way off the tiny baby he'd been squashing. The little seal pup shakes its head and bleats for its mother, who nuzzles it in relief, while the male gives a roar of indignation and then flops back down to sleep.

"He nearly killed the baby," I say, horrified.

"Yeah. It happens, sadly. They don't mean to, they're just so big. Fen stays in there a lot to try to stop it."

"Doesn't it bother them to have a human among them?"

Orly frowns, looking at his sister. "I guess not," he says, as though it's a stupid question, and given what we're looking at I suppose it is. "The researchers used to have rules about keeping a few meters away, letting them come to you, you know, just basically not bothering them. But they didn't even try to make Fen stick to those rules. She's just . . . one of the seals."

Which seems a truly bizarre thing to try to contemplate, and I find myself wondering how this could be true, how such a thing could come to be. Why is she down here among these animals instead of living in a house with her family? And why does her dad allow it?

Fen has seen us now and is making her way over to us. We have met before but that feels like part of the fever dream. I take her in properly, watch the way her body moves, completely at ease on the sand and among the animals, strong and graceful in the full wet suit that looks not unlike the sleek dark fur of the seals. Her hair is long and sun-bleached blond, tangled and salty almost to the point of dreadlocks. Her skin is very tanned and freckled and she seems like a wild animal who has stepped free of a life under water.

Maybe Dom doesn't have much choice in the matter of who and what his daughter is; I can't imagine it would be easy trying to keep this creature from the sea.

"Hi—" I start to say before I am cut off by an embrace. I am so shocked and it hurts so much that I don't think to hug her back, and when she lets her arms drop I immediately regret this, wanting to reach for her even through the pain.

"Oh!" she gasps. "Your wounds!"

I grimace. "It's okay."

"Sorry. It's just . . ." Her eyes are filling. "I didn't know if you'd wake up."

I gaze at this girl, realizing all three of these children have shown me the same open warmth, a kindness given freely and without agenda, and I wonder if that generosity is a product of their isolation, of their loneliness, or if it is simply a truth of their characters. Their father is different, he looks at me with wariness, but if that is to protect his children then I can understand it.

I don't want to ask this girl what I've come here to ask her. Not now that I know she will say yes.

"They're beautiful," I say of the seals, and she beams, a smile of crooked white teeth, and *she* is beautiful.

"They are," Fen agrees. "I find it so hard to leave them. How are you?"

"I'm okay."

"You were just a shape," she admits. "Tangled in driftwood and kelp. I didn't think you'd be alive."

I don't know how to thank her, how to convey the enormity of my gratitude.

"Come on," she says before I can try. She leads Orly and me to a wooden hut on stilts in the water. It's a boatshed, with a single rumpled mattress in one corner, a kitchenette with a sink, kettle, and fridge, and a bookshelf bursting with paperbacks. Fen has a row of shells and knickknacks on the windowsill above her bed, the only sign a teenage girl lives here. This all sits alongside three inflatable motorboats, bobbing gently against the timber floorboards. It is cold in this shack, and it feels exposed, and looking at the space makes me feel a little depressed for her.

"Could I use one of these to get back to the mainland?" I ask, gesturing to the boats.

The kids look at each other and burst out laughing.

My hope curls into embarrassment. "Yeah, yeah, what then, what are you showing me?"

"I have an idea," Fen says. "If you're, if you want, I mean."

"Okay."

"Dad told you where your boat is?" she asks.

I nod.

"I might be able to use the Zodiac to reach it. Then radio an SOS."

Turns out I didn't need to ask at all.

The problem is the current. I've heard it from each of them separately: the Drift is perilous. There's no swimming against it, there's barely swimming with it. It dumps you ferociously onto sharp-toothed rocks. If Fen can manage to steer the Zodiac into a calm pocket of water protected by the hull of the wrecked boat, she might be able to climb onto the deck, find the bridge and check the radio, all without getting wet. But if the current steers her too far to the left or right, even by millimeters, she will shoot past the wreck and into the rocks.

The big thing, she says, is not to tell Dom.

"No," I say. "No way."

But she says, "I know this ocean, trust me," with such confidence, and because the selfish, ugly part of me wants to, I do.

She looks at Orly next, the weakest link. We can both see him itching to race for home, worried about his sister but also happy to be part of this. "Can we count on you?" she asks him.

Orly extends his hand and they shake. "You can."

We climb into the Zodiac. I don't want to be in this flimsy boat, or any boat, but despite their clear independence I don't think I should let them attempt any of this without adult supervision. Orly and I will go with Fen to the southern bay and watch from land.

Fen starts the motor and steers us out of the shed. The sea opens up before us.

I train my eyes skyward. If I think about how close the water is, if I imagine how easy it would be to tip over, I stop being able to breathe. I focus on my bum on the rubber, my feet in the boat, my hands tight about the rope rail.

We zoom along the island's coast, cresting waves with big leaps and landing so hard we are thrown up off our seats and slammed back down on our tailbones. I scream with each one. It *hurts*. Sea spray drenches us and I realize too late it's drier to sit at the back. Orly can't stop laughing at my screams.

In a calmer moment I look up at the island, taking it in. It is dramatic, mist shrouded.

"That's a blue-eyed shag," Orly says, pointing out a flash of black passing over our heads. "They're endemic to Shearwater."

Along the shoreline are huge stretches of white, and Fen steers closer so I can see that they are in fact enormous penguin colonies, thousands and thousands of birds in swarming masses. "Royals," Orly says, or, "kings." "There are rockhoppers around here too but not as many."

I think of the life these kids are living, surrounded by such beauty, by so much wildness. This place is a dream. Do they think it's normal? Even my home among the trees was still nothing like this. The animals I shared a stretch of forest with were shy and elusive; if I ever saw them, it was as they ran from me. I'm not even sure I knew places like this island still existed. That a place so *alive* could survive our colonizing.

On the tail of this thought I spot large metal shapes in among the penguins, rising up above them, red with rust. There is a bad feeling in me as I look at them.

"What are those?"

Both the kids go silent.

Then Fen says, "The sealers who came here. When they'd clubbed all the seals they could find, they'd stuff the penguins into those barrels—"

"Alive," Orly adds.

"—to boil all their oils out."

Oh god.

"And they're still just sitting there?"

"I don't think anyone knows whose job it would be to remove them, so they say they're historical artifacts."

I look at the barrels and at the thousands upon thousands of penguins surrounding them. As before, the image is like an intrusion into my mind, I see the men again, climbing out of their wooden boats and wading through those masses, lifting the little creatures into the barrels and ignoring their screams. I am glad when we've passed this particular stretch of coast.

"We see them too," Orly says to me, and I look at him and realize he sees not only the penguins and the men but me, he sees far too much of me.

The bay is deceptively calm. Yen's boat appears as we round some rocks and enter the mouth. It is confronting, to see it so broken, and I find it hard not to go back again to that storm and that swell. He tried to make a Mayday call but the only station close enough to hear us was here, on Shearwater, and nobody answered. I know now it's because the radio had been destroyed and most of the island's occupants had already gone. But we didn't know, he wasted so much time trying to get through and the waves were so big.

"It's okay," Fen tells me softly.

"Sorry." I swallow. "I didn't realize it would be so hard to see."

She steers us closer, then idles the engine and lets us bob in the waves. I can see a change in the color of the water, which must be the Drift. I can see the rocks. I can't see a way to avoid either. I realize we are not getting that radio.

"I'll drop you to shore and circle back," Fen says.

"No," I say, and she looks at me. "We're going home now."

"What? No, I can make it."

I hold her eyes. "We're going home now. It's alright."

Her mouth opens but whatever she was going to say dissolves and her shoulders slump. "But we need the radio."

"It's not worth drowning for."

Fen starts the Zodiac once more and makes a wide turn. It opens up a different view of the rocks the craft is wedged within.

"What's that?" Orly asks. "Stop, Fen, what is that?"

She slows and I make sense of it seconds before they do. I grab

Orly and pull his face to my chest so he can't see. "Don't look," I say to Fen. "Don't look." But she is looking, and a sob leaves her. Because the body barely looks human anymore. Birds have feasted on him. And the rocks. He is not in the shape he should be, his limbs are out of place. Parts of his skin gone.

"Go, Fen," I order her, making my voice hard enough to reach through to her, and she blinks, wipes her eyes, and navigates us out of the bay. Her hands on the throttle are shaking. I am still holding Orly against me, not letting him move, and he submits to it, returns the embrace, I don't know how much he saw.

I face the wreck and the rocks and Yen's body, I watch it grow smaller, I'm so sorry, I'm so fucking sorry, I hate myself.

———

They are waiting for us on the beach. I can see it's going to be bad. Raff's pacing back and forth like a tiger behind glass, and Dom is still as a gum tree, arms folded over his chest.

"Why would you take him down there?" Raff demands the second the Zodiac hits the sand. I realize he's talking to his sister, furious with her even as he helps her out of the boat. Orly is still within the circle of my arms. Dom wades into the sea and reaches for his son; Orly clings to his father as he's lifted easily out. I raise a leg over the side just as a wave hits us and I'm sent into the ankle-deep water. The pain of the impact brings hot tears to my eyes.

"Did you get the radio?" Raff is asking as I drag myself upright.

"We didn't even go for it, nothing happened," Fen says.

"We saw a body!" Orly shouts. He is halfway between terrified and excited. Then he says, a little more subdued, "He was all eaten."

"Oh my god," Raff snaps. Dom places a calming hand on his eldest son's shoulder, while his gaze swivels to me.

"I'm sorry," I say quickly.

"Why would you take my children to a boat wreck?" he asks me, eerily calm. "Where you know there will be a dead person?"

"I—"

"*We* took *her*, Dad," Fen says.

"A nine-year-old and a teenage girl who's been through more than enough already," Dom says, ignoring his daughter.

"What has she been through?" I ask him. "Why does she live alone in that shack, for god's sake?"

"Don't, Dad," Fen says and then walks a few paces away.

"They seemed like they knew what to do," I say helplessly. "That it was simple, and I . . . I just was thinking about that radio, it didn't even occur to me that we would see him . . ." I press palms into my closed eyes. "I mean they run wild around here, how am I meant to know what they can and can't do?"

The question falls into silence, sounding pathetic. The wind leaves me. I am shivering with cold, drenched through. Instead of making excuses I say again, "I'm sorry." And "I really messed up."

Dom's eyes move to his children. "Are you okay?" he asks them.

They nod, but they look pale, and I don't think their father is convinced.

"Everyone up to the house," Dom says. Then to Fen, "Including you."

Orly says he wants to walk with his brother and sister. Dom tells Raff to carry him if need be, and then he and I trudge over to the quad bike.

I grip the seat and peer over my shoulder at the three figures behind us. It's late; the sun is starting to set and I can feel something unraveling inside me. No radio to call for help. No boat on which to leave. No husband here, as he said he was, when he pleaded for me to come. No home to return to, only ash. And I have killed a man and left his body in the sun to be picked at. I have shown him to children, and altered the way they see the world.

I am a tunnel, wind screaming through me.

And into this empty space comes a mad thought, unbidden.

They have killed him. My husband.

Dominic

I am conflicted as I turn off the bike and help Rowan climb off. Half of me despises her. For existing. For being here. For being any part of a stunt that might harm my children. The other half feels concern for her and a reluctant sympathy: she is shivering, her hands ice to the touch. I am aware of what Fen and Orly can be like; I can imagine exactly how they convinced her to go along with the plan, how they made it seem easy.

"Head inside and get warm," I tell Rowan, who seems distant and lost in her own thoughts. I wonder if she's thinking of Hank. And of the boat she couldn't reach, the radio she couldn't retrieve. I wonder what she thinks of us, this odd little family she has found herself trapped with, instead of the husband she came here to find.

I will have to tell my kids who she really is. I will have to warn them that she's a liar. I'm not sure when or how to do this.

I walk back to meet them on the hill track. The sky is charcoal and releases a spattering of rain. I hear the kids before I see them, their voices drifting up and around. They are talking about Claire. Raff and Fen are telling Orly what they remember. Things like *she always had music on, every second of the day*, or *she was really good at gymnastics, she showed us how to tumble and flip*, or *she used to put oysters under her nose and pretend they were boogers*. And though they do this often—he craves the details—it stops me in my tracks because they are always things I'd forgotten and there is something profound about being reminded that they had specific relationships of their own with her.

My kids round the bend and fall quiet as they see me. Once, not long ago, I would have joined them easily—we were never apart, the four of us. Now I am a conversation killer, a mood deflater.

"Fen," I say, thinking to ask if she's alright, thinking no one should have to see a body spat out by the sea, or any dead body. I'll tell her I want to look after her, that she shouldn't be alone. That we will drink hot chocolate all crammed together on the couch like we used to. And that she will forget this. My three kids look at me and something in me panics and instead what comes out of my mouth is, "I had no idea you could be so stupid."

Her face falls. When she replies I almost don't hear it. "I'm sorry," she says, and in response to my callousness Raff is no longer angry with his sister, but with me, he can't believe me, and I agree with him: I am an asshole.

I look at Fen once more and think *my darling girl*.

It starts to rain in earnest as I lead the way home.

I was not meant to have to do this part alone. The teenage part. I was changing her nappies yesterday, and today I am grappling with the reflection of my failures in her too-wise eyes. I am trying to allow her to grow while simultaneously keeping her from drifting away. I want her to know life, its beauties and its complexities, I want her to take risks and make mistakes and know love as we all should, and yet those things feel too big, they are dwarfing us, she is just a baby and I really need my wife.

Fen

As she follows her family up the hill in the rain Fen thinks about bodies. The dead sailor's, of course, and all the missing bits of him. She is surprised most about the . . . *disregard* he's been shown. That sounds stupid in her own mind but it's the word she can't shake. She has seen plenty of dead seals and always meets the sight with sadness and a sense of nature's disregard for fairness or dignity. A sense that the world shows no pity for animals. She sees the way they eat each other, eat the worst bits of each other. Somehow she's imagined people to be exempt from that disregard, but she knows now that she was wrong.

Thinking of Yen's body leads her to think of her mother and to wonder if Claire was left in such a state. Was she peeled open and spilling before she was incinerated? Were her eyes open or closed? Did she look peaceful or monstrous? Were they careful with her, or rough? She is crying silently as she walks. Fen feels too much, always bursting out of her body.

If she was alive, would her mother's body look like Rowan's does now? Would they be the same age? She tries to work it out. Sees again the way Rowan looked as they undressed her, as they warmed and stitched and bandaged her. And more privately, later, as Fen washed her under the shower, dried and clothed her once more. She has never been naked with another woman before. She's never seen another woman's body, except in movies. Fen feels so much tenderness for this poor battered form. She feels, for the first time in her life, a connection to her own woman-ness—it felt right to gather up this body and try to care for it the way women have been caring for each other since the beginning. It made Fen feel more . . . *herself* than she has in a long time. More of the woman she wants to become. There are other ways for bodies to be treated, but she does not want to think about these.

At the lighthouse they eat together at the table, a basic dinner of sausages, mash, and steamed greens. Rain lashes against the windows, and wind screams through tiny openings and under doorways.

Fen sees her father watching Rowan. She sees the way he is unpicking her with his eyes. She knows he is shaken by her arrival: he doesn't like losing control, and this new person among them isn't controllable.

After dinner he disappears upstairs—he will be doing some chore, some repair job, it will be hours before he'll let himself stop. The pipes in the bathroom have been making weird noises lately so probably that. Raff and Orly go into the living room to fold laundry and then work on their latest Lego project, which is just about the only form of entertainment they have these days, since all their books have been read a dozen times each and there is no longer any power for movies. Fen and Rowan clean up the kitchen and do the dishes.

"Are you okay?" Fen asks.

Rowan glances at her as she scrubs a pan. "Don't ask me that. I'm asking you that."

"I'm fine. You're the one who knew him."

"I didn't know him at all. I just spent a few days at sea with him." Rowan pauses, then murmurs, "I'll have to find his family when we get back."

Fen knows how the people in that family are going to feel when someone says the words *he didn't make it*. That's what her dad said when he came to find them, dressed in surgical scrubs: *she didn't make it*. As though it had been a journey their mother had gone on, one she just couldn't make her way to the end of. Though she would have tried very hard, Fen knows that much about her mum.

"Hey," Rowan says. "It's okay, I'm sorry."

Fen wipes her tears quickly, embarrassed, god she is *always* crying. "Why did you cut your hair off?" she asks.

Rowan absently runs fingers over her shaved head, leaving trickles of soapy water to trail down the back of her neck. She grimaces and tries to shrug the drops away. "I wanted to feel lighter," she says.

It is an answer Fen understands.

Later Fen goes upstairs to find Raff in his bedroom. He is sitting on the floor in the corner, mostly hidden behind the bed. She's in time to catch him shoving something under his legs.

"What are you doing?" she asks.

"Nothing."

Fen flops onto his bed, propping her head on her hands. "How have you been charging that? Does Dad know?"

Raff sighs and pulls out the phone he tried to hide. It's on, and he shows her a quick flash of what he's been looking at. A photo of him and Alex.

"Raffy," Fen says.

Her brother turns the phone off. And throws it hard into the wall. The phone cracks down the middle and falls with a thud onto the rug.

"Hey," she says. "Can you play me something?"

He shakes his head. He can't talk, really, when he's like this, though he doesn't talk much anyway. If he would just play his violin, Fen knows Raff would feel better, but he hasn't touched it since Alex. He rises with explosive power and mutters, on his way past, "I'll get to the bag." And then he is gone, and she's failed him.

To busy herself, to not think about how much she hates being in this building, Fen makes tea and hot chocolate for everyone and carries a cup up to her dad. She is about to knock on his door when she hears his voice from within. She knows from the low tone, the intimacy of it, that there's no one else in the room with him.

She leans her forehead on the door and listens to the rumbling sound of his voice. She feels too old for her life. Doesn't know how to save him from this. She will cry again if she keeps listening. So she knocks loudly and pushes in.

"Cuppa," she says.

"Thanks, darlin'." He's been standing at his wardrobe, looking at the precious things hidden within, talking to them. But he shuts the cupboard door quickly upon her intrusion.

Fen is about to ask him if he's ever seen a dead body, wanting maybe to express to him what she felt today, the strangeness of it and how it has imprinted like light on the backs of her eyelids, but then she remembers everything at once and feels like an idiot. "Raff's gone to the bag," she says instead.

Dom breathes out heavily. "Righto. Thanks." He takes his tea and pauses long enough to give her a quick kiss on the forehead, then heads up the stairs to find his son.

Fen waits until his footsteps have disappeared and leaves the door wide so as to hear any approach. Then she crosses to Dom's wardrobe and opens it. In the top drawer he keeps an array of items that once belonged to Claire. There are pieces of jewelry, trinkets or knickknacks that were sentimental to her, smaller items of clothing, like the silk scarf Claire's mother gave her when she was Fen's age, a bottle of her perfume, and several of her favorite books, which she'd annotated with her thoughts. Fen picks up one of these last, Claire's battered old copy of *Jane Eyre*. She opens the worn and yellowed pages to see words underlined in pencil and notes scrawled in her mum's handwriting in the margins. It makes her ache, to see this handwriting, to read the neat little thoughts.

Dom has brought these items from the mainland. He collects more each time he goes back and visits Claire's parents. It has been nine years since she died, but he is still collecting, still carrying things across an ocean, still hoarding them privately in this drawer. Fen feels hopeless when she sees these things, proof of her father's obsession, of his prison. These are what keep Claire alive, what bind her spirit here—Fen is sure of it. They are a prison for both her parents. So she slides *Jane Eyre* into the waistband of her jeans. She only ever takes one item at a time, so he won't notice. One day, when they're all gone, he will know, but by then it will be too late.

Everyone is going to bed now. Rowan protests a lot but Fen will sleep on the couch. She sits quietly as the others head upstairs, feeling the hard edges of the book pressed to her body. She watches the window, a long pane of curved glass that opens onto the headland. The sky is a wash of dark clouds. Not a storm, exactly, but heavy rain.

She won't be able to sleep on this couch, in this room. Not next to this window. Because she is quite sure she's just seen someone walk past it.

The terror this figure fills her with is profound. It drives her up and out into the night. Her windbreaker will have to be protection enough against the weather, until she can make it to the boathouse. It's very cold as she descends the hill, though her stolen treasure sits warm against her spine and the little green lights dance ahead to show her the way.

Raff

The heart of a whale is the heaviest on the planet. It is big enough for a human to swim through. And it is very slow. These are the things that occupy Raff's thoughts. He thinks of that weight and feels overwhelmed by it.

In the communications building on the island he keeps a hydrophone, a prized possession second only to his violin, which was a gift from his mother and which, at the time, was too big for his little arms and hands to wield but which he has grown into like a fifth limb. The hydrophone was from his dad for his fourteenth birthday, and he is aware that it cost a lot of money and that his dad had to save up for it, he is aware that he loves it almost as much as the instrument but without the entangled pain.

When he can find enough time among chores and schoolwork, Raff sets up his waterproofing and dives beneath the surface of the ocean to capture whatever sounds he comes across. It is best in deep water because there is less noise pollution, and sound transmits better in cold water. The sounds aren't what he first imagined they'd be, they aren't what you hear in movies. There are no friction-based sounds, which can occur only when you add wind or sand or plants into the equation. But for Raff this is the thrill. The discovery of the unexpected. And while he enjoys it all, from the bubbles of air popping on the surface to the swish of a nearby seal fin, what he wants more than anything, what gets him out here at the crack of dawn, even in freezing temperatures and miserably windy conditions that skew the sound results, is the possibility of hearing the song of a whale. He was born the day he first heard the song of a whale, and he has been finding ways to record them ever since. In one moment high and squeaking like the top note of a violin, in the next guttural, echoing, some space between the moan of a cow and the trumpet of an elephant. Sometimes joyous and playful, sometimes mournful and searching. Sometimes with a trill or a creak or a rumble. A question, a call, a love letter.

After these lucky moments—and there have been only a few—he inevitably finds his way to the boxing bag, where he punches his body empty of the white-hot rage he feels at the thought of his mother not being here to experience the sound with him. What he is left with when that is punched out is loneliness.

Which is how he's feeling on the day he first meets Alex.

He is in the comms building, up at the peak, and he is playing his fiddle over the top of the humpback music he recorded last month. The audio file floats from the shithouse laptop speaker; it's all he has. He has been trying to compose something that will complement the whale song, that will translate and magnify it, but everything he adds only distracts from it. He is growing frustrated by his ineptitude. A stray G sounds discordant to his ears and he drops the bow, closing his eyes, letting the last notes reach their crescendo and fade out. He needs something more ambient, something to create atmosphere, not battle for the lead.

"That was incredible," an American voice says.

Raff opens his eyes and sees a young man. He is short, Black, handsome. He wears round glasses, which look to Raff in this moment impossibly cool.

"Sorry, I'll get out of your way," Raff says quickly, fumbling to pack up his violin and sound gear.

"Hang on," the man says, the researcher, for that's undoubtedly what he is. "Can you play some more?"

"More whale song?"

"Both, like you were just doing."

Raff shakes his head. "I was just messing around."

"I loved it," the man says simply.

And that's how it starts. A soft unfurling, a discovery. His name is Alex and he has come to study the fur seal population. His older brother

Tom is here too, a meteorologist. Raff goes into the field with Alex and learns about the fur seals, about their extraordinary recovery from almost total annihilation. They take Fen with them when they tag the creatures, wrestling with the big bulls, and Raff is glad to see a friendship blossom between Alex and his sister, too. Sometimes Raff takes Alex diving for whale song, and while they don't catch many whales they do get other interesting sounds that, with Alex's encouragement, Raff works into his music. For the first time in years he doesn't feel lonely.

On the day they first kiss, Raff's heart does not speed up; instead it seems to slow right down, it beats so hard and so slow that he thinks of the whale heart. Of the humpback, and the enormity of that heart, of its chambers a person can walk through.

———

Those days are long past. Alex is gone and there is no slow. Raff can't touch his violin, hasn't reached for his hydrophone. Now there is only the bag for when he needs calm, and such moments are coming too often.

He felt it as he paced the beach, waiting for his sister and brother to return, wondering if he'd lost them to the Drift. He should have been there, keeping them safe. That she tried something so dangerous without him is terrifying.

After, Raff tells himself over and over that they're safe, that nothing happened, that there's no need for this fury in his chest, in his fists, but the swell of it is more powerful than any thought, and not even the photos of Alex are enough to calm him down.

He takes the stairs two at a time. All 219 of them, winding stairs he knows well. He knows where muscles start to burn and where the second burst of energy is needed. He knows the exact step at which to tell himself there aren't many to go, he's nearly there, and he knows that stopping to rest at any point is a mistake.

It used to be called an observation deck and maybe that's a better name; they just call it the light room even though there's been no working light in it for a long time. Just a bag swinging eerily in the stray tendrils of wind that creep through the windows.

Raff uses teeth to pull on his gloves, and as he sends blow after blow into the boxing bag the pain builds within him until he is throwing everything into his punches, his whole life. He is letting things unravel, he should be holding his family together as he has *always* done, but they only grow further apart and he hates himself, he is useless, the only thing he can do is punch until he can feel nothing and is nothing.

Dominic never intended on teaching Raff to box. Certainly not the way Dom's dad and granddad taught him, with bare fists and bloody knuckles and broken ribs and noses and never a single day of rest. Dom even went pro for a few years until he met Claire and gave it up cold turkey, but he always kept a bag hanging, a way to stay fit. He didn't *need* the bag, because Dom, unlike Raff, has no temper whatsoever.

Raff would ask him, as a young kid, why he wasn't allowed to train with him, and Dom would say he didn't want Raff's childhood to be full of hitting things.

Until one day Dom just . . . changed his mind. He brought Raff up here to where the bag hung, and he made Raff punch until he could barely feel his arms anymore. Until he was liquefied. Calm. Raff realized over time that they only ever came up here when he lost his temper. A broken glass, a kicked door, pages he was meant to read, torn in deepest frustration when he couldn't. Get to the bag, get it out of the body. And so there came, for Raff, a dawning awareness of a kind of peril within him, one his father had recognized far earlier and sought to subdue.

Dominic

I look in on my boys before I go to bed. Raff is rolled over to face the window, no doubt exhausted by his session with the bag, but Orly is huddled over a book lit by a single candle, trying to ignore the weather outside. He makes room for me to climb in next to him, relieved, probably, to have some company during the storm.

"What are you reading?" I ask softly, not wanting to disturb Raff.

He shows me the graphic novel and tells me a little about its story, but he seems distracted.

"Nice," I murmur. "You can sleep, you know. I'll stay with you."

"I'm not tired," he says.

"Are you bothered by today?"

"No." He glances at me. "Should I be?"

"Things affect people in different ways."

I wait for him to find the words to tell me what's wrong, or to decide he is sleepy after all.

"This morning," he says haltingly, "before we went to the boat."

"Yeah."

"Rowan was asking me about Hank."

My stomach plummets and I am back to despising her, for putting him in that position. Then again if we didn't have anything to hide there wouldn't be an issue with it, I suppose. It feels like a game of chicken with her. One of us will have to break first and admit we know that something is wrong, that one of us is lying. Or that we both are.

"What did she ask?"

"If you and him were friends. I said no, because you weren't, right? Even back at the start. Was that wrong?"

"No, mate. It's fine." I pull him into me and open the pages of his comic. "Don't waste another thought on it." I ask him to read to me, and while he does I glance at his older brother to see that Raff is awake and watching us. His eyes meet mine, filled with the same sense of impending disaster.

Orly

The buzzy burr, at its heart, is a stowaway.

The dandelion shows us how important plants and their seeds are to the animals around them, but the buzzy burr proves that the opposite can also be true: many seeds rely on animals for their survival.

This buzzy burr's story starts right here, on Shearwater. It's a flowering plant, and it looks pretty similar to a dandelion, actually, only its flower is less delicate, more wiry, and a dark-purple color, while its seeds aren't attached to flying propellers that carry it on the wind. No, the buzzy burr's seeds are hooked like talons. They don't fly—they cling. They grab. And they particularly love to clutch onto feathers.

This spiky little seed, you see, is a world traveler, or would like to be. And who better to hitch a ride with than the mighty wandering albatross itself?

The buzzy burr seed, compelled to spread, to propagate, to live on, grabs onto the albatross with its hooks, and one day, when the albatross is ready to leave its chick, it lifts into the air with its impossibly wide wings, wider than any other bird's, and it sets off on an immense journey around the south of the globe. This albatross doesn't just circle the globe once, carrying the seed and showing it long stretches of ocean, showing it the world. No, it circles the globe *three* times in a single year. Only on this third trip around does the albatross set down on the coast of Argentina, in the alpine reserve among its glaciers and fjords, and deposit the seed into its new home.

Maybe the albatross knows it carried this little life across continents, across oceans. Maybe its long flight this year was to show the seed as much as it could. Maybe now it says *live well, little flower*, as it lifts back into the air on its wide and snowy wings.

Maybe the seed says *thank you*, as it watches the bird fly away.

Rowan

I don't like being in the house alone with Dominic. He is so quiet. The man I lived with for a decade never stopped talking; I grew used to the constant sound of Hank's voice as a steady hum in the background of whatever I was doing, without much need for me to reply. This silence, with only the wind to pierce it, makes me almost long for the loathsome noise of a TV. I ask Dom what I can do to help out, but he tells me to rest and then doesn't speak to me again. I find some cleaning supplies in a cupboard and clean the bathroom, which takes all of half an hour, and then I am stumped. I am directionless. Pulled to a painful halt, the momentum I had in getting to Shearwater stalled. With no hope of rescue or escape, I don't know what to do.

The dining table needs some attention. At least that is something I am capable of. Under the chipped white paint on its surface I can see that it's actually a rather lovely piece of old Tasmanian oak—whoever painted it should be sent to prison. I raid Dom's tool trolley for a few different grades of sandpaper, some turpentine, and some tung oil. I can't find any paint stripper, so I start with a coarse 80-grit sandpaper, knowing this will not be an easy task without a power sander but happy to have something to concentrate on for the next few hours. The paint is so old it chips away easily in most places, especially when I use a metal scraper, but it's harder to work free in others. I am careful not to apply so much pressure that I damage the wood beneath. The movements of my arm are so familiar to me, the scent of the fine wood dust so visceral that I feel, for these moments in time, unburdened. By memory. By responsibility. By loss. The way it's always been. A homeplace, working with wood like this.

When the paint is gone, my shoulder and arm are aching but even this is comforting. I clean the table, then take a medium-grit sandpaper to it, working carefully and consistently. It's a simple piece of furniture, there aren't any curves or grooves for me to worry about, no delicate detailing or carving, so it doesn't take too long before I can move onto the finer sandpaper. The smell again, god, the calm it brings me. But I come all too soon to the end of what I can do today. Once I have wiped the table down thoroughly and applied a coat of the tung oil, I have to leave it to dry overnight before I can do any further sanding and coating. I stand back and look at the table. The pale timber is gorgeous, with its intricate white grain. I force myself to leave it, and then I am back where I started, with too many hours left to fill.

It strikes me that I haven't seen the kid all day, and—despite having wished he'd leave me the hell alone—I miss him. I also want to check that he's okay after yesterday. I find him in a fourth bedroom I haven't yet explored, a study. There are three small desks crammed awkwardly against the curved walls, and here is the tech I wondered about—each desk has a computer connected to speakers, and there is also a phone sitting on a tripod, its camera aimed at a desk. Orly isn't using any of it, he has a pencil and workbook. Spread before him are dried plants, flowers and grasses he's pressed between the pages of a book and is now drawing.

"I thought you were on holidays," I say as I enter the room.

"Summer homework," he says.

"What's this for?" I touch the phone on the tripod.

"Our distance ed classes. During term we had to video call in once a week, and there were a bunch of presentations we had to film and send. They're all dead now, batteries are done."

I nod, wandering the room idly. Orly watches me. In glances I try to ascertain if he seems bothered at all by having seen a dead body. "Wanna do something?" I ask.

"Like what?"

"Anything. Show me something I won't see anywhere else in the world."

"I'm meant to be doing my work."

"You're on holidays! Take a break, kid. If your dad asks you can blame me." Dom already hates me.

"It's pretty self-serving of you to distract me from my education purely because you're bored, Rowan," Orly says.

"Oh." I am crestfallen.

He laughs. "Just kidding. Let's go."

"So what's going on with your dad and your sister?" I ask as we walk.

We are headed, not down the hill to the pinch and the beach, but inland, into the mountainous center of the southern island. I told Orly I couldn't manage any extreme hiking or climbing, which means this relatively easy walk is our only option.

He doesn't seem eager to answer my question. "I don't know," he says. Eventually he adds, "They disagree on a lot of things."

I am starting to worry about Fen. I don't think Dom should just be letting her live in the boathouse on her own. Something's happened but it's clear they don't want me to know about it, and it's far from my place to get involved.

Orly leads me up a small incline and tells me to lie down on my tummy and crawl to the edge. Grasses tickle my face as I awkwardly commando forward. After a few centimeters of this it's too painful and I have to sit up and edge forward on my bum. The ground drops away before us, a series of sweeping hills and valleys. Orly points to the hill directly to our right, its slope intersecting with ours to give us a perfect view of what sits among its silvery grasses.

It's an albatross. Close enough that I can see the soft, snowy plumage of its neck and face and head, the speckled gray on its wings, its pink hooked bill and dark eyes. It is sitting on a nest, I think, and it's huge. I have seen David Attenborough. I know what they look like. But I could never imagine the majesty of them so close; the true size of this bird is dazzling.

"Is this the one you told me about?" I ask softly. "With the seed?"

Orly smiles. "Maybe. That's Ari. She's got an egg under there. Nikau is at sea. He'll be back sometime soon to take over on the nest."

The moment is so peaceful that I could lie down and stay here with her forever. I feel all the restless, panicked threads of me calm.

"Did you know they spend most of their lives in the air?" Orly says. "They can glide without flapping for hours at a time."

I imagine this easy, lazy flight. I saw it, on that first walk down to the beach, I sat in the tussock and watched Ari—or maybe it was Nikau— soaring almost motionless through the air, so different from the other birds that it's impossible not to recognize.

The wind picks up a little and I lift the hood on my windbreaker (Dom's windbreaker). Orly doesn't have a hood today, and his long pale hair is whipping around, getting in his face. I gently comb the threads with my fingers and start braiding it tightly. I haven't done this since my sisters were little but my hands remember it well. While I braid, Orly tells me more about the wandering albatross. He explains how they only lay an egg every two years and how the last time Ari and Nikau did this, for her senior biology project Fen tracked and studied the process, from laying the egg and then incubating it for eleven weeks, to the egg hatching and then the growth of the chick. She set up a camera that recorded the chick, named Tui, for the months he sat in that nest, waiting for his parents to return and feed him. They watched as he practiced building his own nest by collecting mud and vegetation into a mound, and they were here when Tui finally took to the sky. Orly says his sister sobbed, knowing she would probably never see the bird again but also knowing this was a triumph, that he'd made it to maturity when not all chicks did. They are old, Ari and Nikau, nearly fifty years old, and they don't have many more breeding years in them.

"We might see this egg hatch," Orly says. "Before we leave."

"I hope so."

I finish Orly's hair but neither of us moves; instead he leans back into me and together we watch Ari tilt her head and lift her beak into the sky, we watch her spread her extraordinary wings as though to show us her beauty.

———

"This your doing?" Dom greets me. He's standing by the sink, gesturing to the dining table.

There is a brilliant pink and mauve sunset tonight as Orly and I get ready to brave the walk down the hill. We plan to join his brother and sister on the inky sand of the beach.

I nod.

"Why?"

I don't know if Dom's pissed off, but he is studying me closely, trying to work me out. He certainly doesn't seem *pleased*.

"It was a travesty," I say. "And it'll need a few more days of work before you can use it."

"So where are we meant to eat?"

"On the couch, like normal people."

This irritates him, and I try not to smile.

"Come down to the beach with us," Orly begs his dad.

Dom drags his eyes from me long enough to tell his son, "Can't, mate, I got things to get done around here."

I see Orly's shoulders slump and I wish his dad could see it too.

By the time we reach the pinch, Raff and Fen have already made a fire of driftwood. The world outside these flames disappears into shadow, but I can hear the constant snorts and scuffles of the seals, hundreds of them all around us.

Fen uses a blade to cut open the rubbery orange kelp, the texture and look of which makes my skin crawl, it is so alien, and then she places a fish inside it and puts the package on the fire to cook.

"You feeling okay today?" I ask Fen while the boys practice boxing moves by the water.

She nods.

Raff is about four times the size of his little brother, and he is laughing as Orly feints and weaves around him, his feet moving in swift dance steps, a twirl here, a pirouette there.

"I'm picturing it a lot," she admits.

"Me too. You're seventeen, right?"

"Yeah."

"And you've been here since you were nine?"

She nods. "We've been back to the mainland a couple of times to go to the doctor or the dentist, but that's it."

"That's . . ." I shake my head. "Crazy."

She shrugs. "I guess."

"Do you like it here or would you prefer to be in the real world?"

"This is real," she says, and leaves it at that. A while later she asks, "Do you have kids?"

I shake my head.

"How old are you?"

"Forty."

"Then how come you don't have any?"

"I don't want any."

"Why not?"

"Fen." I laugh.

"Sorry," she says quickly. "Was that impolite? I have nightmares about getting back to the mainland and offending everyone because I don't know how to talk to people."

I shake my head. "You're fine. You'll be fine." We are quiet a moment, and I think about her question. "The world's not a good place for a child."

She frowns. "That's not true. Look around."

I do. And wonder what she can see that I can't. What I can see is an ocean rising so swiftly that this extraordinary island, this home, will be gone in the blink of an eye. A place so unsafe that most of its occupants have already fled.

I meet Fen's gaze. She is all the hope and wonder and optimism of youth, and that's good, I guess, maybe she should try to hold on to that for as long as possible, until the world and other people take it from her. But I find myself wanting to warn her of what I wish I'd known. "It's not a good idea to fall in love, okay?" I say softly. "Not with people, and not with places."

Fen looks surprised by this.

"I loved a landscape and watched it burn," I say. "This island, you can see what it will look like, there's a film over everything. You can see it disappearing. There's no stable ground. Not here. Not anywhere else."

"And you'd want to try and survive all of that on your own?" she asks.

"What that instability does to relationships—what constant danger does to them—is devastating. It's unraveling."

I can see she doesn't believe me but I don't push the point. She will see, one day. Loving a place is the same as having a child. They are both too much an act of hope, of defiance. And those are a fool's weapons.

"Your dad," I say. "He's pretty tough, huh?"

Fen nods.

"What's his deal?"

"Like why's he so strict?"

I mean I guess he is and he isn't. He has strict routines for his kids, he works them hard, but he also lets them roam, he lets Fen live down here. It's a contradiction, but rather than trying to articulate this I just say, "Yeah."

"He just . . . It's not easy to raise three kids alone on an island," Fen says.

"So why is he doing it?"

"He was pretty messed up when Mum died. I think he wanted to be somewhere he felt he could contain things."

"He made it so hard for himself."

"Well, he had me and Raff. We helped with Orly a lot. And we had systems, you know. You all just have to stick to the systems and things hang together."

"Sounds boring."

She smiles. "It is."

"Is that why you're down here now? Is this your youthful rebellion? Running away from home?"

"It's not much of a rebellion, right?"

"It's pretty good, given the circumstances."

"What was yours?"

"God it feels like a long time ago. I didn't really have one, I don't think. I couldn't; I was too busy looking after my sisters."

"Oh."

"Any rebellion I had was just this . . . quiet anger. Always swallowed down."

"Who were you angry with?"

I recall those painful years. Feeling either invisible to her or hated by her. "My mum," I say.

Fen's head tilts to the side. "I don't know much about that."

"But this stuff going on with your dad. It's all the same. Parents. Trying to impress them or enrage them."

She is quiet for a moment, and then she says, "I know Dad loves me. I just don't know if he can see me."

Raff and Orly tumble down beside us and we eat the fish with our fingers; it falls apart, moist and rich and full of flavor, and the sky is enormous and pricked with stars, and I think it is an astounding life he has brought them here to live, and a lonely one.

———

I walk the boys back up to the lighthouse and it seems wrong to be leaving Fen on her own. I can see that it pains Raff, too, but he doesn't say anything and so neither do I. When it's just the three of us, struggling our way up the hill in the dark, he says, "She'll go to the boathouse. She's not allowed to sleep outside." Which makes me feel a little better.

It's the first time I make the walk up the hill. So far I've had the quad bike to carry me but tonight Raff doesn't offer it and I don't ask. I just take one plodding step after another. And with each of these steps I feel a sense of achievement. It hurts, and I can barely breathe, but I'm going to make it. It's not going to kill me.

Because it's late and Orly is tired, Raff carries him the last part of the journey, and then up the lighthouse steps, and I watch from their bedroom doorway as he settles his little brother into his own bed. "He sleeps better when he has company," Raff explains, though I didn't ask. I am well acquainted with Orly needing a bed buddy.

"Night," Raff adds, dismissing me, and I make my way carefully up a few more stairs to Fen's room. It's dark, and I don't bother turning on a light, I just unbutton my jeans, intending to fall into bed.

A voice clears its throat and says, "Sorry."

I jump halfway out of my skin.

"Sorry," Dom says again, but he doesn't sound it.

It annoys me—I don't like feeling as though he could enter my space whenever he wants. "You don't need to sit by my bed anymore, okay?" I say. "I'm alive. You want to talk to me, you knock."

He nods, an acknowledgment.

As my heart slows, I sink onto the end of the bed. He is mostly in shadow. There is something coming, he is building to it. An admonishment for distracting Orly from his schoolwork today, maybe? Something about the dining table?

He says, "We had Raff and Fen quite young."

I wait, unsure if he expects me to answer.

"We didn't want to waste time. Life seemed so short."

"It is, I guess," I murmur.

"It doesn't feel that way anymore," Dom says. "It feels very long."

"You lost a partner."

He looks at me and I am surprised to see something gentle come into his face. "I learned how to be a parent from her. I watched her with Raff and Fen. So I knew what I had to do when Orly came. I don't mean to say I did well, or that I was good at it, but she'd shown me the way and there isn't a minute I'm not grateful for that."

"Okay." I am nervous about what he's trying to say.

"I know what a spouse becomes. A whole world. So much a part of your life you couldn't untangle yourself from them even if you wanted to. I would have done anything for her." He gets something out of his pocket. Unfolds it. I know what it is without looking.

"You didn't have to lie," Dominic says, handing me the photo of Hank. "I understand. You're the wife, you came here to find him."

My eyes move from the picture to his face in shadow. I try to think through what this means. There are some things I still need to hold close to my chest. There are others to which I intend on getting answers.

"So where is he, Dom?"

"I told you, Rowan. He left. They all did."

"He was asked to sort those seeds and you're telling me he left without finishing the job?"

"He did finish it. He left us instructions. We're just moving boxes."

I study his face, searching for truth or lie, but I can't read him. The words have a ring of believability. Except, "Why didn't he tell me? Why not let me know he was on his way home?"

"I don't know. You'll have to ask him when you see him."

There is silence as I process that. The thought that his absence and my presence could be just one big, ridiculous miscommunication is painful. The thought that this miscommunication has resulted in a man's death is worse. I don't know why Hank would get on that boat without sending me an email to tell me he was coming home. To tell me to disregard his last messages.

Unless he wasn't coming home but going elsewhere. Leaving me for good.

"He didn't seem well," Dom adds more carefully. "In the end. He seemed burdened."

"In what way?"

"I don't know. He was doing a difficult thing."

Burdened.

Hank is the most self-confident person I have ever known. He is arrogant. Single-minded, certainly. Could that have turned to something else? Obsession?

"This place," Dom says, as though reading my mind. "It's extreme isolation, Rowan. You don't understand it yet, but it takes a very real toll."

Then he says, "What I don't get is why you felt you had to come all this way to see him."

⁓

It's the heat of the water, and the steam within the shower. I am sitting beneath the downpour, feeling the burn on my cheeks, and then I am returned, speeding along the bubbling bitumen of the road, trying to outrun roaring flames beneath a sky so red. Beside us I watch the running shapes of three horses, swallowed by a cloud of smoke.

"Rowan."

My sister. She is turning off the shower and helping me upright, wrapping me in a towel. "Jesus, you've cooked yourself," she mutters, of my bright pink skin.

"Sorry," I say. There is still so much steam. "I'm fine."

"Rowan, you can't—"

"I'm fine," I repeat, meeting her eyes. She is scared. I see this fear in her face whenever she looks at me: she has never known me like this. To Liv I have always been rock solid, the most reliable thing she has ever known. I made myself this way, for her and for our sister Jay. I had to carry them. And now I am unraveled and she's frightened and I don't know how to tie my pieces back together. I have lost too much and am too much lost.

When I can convince Liv I'm not a threat to myself and shuffle her out of the bathroom, I get dressed and return to my bed. After the fire (nearly a whole year ago now), Hank went to Shearwater and I, with nowhere else to go, came here to Liv's spare bedroom, which, in a month, will be a baby's room. I open my sister's old laptop, and the emails are waiting for me at the top of my inbox, three of them.

When Hank first got to Shearwater, he would tell me at length about his colleagues on the island and what they studied and how the base worked. Though he was there to study the ecology of the island, he also liked to go south and visit the vault and learn about the seeds stored there. He would talk about the specimens, about the nature of the vault itself and how extraordinary it was that it boasted such diversity. He told me of the weather on the island, the storms, the rain, and the wind. He said the wind was alive in a way it isn't elsewhere; he said he'd met a boy who spoke to it.

Hank's life was full, it was rich; in the wake of our loss he had found purpose, he was *thriving*. My life was the opposite. I was—*am*—dispassionate about everything. Barely able to find a reason to get up in the morning. Alive with envy for Hank's purpose and his passion, which now evade me completely.

Then things with Hank changed.

He told me the seed vault was being shut down. He said the island was too hazardous—weather events getting worse, sea levels rising with alarming speed—so the seeds were being moved off island to a much smaller vault. The UN was streamlining funds into identifying and storing only the seeds needed to feed humanity. There were fires and floods, there were wars, diseases, food shortages—they were going to need to feed people.

As the only botanist already working on Shearwater, Hank was asked to make these decisions. To do the sorting. To choose what would have a place in this new vault and what would be left on the island to gradually be surrendered to the sea. He told me it was utter stupidity. Shortsighted, linear thinking. The world, he tried to explain—to his bosses and also to me, on the other end of the video call—needed biodiversity more than it needed any other thing, and he said this as though we didn't already know it, except that we all did. And still, he had to decide on half. Which means that when the fires rage and the seas swallow and the bombs destroy, there will be no backups for the thousands and thousands of lost species. No way to replant. They will simply be gone forever.

At this point Hank stopped video calling me and switched to email, and these emails read differently. They were short, erratic, full of errors. They changed subject midsentence. I could see him spiraling on the page but I couldn't get through to him. I tried to get in touch with his colleagues to check if he was alright, but no one would get back to me.

And now. Finally, today, he has sent me three emails.

The first is this.

I need help. It's not safe here for me anymore.

And then this.

They don't understand what I'm trying to do. They fear what I have realized and they fear me for knowing it.

And then this.

I am in danger. Send help.

I don't sleep. I let the words turn over in my mind. I let them stir some dormant part of me. A little after dawn I stumble into the kitchen, startling Liv, who is not used to seeing me at this hour. She's drinking coffee in her dressing gown, which is barely closed over her enormous eight-month-pregnant belly.

"God, you look . . ."

I am aware that I must look deranged. I put the laptop in front of her, open to the first email.

"What is this?"

"It's from Hank. These three. Read them."

She frowns as she does so. Then looks up at me. "This is . . . Jesus. He doesn't sound . . . well."

"No."

"Should you call the police?"

"The police? What the hell are they gonna do? He's thousands of kilometers across an ocean."

"Well, what about his colleagues out there?"

"Nobody's getting back to me."

"So we just . . . stay calm, okay." She reads the emails again.

I start making myself a coffee with trembling hands.

"We'll go through the right channels," Liv is saying but I'm barely listening. I am vibrating. My mind is working with a clarity it hasn't known in a year, making swift plans. I feel woken from a dream.

"Rowan."

I look at my sister.

"Don't do anything stupid, okay?" she says.

But the answer is simple. "He's my husband," I say, "and he needs my help."

And so. I should have waited. Pursued other avenues first. But the messages did something to me. They brought me back to life.

Raff

Raff is up early, and walks the hill track to find his sister. She is on the beach, as always. He wonders at the kind of person you'd have to be to hate shelter, to want only exposure. The same, he supposes, as someone who has to punch and punch and punch. Longing takes on different forms.

Fen is using a thick chunk of driftwood to mark the height of the high tide. The seals are farther down the beach, honking and barking and bleating. He can't spot any penguins today, but the shags on their rock are like a dark cloud, rising and falling. Fen waves to him and waits for him to reach her.

"Higher again?" he asks.

"Higher again."

Soon there won't be a beach here at all.

They go to her little campsite and he takes out the container of food he's brought. Last night's leftovers, unheated. He stokes the campfire, searching for coals, but Fen doesn't bother heating up the cold steak. She eats it with her hands, juices running down her chin like the wild animal she is becoming. Though truthfully she has always been a bit fey, a bit *other*. He flicks her forehead. "Savage."

Fen smiles.

"Come back with me."

"I can't, Raffy."

He does not understand why. Not truly. He knows she has been frightened badly, and he knows his dad is not a man capable of acknowledging fear, except to tell them to get it out of the body, to physically force it away, which is not how Fen copes, and so she has come down here to be alone with the animals and the ocean. Raff misses her as he would a limb cut off. That's how they've spent most of their lives, joined heart and mind. He is scared of what leaving this island will do to that connection, but maybe that's stupid; it existed before they came here.

They spot Dominic and Orly headed down the hill, just two little shapes in the distance, a wide gray sky at their backs. After a while the larger of the two swings the smaller one up onto his shoulders.

"How will either of them survive on the mainland," Fen says, not really a question.

None of them, Raff included, know how to imagine another life. Still, he thinks, Fen needs people her own age. Raff wants for her the things he was lucky enough to have found, by some miracle, with Alex. He wants her to forget Shearwater.

He knows, as his dad does, that he's failed to protect her. That he got wrapped up with Alex and forgot to look after his sister. He wakes in a cold sweat sometimes, thinking about this, hating himself.

But she is still here.

"He doesn't want to leave," Raff says, of Dominic.

Fen frowns. "Don't we have to?"

"What would you want, if you had the choice?"

He watches his sister contemplate this. She is looking at the seals farther down the beach. "When I think about leaving," she says, "I almost can't breathe. But staying here is killing us."

"So it's shit either way."

Fen smiles. "We'll be okay. There'll be somewhere else."

But will there ever be, he thinks, another home for the four of them to share? The second they leave Shearwater, Fen, who is younger than Raff but who has finished school years ahead of him, is going to leave them to start her new life, and Raff doesn't know what he can do to stop this. It has always been his job to keep them together, to keep them strong.

"What if Dad won't go?" he asks.

"We have to make him," Fen says.

That's all well and good but there's no making Dominic Salt do anything he doesn't want to do. Stubborn is too small a word for what he is.

"I know you're sure that leaving Shearwater will fix the problem," Raff says, the problem being their mother. "But what if she just goes with him?"

Given that Claire is not an actual ghost but their father's grief and loneliness made manifest, this seems likely to Raff.

Fen looks at her brother, shakes her head. "No, Shearwater is a bridge."

He is impressed by her certainty, but then she's always been this way, sure of things, sure of herself. She has a pure and simple belief that there are ghosts on this island. Orly's the same. He doesn't know what goes on in his dad's head but he's heard Dom talking to thin air. Sometimes Raff feels like the only sane person here.

Orly arrives first, barreling into Raff so their bodies go down in a tangle. Raff laughs as his brother tries to pin him. Fen comes to his aid, wrestling Orly onto the sand, tickling the boy mercilessly. All three stop and brush themselves off when Dom arrives. He looks very serious this morning. What, Raff thinks warily, has gone wrong now?

"I've learned something about our guest," he says calmly. It seems to take him forever to go on. "She's Hank's wife."

Fen looks startled and it reminds Raff of how their dad always says this expression is their mother's. Claire wore a look of perpetual surprise. Raff doesn't remember that, but he remembers his mum's hands very well, the neatly manicured half-moon nails and the slender length of her fingers, even the smell of the hand cream she used to wear. He thinks of this, right now, in this moment, as a way of not spiraling into panic.

"Why's she here?" he asks.

"She's come looking for Hank. I don't know why."

Fen sinks to the ground and rests her head in her hands. "Oh my god."

"It's alright," Dom says. "It doesn't matter. We carry on."

"What if—"

"All we need to do," he says, "is keep our mouths shut."

Raff marvels at his dad's even keel. He is always even, always calm. Raff knows, in this moment, the way he sometimes knows what his sister is thinking, that Fen is imagining the same thing he is: that sudden, calm violence Dominic Salt is capable of, and the damage it can do.

Dominic

The weakest link, of course, is Orly. Keeping the truth of what's happened from a woman with whom he is hell-bent on spending all his time is not going to be easy. I have a conversation with him about what this means. It means slowing down, it means thinking about what he says before he says it. "Is that sinking in? Say it with me, mate: *think about what you say before you say it.*"

But it's not just Orly. We all need to be careful not to slip up, we can't give her any reason to doubt. And what's more, we have to keep her in sight.

Unfortunately there's still the running of the island to deal with, and this morning I need to get a new roof over the remaining solar batteries so we don't lose what little power we have left.

"I can help," Rowan says. I must be looking at her in a certain way, because she adds, "I'm handier than I look."

I consider saying I've had well-wishers offer to help me before and each has been a total failure, the struggle to teach them basic stuff chewing up more time than the task itself. But if she's helping me, I'll at least know where she is.

I take Rowan to the storage shed, a warehouse down at the base that sits a little higher in altitude than the other buildings and thus isn't so wet. It takes me a few minutes to roll open the door because there is a particularly large elephant seal lying directly in front of it, and I have to reach awkwardly over him.

Rowan gasps as she sees what's inside. "Wow."

I had the same reaction when I first got here. It is easy to assume that a remote island would not be so well stocked, but this is a wild place that houses a couple of dozen people and has to be completely self-reliant—I can't duck down to the hardware store if, say, a roof blows off a building—so tools are the one thing we do not go without. At one end of the shed are the basics: hammers, saws, screwdrivers, wrenches, shovels, and so on, with a wall of boxes containing any size or type of screw, nail, bolt, nut, hinge one could think of. Then there are the power tools: drills of all kinds, saws of all kinds, routers, sanders, chisels, a jackhammer, and a welding torch. There is safety gear, goggles, gloves, masks, helmets. There are ladders and wheelbarrows. Painting gear. Cleaning equipment. Light bulbs and electrical supplies. A huge area for materials like timber, glass, cement, bricks, steel. I have work benches covered in sawdust and wood chips and metal vise grips. There is a repair pile and a junk spot. And at the other end of the warehouse is the heavy machinery. Our amphibious vehicle—the Frog—lives here, as well as the quad bike and the tractor, with its various arm attachments.

"Oh man," she breathes. "It must be killing you to leave all of this."

It really is.

I take an angle grinder off the shelf, place it near the door. A couple of ladders, a couple of drills. Rowan is looking through the screws and bolts, making a selection of what we might need. I feel an urge to double-check.

She sees me looking and shows me. "These okay?"

I nod: she has gathered what I would have collected myself. Next she fills a couple of tool belts with the basics—screwdrivers, hammers, protective wear, and so on—then hands me the belt that is clearly mine, the leather old and soft and worn down almost to felt. She tightens the second, newer belt around her hips.

We put our equipment on the back of the quad bike and I drive it over to the sleeping quarters of the research base. There's an almost-new metal roof on this building, and no one lives here now, so I figure it's the best choice.

I send Rowan to one end with a ladder and a large socket wrench, asking her to loosen all the nuts holding the last sheet of metal in place. "You comfortable getting up on a roof?"

She doesn't reply, just heads that way.

I climb up my end and start working on the nuts. They won't budge, as I suspected they mightn't; the salt air here gets into things and rusts them tight. I use my angle grinder instead, cutting through them one at a time, and with each one I am expecting to hear Rowan calling for help. I get through an entire sheet before I stop and look for her. She is at the end, head down, doing something or other. I lower my tools and stomp my way over to her, thinking to tell her not to waste time, there's other stuff she can be doing, only to see that she's got a pile of loosened nuts and bolts.

"How'd you manage that?" I ask, stumped.

"What do you mean?"

"Damn things were rusted on tighter than a duck's arse."

She frowns. "You asked me to loosen them so I did." She shoves her hands into her windbreaker pockets but not before I've seen that some of her fingers are bleeding.

I stare at her with the creeping realization that I have underestimated her. Beyond my wariness there is a tinge of admiration. My mind darts ahead to all the things I have been putting off, things I could accomplish with the help of someone who knows her way around a tool.

I am also aware that this willfulness makes her more dangerous.

Once we have the roof free, we tie the metal sheets together and attach them to the back of the bike, then begin the slow process of dragging them up the hill over the tussock grass. Rowan doesn't know how to drive the quad, so I do that while she walks behind, lifting the sheets out of any tussock they get caught on. It's a painstaking process and she has the harder job. By the time we get up to the solar batteries the day is wearing on, but we stop for a sandwich, both of us ravenous.

"You in construction or something?" I ask her.

"I was."

"Chippy?"

She nods.

"You don't meet many women chippies."

"I've met plenty," she says.

"Was your dad one?" I ask.

"No." She chews and swallows another mouthful. "I like building things."

"Fair enough."

She runs a hand over her short hair, and, watching, I have an urge to run my own hand over it. It takes me by surprise and I look back to my sandwich. Where the fuck did that come from?

"When I was a kid I decided I wanted to build a house," she says suddenly. "So I did what I had to do to learn how. And then I built one."

I stop chewing midmouthful. "You yourself?"

"Me myself."

This casual statement astonishes me. It is the one thing I've always thought I'd love to attempt if we ever left Shearwater.

"That must have been satisfying," I say, and it is an understatement, but I can see she knows what I mean, and that it's enough, for she smiles and nods.

"How about you? Always been a caretaker?"

I shake my head. "I've done bits and pieces of different things. Always been handy, so I take on whatever I can."

"Jack of all trades," she comments.

"Master of none," I finish, and we both smile.

I bite, chew, and swallow, then say, almost reluctantly, "I boxed as a young fella. All the men in my family did."

Her eyebrows arch. "Where are your cauliflower ears?"

"Got lucky, I guess. My dad and granddad both had beauties." I smile, remembering their misshapen bulbous ears.

I stand and brush the crumbs off my jeans, reaching for my tool belt. "Anyway. Day's getting on."

She hesitates. "I don't think I should, I'm sorry."

"Why not?"

She stands and lifts her three layers—wool pullover, shirt, and thermal top—to show me her side. Blood has drenched the bandages around her torso, and I can see it trickling down her hip and under her pants.

"Shit," I say.

"I guess maybe this body wasn't as ready to work as I was." She seems genuinely embarrassed.

"Sit down. Don't give it another thought."

"It'll take you twice as long on your own."

"Yep. I'm used to it." I set up the ladder and climb onto the roof to take my measurements. "The worst part is the lack of company, so you can talk and I'll work."

I spend the afternoon replacing the roof sheets, removing old screws and bolts and tightening in the new, and she tells me about this house of hers.

She describes the shape of it, and the outlook, how she designed it to have windows that would face the sun no matter the time of day, that she wanted a light palace on the hill that would look down over the mountains and the forest, that in this way it sat above like our lighthouse does. She describes the materials she used and the ways she got around not having the strength of several men, how she came up with ropes and pulleys to serve her, how she would do almost anything before she hired another set of hands for the day. She talks of laying the slab, of framing the walls, tiling the bathroom, carving the kitchen benches herself out of timber from the property. She wanted the house to be so well designed and insulated that it would hardly need heating or cooling, making it as sustainable as possible.

I don't realize at first that I am smiling as I listen to her voice. There is incredible love in every word, as there must have been in every movement of her hands, every nail she hammered. I am taken from this bleak and stormy island to live for an afternoon among her snow gums, I imagine myself waking to the morning fog and the sun rising over the hills, the glorious view from her bedroom, and before I know it I am in her bed, and then, accidentally, she is in this bed beside me.

I'm uncomfortable with the intimacy of this thought. Haven't done much thinking of women in that way since I met my wife, and that was a good twenty years ago. Fuck, I've been out here alone too long. I don't even find Rowan attractive.

(Is that true? She wasn't attractive when she was unconscious and had ribbons scraped off her flesh. You'd have to be some kind of sicko to find that attractive. Nor was she particularly appealing after she took two of my children to look at a dead body. But today she is speaking to me in a language I have not spoken in a long time, my mother tongue, a homecoming. Today she looks long and lean and strong in the sunlight. Maybe the truth is more uncomfortable than I'd like to admit, that I don't *want* to find her attractive because I dislike her, because she is a problem, and that I need to be careful of this woman, lest she creep her way into more of the rooms in my mind.)

I ask everything I can think to ask, not wanting her to stop talking, but eventually she says, "Is it something you've thought about doing?"

"It is," I admit, though I've told no one else this.

"Tell me about the house you'd build," Rowan says.

And so we do that instead, I take her to the coast and I tell her of the beach house I have sketched out in my head. I describe its shape and form and what it's made of.

She says, "It's perfect." Then she adds, "But if you build it by the sea, that house will be underwater in no time."

I give her a lift back to the lighthouse on the back of the quad bike because she is bleeding a lot and I'm not sure she'd make the walk. The ridiculous thing is that I do consider it first. I think of the amount of diesel it'll take to drive the bike farther up the hill and then take it back down to the warehouse. I think of what that might mean we can't use it for in future. That's how obsessed I have become with the rationing. That's how frightened I am of running out of supplies. Without a radio to the mainland for help, every single decision is weighted differently, every moment I stand on the edge of that drop, so close to falling.

We arrive at the front door. "I'll get you some fresh bandages. You lie down."

"I'll take a shower first. I feel disgusting."

"Two minutes," I remind her.

"You're kidding. All it does is rain in this place—there can't be a shortage of water?"

"It's not just the water, it's also the power it takes to heat the water. Do you need help?"

"No." She is taking the stairs slowly, with a short rest between each.

"I could carry you, if you—"

"I'm fine, Dom."

"Righto, give a shout if you change your mind. I won't peep at you or anything if that's what you're worried about."

She snorts and goes into the bathroom, closing the door.

A couple of hours later I am cleaning the windows. It's late in the evening but the light carries on for hours yet, and this is a big job, I can't let it get out of hand. Every bit of glass in this place gets covered in thick layers of salt. This salt gets everywhere, into everything, and cleaning it is tedious beyond belief. Along with the wind, it's extraordinarily harsh on buildings. It works away at the windows, at their edges, and despite my almost obsessive efforts, there is always wind whistling its way through somewhere.

"Do you have a needle and thread?"

Her voice startles me and I drop my cleaning rag out the window. I watch it flutter four stories down to land in the grass. I turn my eyes to her, unnerved at how quiet she was and wondering how long she's been standing there. "Yeah, why?"

"Am I obliged to tell you everything I'm doing?"

"Yes."

"So I'm a prisoner, then?"

I step down off my stool. "Think of the island like a military base. Everyone and everything has to be accounted for. Or it all falls apart. Nobody's exempt."

She considers this. "What happens if someone steps out of line? Do you dole out the punishments, Dom? Judge, jury, and executioner?"

I level her with a look. "You're wasting my time."

Rowan grins. "God forbid we waste time! Some of my stitches need redoing."

"And you were just gonna go at it yourself, were you?"

"Yes."

It is my turn to laugh. "Go and lie down. I'll be in to you shortly."

The wound is on her hip, and it's deep. It is the shape of a bite, a large flap of skin unattached to the rest of her. Dark blood is smearing from it, even still, and I wish she'd told me the stitches had busted—at this rate it's bound to get infected and I shudder to think how much blood she's lost.

"Do you know how to sew?" she asks me. She's leaning up on her elbows, looking at the gash.

We've run out of rubbing alcohol—I'll have to get some more from the base, but for now I dab some vodka on the wound to make sure it's clean. "I do."

She winces at the sting. "You ever sewn skin before?"

"Who do you think did all yours? Lie back and don't look." Until now there's always been a doctor down at the base for when the kids needed stitches, and for the one time I nearly sawed off a thumb. Rowan's wounds were my first attempt and I guess I didn't do a very good job. It's not like sewing fabric. Her skin is thick and almost rubbery, and I have to really force the needle through. Rowan makes a sort of growl and reaches for the alcohol.

"That's not for drinking."

"Fuck off, Dom," she says, and drinks it anyway.

When I've finished we both look at the Frankenstein patch job.

"Fine, subtle work," she says, and it makes me laugh.

"You'll have a scar," I say, as I smear petroleum jelly over the wound. There's no avoiding it, given that butt-ugly stitchwork.

"It's just a body," she says, and as I dress and bandage the wound, I am all too aware of this body, and of my hands on the warm skin of her navel, her waist, her ribs. The flesh of her, the *realness* of her. A powerful wanting comes over me and I could lower my mouth to this body right now, I could taste her, and then I think *don't do this, don't start thinking this way, she's dangerous*, and also *she's married, for god's sake*, and then I think *I'm married*, except I'm not, am I?

"You'll need antibiotics," I say.

"I've already been taking them."

"We'll remove the stitches when the wound's closed. You let me know." I head for the door, taking the medical rubbish with me.

"Thanks, Dom," she says.

I wasn't expecting it, or the sincerity of it, and I force myself not to look back at her.

But she ruins it anyway by adding, "And not even one peep! What a gentleman!"

Because we both know I looked.

I wake in the night to the sound of crying. It is not unusual but it kills me just the same. I sit up and put my arms around my oldest son, let him rest his head on my shoulder, and though I love holding him like this, I am panicked at the thought of the inertia within him. If he asks me something, if he wants to talk, I will have no way to help him.

"Let's get to the bag," I say.

"I can't. I don't want to."

"Come on." I pull him up from the bed the two of us have been sharing with Orly; the little fella is still fast asleep as I drag his brother from the room.

It's very cold in the night; the stairs will do us good. Raff stops twice on the way up, leaning against the wall for support, his grief a physical presence he must fight. "Keep moving," I order him, and he does so, putting one foot in front of the other until we've made it to the top.

His punches are weak and listless and no matter what I say I can't stir within him the energy it takes to rid his body of the poison. He is too sad, and I don't know how to help that. I'm good at dealing with his anger, but this sorrow frightens me.

"Dad, I miss him," he says, forehead resting on the bag.

Panic flails again. If I open my mouth I will make it worse. I need his mother here, she would know how to ease this, but I look and look and can't find any version of her, and I am useless.

"Keep punching," I say, and turn for the stairs.

"Dad," he begs, his voice breaking, but I don't know what else to do.

I dream of that punching bag, of holding it like an embrace as it swings gently in the wind. Only it isn't the punching bag I am holding, no, it is a body hanging by its neck from the fuel tanks, its weight almost tender against me as it falls.

———

I wake a second time to a different son wailing. Raff hasn't come back to his room—it is Orly who sobs wildly beside me. I shake him gently awake and then hold him close while he cries. I wonder why I am able to do this with him but not with his brother or sister.

"Just a dream," I tell him. "It wasn't real."

"But it is."

"What is it? Tell me."

I am expecting a body, eaten by fish and birds. It takes some time to get it out of him, but eventually I am able to establish that he has dreamed of a bushfire, and lost in its flames were animals and plants alike. He's never had this dream before; I ask him where it's come from. He explains it is Rowan's land and house that have burned. And I sit in the dark as every piece of timber she erected turns to ash, and that house I inhabited for an afternoon is gone from around me. Orly says, "Everything will burn or drown or starve, including us." And it is as though she has brought these deaths with her from a land so hostile I don't know how I will ever deliver my children back to it.

Rowan

I am greeted, at breakfast, with "You got a screw loose?"

"Huh?" I fumble with the coffee percolator because I have a sense I'm going to need it for whatever this is.

"Telling my nine-year-old that if he doesn't burn or drown he'll starve."

Oh.

I get the coffee onto the stove and light the gas. Then turn to face the simmering man seated at the kitchen table. "That's not exactly what I said. And I told you not to use this table yet."

He lifts his hands to show he hasn't been touching the table. "Why'd you say anything remotely in the realm?"

"He asked. He's curious."

Dominic stares at me, astonished, and then he rubs his eyes. "Jesus," he mutters. "Okay, you don't have kids."

"No."

"Let me explain. You don't just say to them whatever dark bloody thoughts pop into your head."

"He's smart, Dom."

"Yeah and he's a child. You think he's able to cope with the image in his head of animals burning?"

"None of us can cope with that."

"Too right. He woke up screaming."

My insides plummet. "Shit. I'm sorry." I sit down opposite him, holding the coffee mug in my lap. I try to make sense of what possessed me. "It felt wrong. Not to tell him the truth. He hasn't seen the way the world is but he will. He needs to be prepared."

Dominic contemplates this, his eyes fixed on the sky above the sink.

"How do you know what to say and not say?" I ask.

He looks back at me. "Bit of common sense'd do the trick."

I look down at my hands, chastised.

"And just so we're clear. They're mine to prepare—or not—in whatever way I reckon."

"I know that, of course."

There is a long silence.

"I thought it would be the body," I admit.

After a moment he says, "So did I."

—

You think there will be time, but there isn't. You get the sprinkler systems going to drench the ground between the forest and the house, the firebreak or so it's called. You get the hoses ready to fight the flames by hand if you have to. You check that the gutters are clean, you soak them yet again. You pack bags. You pack everything that means anything to you. You think there will be time to pack more but it's already arrived, tearing through the hills. You think you will fight it but you can't, you can see that now. There is no stopping this blaze.

I'd set up the property well. My firebreak was wide enough that it should have saved the house. The materials I'd chosen to build with were about as fire resistant as you can get. I had several huge rainwater tanks hooked up to the sprinklers.

But there were eucalypts, three of them. My favorite trees on the land. They were a fraction too close to the house, but I couldn't cut them down for that. I loved them too much.

In the end everything burned for those eucalypts. Because the flames, they leaped. They flew farther than I'd ever imagined they could.

—

I am going south with Dom and Orly to the seed bank. It requires a look-in every few days—we have to check the temperature now the power's out, on top of which they have this sorting and packing task

Hank left them. I've told them I'm coming, regardless of whether they want me to, regardless of how much it slows them down. We are going to sleep the night in a field hut, which is where Hank mostly lived. I want to see for myself where my husband spent his time. I want to sniff around a bit. Can't shake the feeling Dom's not telling me everything.

If Hank has indeed gone home (there is no home, there is nothing left, where will he go?), then I'd like to know what he went through in his final months here, and why he was so disturbed he sent me those last three emails. They tell a different story.

I think my body is starting to get used to the walking. I suppose it has to. The stitches have helped: there is no fresh blood. This improvement bolsters me.

We make our way south. Dom quizzes Orly on his maths. The kid makes swift work of it, then turns the conversation to the land we walk through. Much of the trek is difficult, and there are stretches so steep we need ropes to help us walk up the inclines. But there are also long tablelands of grasses, with mountains rearing up on either side. Sloping green hills and valleys. Mossy mounds. Rocky sea cliffs. And crystal-blue lakes nestled within it all. It is like walking through an ancient, untouched paradise, and I begin to see the island differently, now that I have trespassed within it. From outside, from the ocean, it is dark and dramatic and uninviting, but its center is quiet, it is peaceful. I can see why they love it here so much.

We reach a lake and above it circles a giant, snowy albatross. "Is it Ari?" I ask. "Or Nikau?"

Dom and Orly peer upward, studying the graceful, gliding arc. "It's Nikau," Dom says. "Males have less gray on their wings."

We watch the bird for a long while. His flight is mesmerizing. I breathe in the cold, crisp air and it reminds me of home.

"Dad calls them the teenagers," Orly says, "'cause they only wake up and start flying around at midday." He seems to think this is hilarious.

"You can swim here," Dom tells me. "If you dare."

"Feel it," Orly urges me. "Take off your glove and put your hand in."

"No way, I'm not that stupid."

"Come on, please? Please, please, please."

I take off my glove, mostly to shut him up. Walk down over the rocks to the clear water. The albatross glides through the crystal reflection on the surface. The cold, when I feel it, hits me in the guts. For Orly, I let out a mighty yowl. He cracks up, goes to his knees laughing, and his dad and I are chuckling too, if at nothing else than his pure delight.

We walk on, skirting a valley so green it's almost neon.

"That's bog," Orly tells me. "Don't go down there, whatever you do. This is a type of fern." He points to a vibrant green plant with many tiny fronds. "I can't ever remember its proper name . . ." He gives his head a hard knock with his fist, looking desperately disappointed in himself.

"I forgive you," I say. "What's that one?"

"These are megaherbs, they don't grow anywhere else in the world except on these subantarctic islands. This one's the *Stilbocarpa polaris*, and it's got loads of vitamin C. The sealers who came here used to eat it so they wouldn't get scurvy." The plant in question looks like a big green cabbage with fanlike leaves, and there is another one beside it with a long stem to hold a bright-yellow flowerhead. "And see this mossy-looking stuff?" Orly says next, indicating a large round patch of what does indeed look like moss. "It's called *Azorella*, and it's a perennial herb, but it's interesting because it gets really windy here—the wind can get so savage, you haven't even felt it yet, Rowan—and this plant has evolved to get pulled underground by its deep roots, so it can survive the harshness of the conditions. Oh, and look! This one here, this pretty one"—he is touching what looks like a purple spiky dandelion—"this is the one I was telling you about, the buzzy burr. Its real name is *Acaena magellanica*. See these tiny little hooks on the seed? This is how they catch onto bird feathers and get carried around the world. A lot of the plants here are like that, they've had to find ways to survive an unsurvivable place."

I peer around at the vegetation. "They're pretty special then, huh?"

He nods proudly, and though I had thought this island's botanicals were sparse and bleak, I realize I just didn't know how to recognize their abundance.

It gets colder as we travel farther south. I see frost covering the ground, and one of the southernmost mountains is completely covered in snow. Cresting a rise brings us out onto a kind of grassy plateau, and Dom tells me I have to move quickly along the worn footpath, because there are baby giant petrels nesting. I do as I'm told, following his pace and letting Orly bring up the rear, and as we walk I catch glimpses of them, fluffy gray dodo-type birds, completely adorable in their little nests among the tussocks.

The freezing wind is whipping against my face, icing my eyelashes and making my teeth chatter. This wind is a high shriek through the snowy grasses and the megaherbs; it is almost wordlike. I hear Orly say, "We aren't going that way, I promise."

I look back at him, thinking he must be talking to me, but I see him gazing into the sky and something about it chills me.

"Keep moving," Dom orders me, voice low, and there is an urgency I'm not expecting. I find my pace again, a little more quickly now, and my heart is racing, I can't help hearing Orly's voice in my mind and the wind is lifting—

We climb down over the edge of the plateau onto a set of wooden steps, and the second we are protected by the cliff face the wind is gone and my panic with it.

What I am met with, instead, is an entirely different world.

A cacophony of sound. A universe of it.

My god. If I thought there were animals before, it's as nothing to this place they've brought me to. Thousands of penguins, both royal and king, squawking and screeching and chattering. Huge elephant seals flopping about, either lying on the sand, using their clawed flippers to scratch their fat bellies or throw sand over their fur, or rearing up in the water, practicing their fighting with great bellowing honks and gurgles. The racket is mind-blowing; I have never heard anything like it. Not eerie and haunted like the wind was but wild and boisterous and full of life. I can't help laughing in astonishment, in wonder.

Even the color here feels richer, the black sand blacker, the mountains a deeper green, the kelp bloodier, and the bursts of color worn by the penguins so intense it's like they're waving flags at us, joyfully calling *here I am!*

"Welcome to South Beach!" Orly announces, flinging his arms wide.

I shake my head, lost for words.

We walk along the water's edge, and unlike up at the pinch, where the westerlies ravage and batter the beach and base, here we are protected, and the water of the bay is quite calm. I can see penguins diving, their sleek little bodies launching in and out. Here and there in the shallows are more fighting seal pups. Chunks of ice bob in the dark water and sit on the sand, and there are spatterings of snow upon the ground. Dark cliff faces rise up on either side of us, shrouded in mist, and again, at these coastal points I feel a sense of the dramatic, but this time I don't feel so uneasy. I feel moved by the beauty.

"Wait here, please," Orly tells me in an imitation of a traffic cop. He uses hand signals to gesture to the penguins and I realize there is a steady stream of royals waddling up and down this particular path between the water and the steep craggy cliff face. They start leaping up the rocks and disappearing behind a curtain of the big green cabbage. "The royal highway," Orly tells me. "They head up through there to their nesting ground, way up in the hills. This is the only place in the whole world where they breed! We can go and look at the colony later, there's still some chicks up there, they're so cute. But you have to keep the road clear for them, so when we get a break in the traffic . . . we go! Go!"

I realize he is waving me through and I trot forward over the highway, past the waddling creatures with their stylish yellow eyebrows. The kings are quite different, much larger and more elegant, with a graceful curve to their long thin beaks and a rich velvety collar of yellow at their throats. One of them waddles right to my feet and looks up into my face, inquiring as to my presence here, maybe saying hello. I gaze down at it, trying to communicate silently, trying to tell it how lovely I find it, but it grows bored and wanders away.

A massive bird angles down over my head and I duck, startled. As it nears the bay it flings its huge flippered feet out and runs along the surface of the water, flapping for balance and then plonking down. It's quite the landing.

"That's a stinker," Orly says, following my gaze. "Rats of the skies."

"That's nice."

"They deserve it," he tells me with a wrinkle of his nose. "They'll feed on anything, the giant petrels. They'll peck out the eyes of baby seals!"

I can't help laughing. "You sound excited by that, you little freak."

"Don't get too close to them, okay, they have a special defense mechanism you don't even want to know about."

"Roger that."

"They spew fish vomit on you!" he cries gleefully.

My nose crinkles. "I thought I didn't want to know."

I've been building to something but I'm not sure how to frame it, Dom's instruction about using common sense forefront in my mind. "Hey, I'm sorry I scared you with the talk of the fire . . ."

"You didn't," he says brightly, then skips ahead.

Righto.

I hurry to catch Orly and we follow Dom, who now waits by the entrance of a cave. It seems to sit at the base of the snowy mountain I could see on approach, and it has, I see as I draw closer, a man-made floor. It's not a cave, it's a tunnel.

The long dark tongue of a tube snakes out. From its end trickles a steady stream of water, making its way down to the sea. He's got a pump in there somewhere.

"Why's there water, Dad?" Orly asks, sounding panicked.

"It's alright, mate," Dom says, not looking at either of us but turning to lead the way down into the dark. "Just the storm."

"But that was nearly two weeks ago," Orly says, and is met with silence.

We follow the piping. It gets a lot colder as we descend the tunnel. The heavy snow parka that was too hot for hiking across the island is now necessary against the icy air. Up ahead, Dom switches on a string of lights; I imagine this would be a terrifying walk for those who suffer claustrophobia. I have never been bothered by small dark spaces, but there is something unnerving about walking down into the depths of this island, with its whispering winds and its ghosts. Easy to imagine there is something very old waiting down here for us. And with the orbs of light to guide the way, the shadows seem ever deeper.

"How long is the tunnel?" I ask softly, not liking the sound of my voice but needing to get a sense of our depth.

"Hundred and fifty meters," Dom says.

I was expecting the water to have dried up, but in fact by the time we get down to the chamber door our feet are submerged. The pump is working away, siphoning out as much as it can, but it already seems overloaded.

"Don't let it get inside!" Orly exclaims.

"I won't, it's okay," Dom says. But there's not much choice, really. He pulls the heavy door open and the water runs in. We're in a kind of antechamber, its walls covered in ice. There are special subzero suits hanging in this chamber and we each pull one over our other layers. They have built-in gloves and hoods that cover most of our faces, but as we open a second door into the seed vault I feel the cold striking straight to my extremities. My fingers and toes, my ears and nose all start stinging.

As an afterthought, Dom asks, "You don't have any heart conditions, do you?"

I stare at him.

"The cold," he explains.

Jesus. I shake my head.

We are in a cavernous space, with tall rows of shelving. The walls here too have thick layers of ice, as in a giant freezer. And that's really all it is. For all of Hank's descriptions, for his passion about this room and what it holds, I never thought it would be so . . . *plain*. It is just a very large, very cold storage unit. I try to hide my sense of anticlimax from Orly, who is gazing at the place as though it's a royal Egyptian tomb filled with riches.

Our breath makes clouds in the frigid air.

"It wasn't purpose-built?" I ask Dom.

"No, this cave has been here a lot longer than the seed vault. It was used by the nineteenth-century sealers. A storage room for their catches."

Meaning once upon a time it was filled with the dead. I can see them laid out before me, all those creatures we passed outside, hundreds of them now lifeless, and it isn't the first time I have resented the vividness of my imagination. I don't like this room. I don't like being down here. Hank told me he was all but living here at the end, and the thought is a crawling thing.

"There's an air shaft at the back," Dom tells me. "I've always thought it was pretty amazing that they were able to drill through the mountain with whatever tools they must have had available to them in the eighteen hundreds."

"Can I've a look at it?"

"Nah, we try not to open the door so we don't lose air temp."

"What is it now?" Orly asks worriedly.

Dom peers at the gauge. "Minus sixteen. It's holding pretty well so far."

This doesn't seem to ease Orly's concern. "That's two degrees warmer than it should be," he points out.

"It'll be fine, mate. There's some tolerance."

Orly and I make our way down a few rows. To distract him, I ask him questions, and as he talks me through what we're looking at, I peer at the containers, all sealed so I can't see what's inside. With a jolt of familiarity I see that some of the labels are in Hank's handwriting. *There is not one without another.* His mantra, and how he taught me to garden. The trick is in working out which plants go together and which compete. A patchwork, a collage. Try this here, try that there. In the vault I take in the vast volume of seeds waiting to be plants and wonder how they would go together, know that nature's experiments are far more sophisticated than ours, and far further reaching. These seeds, given a chance, would all be able to work out how to coexist across the globe, how to feed and help and sustain each other, and there is something truly wonderful about that.

"Dad told me you're married to Hank?" Orly says.

I glance sideways at him. "Yep."

"He was nice, he talked to me about the seeds. We did lessons with him sometimes."

"He told me about you," I admit. "In our calls. He said he'd met a very smart boy with a passion for botany."

Orly beams. It's easy to see how much this means to him. "He told me about you, too."

"What did he say?"

"Just that you guys had a garden."

I smile. "I suppose it was kind of the main thing to say about us."

"What was in it?" Orly asks. "In the nature corridor?"

I don't know where to start, so I begin with the trees that were already there, the snow gums of course, but also the mighty ashes, some of the tallest in the world, and the old-growth alpine ashes, the manna gums, the eucalypts. I talk about the long silvery grasses and heathlands that cover one hill, and I tell him about the wildflowers Hank and I planted from seed to cover the entire stretch of meadow. Yellow billy buttons and white or lilac snow daisies, purple native violets and alpine *Podolepis* with their yellow petals and blood-red centers. Vibrant bottlebrush for the bees and the birds. The alpine mint bush we planted has the most incredible hairy flowers, with geometric designs of yellow and purple on their white petals. I tell Orly about the mosses and the tree ferns that bordered one side of the house, making a kind of rainforest that led down to the stream, where the platypus lived. A delicate silverdollar eucalypt, my favorite of all, right outside my window where the rainbow lorikeets came in pairs to feast. And on and on. So many plants over the years. So many experiments. "The climate there's a challenge," I say. "Not as bad as here but still tricky when you're thinking about what to plant."

"Did things die?"

"Of course."

"Wasn't that upsetting?"

I think about it. "I mean, yeah, a bit. You get disappointed, for sure. But that's the life of a gardener. And it's the life of all plants, right? Of living things? Nothing lives forever."

He frowns and walks on, contemplating that.

I stand beside my husband's handwriting for a little longer. *Rhodo-dendron campanulatum*, he has scrawled on one of the boxes, *Himalayan region of Nepal*. Nearby is *Calluna vulgaris (heather), from Scotland*, and I wonder at how they are organized, as it doesn't seem to be by region. I then wonder at the fate of these two plants. Have they been chosen for life or for death?

It comes over me like the mountain we stand beneath. Now that I am here among them, contemplating the scale of these seeds—there are *so many* of them—I can feel the weight Hank must have been under, I can feel the burden Dom spoke of. How to let go of plants and trees and flowers and shrubs, how to let go of the most exquisite, the most unusual, how to let biodiversity die in favor of what humans can eat. Not only do I feel this weight, I see the future laid out before me. A vast stretch of crops and nothing else, nothing wild or natural, and even these neatly planted rows threatened on all sides by flame and flood. All of earth, a wasteland.

I turn and follow Orly because I don't want that image in my mind any longer.

Father and son explain to me what we are doing with the seeds, how we are referring to the list Hank has left us (so long it is collated in a thick binder), collecting the species on this list and moving them into a new area, then packing them carefully into travel cases. They explain how to find my way around, that the seeds are categorized by taxo-nomic classification—by their scientific family rather than their location. The aisles have letters and the rows within the aisles have numbers, like in a library. As I understand it, the seeds are cleaned, dried, and frozen before being transported, and nobody here can open the sealed con-tainers once deposited. They also explain that we need to work quickly, because the cold is not cooperative; we have a limited amount of time down here before we have to get ourselves somewhere warm.

We work in silence. A malaise has come over all three of us. At one point, feeling exhausted by the scale of this task, I ask Orly through chattering teeth, "How many seeds are in this vault?"

"Oh, I'm not sure how many *seeds* there are, but there's at least three million varieties."

I feel sorry that they have to live in darkness, in this place of death, instead of bursting to life up above as they were meant to. I feel sorry for all the boxes we are leaving on the shelves.

Our time runs out and we head for the exit. On our way my eyes go to the nearest wall. There is a large patch where the ice has melted away, leaving the concrete exposed. That alone is cause for concern, but I can also see that the concrete is flaky. "You're getting concrete cancer," I tell Dom.

He follows my gaze. "Meaning?"

"Meaning moisture. Sooner or later that wall will come down."

"We only have to worry about the next five weeks," he says, dismissing it, but I don't know if that wall's got a month left in it.

There is wet snow falling when we emerge from the tunnel. We lift our hoods against the freezing needlepoints but even this weather is a relief from the cold of the vault.

"You said you're not in construction anymore?" Dom asks me as we walk. Orly is at the waterline with a huddle of king penguins—he is crouched among them, almost the same height as they are—so for the moment we are alone. "What do you do now?"

"Nothing."

"What do you mean?"

I shrug. "I took jobs here and there, but mostly I just . . . worked on my house."

"The house that burned down."

I swallow and look at him.

"Why didn't you tell me?" he asks, and I am surprised to hear betrayal in his voice.

My immediate reaction is to reply that I don't have to tell him anything, but I know how much genuine pleasure he took from hearing about my house, and to be honest I took a lot from describing it to him.

So I try to find better words. "I wanted to pretend it hadn't happened. For an afternoon."

He scratches his stubbly beard. There is a long silence as he thinks about that. "So now what?"

"I don't know."

"Build another house?"

"No."

"Why not?"

"What's the point?"

Dom frowns. "So you have somewhere to live?"

I don't reply. He hasn't understood.

But then he says, "Look, you just have to keep going. That's all. There's nothing else."

"I spent decades working for that house," I say. "Now I just want to rest."

"And what's that then, lying around?"

"I dunno, maybe. Why can't I just lie around? I don't owe anyone suffering or working. So much fucking *working*."

"I have no idea what you're on about," he says flatly, a man who has clearly never not worked a day in his life.

I spread my hands. "Look, I get it. I was the same. I dropped out of school when I was fifteen so I could get a job to support my sisters. My dad had bailed and my mum was . . . She couldn't work. So I did. It's all I did. Backbreaking labor for years and years. I had this insane drive to build a house that would keep my sisters safe. But it was stupid, and I'm sick of trying to make things that will survive this world because nothing can, anymore."

At first I think he's done with the conversation, that he will let that be the end. But then he says, "Most of what I do with my days is repair things that are gonna break again soon. I just fix them and then when they break I fix them again. It's like pushing shit up a hill."

"So why do you do it?"

"Because someone has to, or everything just stays broken."

He walks a couple of steps ahead and I take the moment to watch him, watch a droplet of water run off the tip of his nose, watch another slide down into his beard. I imagine the taste of it, of his skin on my tongue. It startles me, and my foot glances off the edge of a rock and I stumble.

"You okay?"

I nod but I'm not. I know the curl of desire when I feel it.

~

There are two field huts: the closest has a blue door, the farther a red. Hank spent a lot of time living in the blue so that's where we go; his room is small and empty. There are no pictures, no personal items. He has cleared it out completely, so that when I sit on this bed where he slept, I feel no part of him, and when I climb between his sheets there is no smell to bring him back, nothing at all, I am alone. I think of how I have felt this way in our bed too, the bed we shared before it was ash.

In the kitchen there is a small gas camp stove. Dom and Orly are already boiling frozen vegetables in pots and searing fillets of fish in a pan when I return from the bedroom. I closed my eyes for seconds and slept without meaning to. In my dream a child was running from me, hiding in the gaps between floorboards where I couldn't reach him. I have had this dream before, but not for many years. It disturbs me that it should return now.

It stinks of bleach in this cabin. The smell seems incongruent to the feel of the place, and I try to work out why. Is it odd that it's been cleaned so recently, given nobody has lived here in weeks? Maybe Dom and his kids stay here regularly when they visit the bank, and like to keep it spotless.

The snow has turned to rain and it batters the windows. I look out at the ocean. "What's that?" I ask, pointing to the water. There is a kind of shadow beneath the surface. A shape. The waves crash over and around it.

They come to either side of me.

"There was a third field hut," Dom tells me. "Green."

"The sea used to be farther out," Orly says. "But it came in."

"It happened in the night," Dom says. "A storm took out the support posts. Ate the outcrops. The hut sank into the waves."

The hairs on my arms stand on end. "Was anyone hurt?"

"No," Dom says, but I catch the glance between father and son.

Later, in the candlelight. In the little living room, on the couches. We have finished our dinner—too delicious to be called a camp meal—of bream on a bed of garlic greens.

"The time is upon us," Orly says dramatically, grabbing a torch and flicking it on and off beneath his face. "Tonight you will learn about the Shearwater Carver."

"Don't waste the battery," his dad says, so Orly switches off the torch with a huff. But his excitement can't be dampened.

"Get ready to be scared, Rowan."

"I'm ready, Orly."

"Many years ago, on this very island, madness reigned."

My eyebrows arch and I glance at his dad. Dom holds his hands up, like *don't blame me for this*.

"It was not long after the animal massacres had ended and the island had been named a wildlife sanctuary, so the feel of all that spilled blood lingered on. The scientists who came to work here were haunted by it, and by all the animal souls that remained."

I don't know who taught him this story, but he's obviously learned the intonation and the pacing as well as he's learned the words, and I suddenly find myself a bit creeped out.

"That haunting worked its way inside a young man called Carver. It whispered to him every night. The souls told him they needed to be avenged, and that any human life would do, but the more blood spilled the better. One night, when he couldn't stand it anymore, he took a carving knife from the kitchen and he went to each of the sleeping quarters, to each of the researchers asleep in their beds, and"—and here he shouts the last words—"*stabbed them all dead!*"

I stare at him in horror. "Oh my god, you little ghoul."

Orly giggles. "I didn't make it up."

"He heard his brother and sister telling it a few years ago." Dom sighs. "Had nightmares about it for a month and then became obsessed with it."

"Well you've done a good job, kid, I feel very uncomfortable." I look at Dom. "Is that true?"

He shrugs.

"Nah," Orly pipes in. "Can't be. The voices are gentle. They don't want anyone to die."

Later, when Orly has fallen asleep in his father's lap, I can't help asking Dom about it.

"Who does he talk to?"

"He says the animals live in the wind. The ones that were killed." Dom shakes his head slowly. "It scares me sometimes but it's not just Orly. We all feel it here. The blood spilled. Don't you think there should be a price to pay?"

I have felt it too. A stain on the island. But I shake my head, for this is not unusual. "We have a debt to pay to this whole world," I say. "We've slaughtered creatures everywhere."

"Only here it sends some of us mad."

"Including you, Dom?"

"Oh, sure." He looks away from me to the corner of the room. It is empty, but he stares at it. "Me most of all, I'd say."

"Do you hear the voices?"

"I only hear one."

I don't need to ask, but I make myself, because I think hearing it from him will help me to banish the thoughts that have started creeping in.

"Whose?"

Dom looks at me. "My wife's."

"It must be nice," I say softly, "being able to keep her close."

"It's nice and it's terrible."

I think I understand. To miss her less and more at once. To grieve for her less and more. She is balm to his loneliness and a symptom of it. His love for her endures, gives her form. Could mine do the same for Hank?

I know the answer to this, too: I would not let it. I have made my love for him weak, designed it to be so, that it should be easier to cut myself free of.

Wind batters the cabin. I listen to it, trying to pick out sounds within it. I think of Orly's promise to this wind. *We aren't going that way.*

What else is out here?

I return to bed and try to shake off the images in my mind, of carving knives in bellies but also of winds that carry ghosts upon them. I want to feel something else, I want to reach for a shadow of the love Dom has inside him, wish to know if I am capable of it. So I imagine Hank's hands on my body, in his bed I try to feel close to him, but it has been so long since my husband touched me that I can hardly remember the feel of him, and anyway a part of me knows he will not conjure the feeling I want. Instead there is another set of hands, a set I spent yesterday watching as they held tools and worked metal, it's these large, strong hands that I can feel on my skin and it's as if where they touch they smooth away pain, they set alight a different sensation. It is easy in the dark to imagine he is not lying in his own bed, thinking of his wife. It is so easy to imagine he is thinking of me, and vividly enough to drive him from that bed and into this one. And when it's over, when I have drifted down the other side, I am myself again, enough to lie here in shame and know how stupid it is to imagine not an ending, but a beginning.

The trip to the field hut and the seed vault has offered no clues as to why Hank left without telling me. Although that's not exactly true, I suppose. I may not have found anything physical, but I felt it, didn't I? The weight of his grief. The terrible haunting of this island and the burden of his decisions. Maybe it was all too much, the choices he was having to make, and so he boarded that last ship with the rest of the researchers and he sailed home to the mainland, but instead of coming to find me, he left me instead. Maybe he has left me.

———

Hank and I don't often fight, and when we do it's only ever about one thing. Tonight we are already in bed, which means I won't sleep for the rest of the night, whereas he will be snoring within minutes.

"The single greatest choice we can make to reduce our carbon footprint is to not have a child," I say calmly; it is very well-trodden ground for us. We have been over the science so many times it feels embarrassing to wield it at him again, but I don't know what else to say. "How many times have we decided together that it means something to us, to live well. Why would the choice to have a baby be based on a different set of values?"

"Because it's different," Hank snaps. He is the first to sit up and put his back to me, which is how I know this is about to go downhill fast.

"I don't get it," I say. "I thought you were as concerned about this as I am. You've always claimed to be."

"Us not having a child is not going to save the planet," Hank tells me. "What's going to save the planet is nobody using any more fossil fuels."

"That's one part of it—"

"No, that's the whole of it."

"So you don't think we have any personal responsibility?" I shake my head. "Bringing children into this apocalypse is selfish and unethical."

"Fuck ethics," he snarls. He turns on the mattress and now I have to sit up too because otherwise he is looming over me and I need the space, I need my own ropes to retreat to.

"I want a child," he says bluntly. "There's nothing wrong with that and I can't stand that you try to make me feel guilty for it."

"That's not what I'm trying to do," I say, even though maybe subconsciously I have been. I suppose I want him to share my guilt; it is a heavy thing to carry alone.

"Your arguments don't hold up," he declares, and in all honesty he's right, they don't. I can feel them falling away, can see that he won't accept the same lines anymore. It is true, what I've said about the cost of children to the world, but it is not the whole truth, not *my* whole truth. That has more to do with the harm the world will do to my children. That is where the deepest currents of fear live, though I can't say this aloud lest he dismiss it as carelessly as he does my other fears.

"I don't want a child," I say. "I have been clear about that from the day we met."

"Bullshit, you've been umming and aahing about it for years, doling out little morsels of bait to keep me on the line. I don't deserve to be treated like this, Row. It would not kill you to do something for me."

I stare at him. In the years we have been together it has become very clear to me that he does not see me at all. I am actually not so bothered by this; what an ordeal it would be, to be known. But the "umming and aahing"? If this is how he has perceived one conversation we had years ago, then I don't know how to make sense of a single communication we've ever had. It was a time during which I questioned myself and came to realize that the problem was not that I didn't want kids, or maybe more specifically didn't want to nurture, to love, to care for, and raise something. The problem, the true heartbreak, was wanting those things and also feeling like I couldn't in good conscience have them. I thought he understood me. I thought he accepted the vulnerability I battled to show him, I thought we were closer for it, but instead of comprehending the complexity of how I felt—and the difficulty of contradictory feelings—he judged me, misunderstood me, and is now using it against me.

A chasm opens up beneath me and I have never felt so lost in this marriage. Never deeply passionate, never a meeting of hearts and souls—I don't think I believe in any of that—it has nonetheless been sturdy ground to place my feet on, it has been strong, it has been joyful to share a vision, to work toward this home we are building, to love this place together. We have made a life here, have grown and raised it.

Having kids has come up before, of course it has, but in this moment I can see what it will do to us. I can see that for him they already exist and that by saying no I am killing them. One day soon he will hate me for them, for the children.

⌒

The trek home from the field hut is much harder than the hike there. The weather turns bad, the wind chill dropping the temperature to minus five, freezing rain burning our cheeks and noses. It is more a mental game than anything to keep walking, and I am in awe of Orly, who carries on without complaint. There is no other option really—we must get home to shelter and warmth before our muscles seize and we start getting hypothermia.

During the last leg of our journey, the wind dies off and we breathe sighs of deepest relief. Instead a thick fog descends over the island. We choose our steps carefully, staying close so as not to lose each other within it. I reach out and my hand almost disappears. It is eerily quiet without the wind, and even the cries of the birds have fallen away. I listen instead to the sounds of our breathing, to our boots on the grass. Dom leads, Orly between us, me last. Which is why it concerns me to hear footsteps behind me.

I stop and turn but there is no one there. Just a wall of white, so thick I can imagine choking on it.

Something touches my hand and I yelp, spinning around, but it's only Dom, looming over me in the fog.

"Hey, it's okay," he says.

"Fuck," I say, trying to slow my heart.

Orly doesn't laugh, he watches me with concern, his pale blue eyes very bright in this light.

"Stay close," Dom says, and I do, shaken.

Is this how it will feel when the world starts to crumble? Like you can't see where you're going, and at any moment you could lose your people and be left to wander alone?

We hear the sound before the lighthouse appears. The long, slightly mournful notes of a violin drifting through the fog to us. Not a light, but a song to guide us home.

"He's playing!" Orly exclaims and runs inside.

Dom pauses to listen, and I stop close behind, still scared of getting lost even within sight of home. We stand in the white and let his son's music wash over us; it is beautiful and strange and familiar. It takes me a little while to identify the sound it calls to mind: it's whale song.

I am about to say something when I catch sight of Dom's face and see that he has tears in his eyes, and I am so frozen, so mortified to have trespassed into this private moment that I am unable to speak or move for fear that he will remember I'm here.

But he looks at me. Shakes his head, and offers by way of explanation, "I wasn't sure he'd play again."

The eerie sounds continue and we stay to listen. It is a searching call and within the notes I can see the whale, swimming a deep and endless ocean, seeking another of its kind. I think Dominic Salt will stand here for as many minutes, hours, days as his son plays. That bond I can see in the man's eyes, that love, the universe of it: I have chosen not to know that.

I thought I had made peace with that fact—I thought I *wanted* it that way—and then I came here.

Dominic

What I miss most is not any of the things I expected. It's having some-one to talk to about our children. The hilarious things they say and do, the insights with which they blow my mind and the ways they change frequently and without mercy. I need her to help me process and de-liberate and delight in. I want to laugh with her. To be awestruck with her. I want her to look at me in wonder, acknowledging what profound creations we have made together.

What I miss is having someone to look at in moments like these, someone who understands not just the talent or cleverness of our chil-dren but the wisdom, the immensity of feeling they hold within. Instead I marvel at them alone.

Raff

He plays for his sister, because she asks. He doesn't want to, might even be a little frightened of it, but the truth is he would do anything for her.

He sits by his bedroom window to tune the fiddle quickly and with an ear honed over years of practice. He tightens the bow strings. He doesn't hold the instrument high under his chin but rests it almost lazily on his shoulder. And then he plays.

Fen is sprawled on his bed to listen. Raff tries something upbeat at first, because the point of this is to make her worry less about him, but soon the music overcomes, it sweeps him away and morphs into something else, an expression of something obscured. He is powerless to it, in the same way he is powerless to his anger. He wonders if this is what he is, all that he is, a leaf battered by one wind or the other.

While he plays, as if conjured by his song, a thick fog rolls in from the ocean, closing them off from the rest of the world. Fen sits up to watch it, but Raff keeps playing. He doesn't need to see them to know where they are. The fuel tanks.

———

There is no fog on the day it happens. Which makes the sight visible from a great distance; you can see the fuel tanks the entire walk down the hill. He makes this walk alone. Numb. Eyes on the swinging body.

When he gets to the bottom, he doesn't know what to do, can't make sense of the problem, so he sits on the grass beneath Alex.

It takes a little while for his family to reach him. Just Dom and Fen; they have left Orly at the lighthouse. Both his father and sister try to hold him, but he can't, he can't be touched. He just needs their help solving this problem because he can't move either, can't make his mind work.

It is Dominic who sorts it out, as he sorts out everything. For a moment Raff reflects on the feeling of safety this has always provided him with, the knowledge that his father can solve any problem, is capable of anything. Except that he can't bring back the dead, can he. There is that. And from this loss, Raff will never feel safe again.

Fen climbs up the metal ladder to the foot railing. She gets down on her hands and knees and reaches with her Stanley knife, and she starts to saw through the rope.

Dom is waiting on the ground, ready to catch Alex. There is only about a meter drop from boots to shoulder, but that will feel like a lot with the entire weight of a body bearing down on him. There is no other way to get him down; he is far too heavy to try to pull back up by the rope, by the neck—

"Here it goes, Dad," Fen calls.

And it's this image that will stay with him. The sight of Alex's body hanging at a distance as Raff made that long, long walk—that will linger for a good while too, it will be there when he closes his eyes, but it will eventually fade. While this moment, right now, will remain vivid until his last breath. The sight of Alex's body slumping down onto his father, who reaches for it, who takes the weight of it upon himself, and Raff can see that Dom is trying to be so gentle, that it is like an embrace, and it's this that sets Dom off balance, that makes his knees buckle under the weight, and they go to the ground, cradled together.

Rowan

It is nice to have Fen here for dinner tonight, but almost as soon as we've finished eating she picks herself up and draws on her cold-weather gear. I admire the obstinacy of it—there's not much that could get me out into that wind at this time of night.

I look at her father, who is watching his daughter with an expression of longing. *Say something*, I will him. *Reach for her. Ask her to stay.*

It's Raff who says, "Sleep here, Fenny."

Fen glances at her dad, then smiles and shakes her head. "I get so antsy up here now. It's the walls. They make my skin crawl."

"Go straight to the boathouse," is all Dominic says.

She nods and then she's away.

It isn't long before Dom goes elsewhere too, leaving his sons and me to do the washing up. When we've finished cleaning, the boys do some schoolwork. The fog has cleared and the evening is long and violet, and I have nothing else to do so I sit and listen as Orly helps Raff with his readings. He has an *L*-shaped card that he uses to block out everything on the page except the sentence he's focused on. Orly reads it to him aloud and then Raff follows suit. He highlights or makes a note beside the text. It's very slow.

On one sentence Raff stumbles, misreads the words, and stops, frustrated.

"You're doing so good, Raffy," Orly tells his big brother, patting his hair like a dog, and it makes Raff smile, and the moment is so tender.

I wonder at the resources Raff's missing out on, the support systems he can't access on Shearwater. Although, to be fair, you could do worse than have Orly as your teacher.

I go into the lounge and sit on the rug to stretch my muscles. They feel tired and stiff after a rugged two-day hike, and the movements pull at the scrapes and cuts, but I know I will feel worse tomorrow if I don't do this now. My thoughts drift around the lighthouse to each of its occupants: to the boys engrossed in their work, to the man somewhere above. They dart down the hill to the beach, to the girl among the seals. I think of parents and children and the choices they make. I think of my mother. I dream of her often, but I don't usually let myself think of her. Right now I can't help it, because I know what it's like to have a parent who chose an unusual place for your childhood, who chose to expose you to something strange. Once, I thought our houseboat was an adventure. I thought we were lucky to chug up and down rivers and along coastlines, to see country and city alike, to explore bays and harbors but also village ports and stretches of forest. But these moments, in reality, were far rarer than the ones we spent moored in smoggy loading docks among freight ships and shouting cargo workers. Far rarer than the ones we spent alone on a cramped and cluttered boat, waiting for our parents to come back from work or making our way to and from school along busy highways, only me to keep the four of us safe, and me not much older than the others. For a while, I looked back on those years and told myself they were idyllic, that we were lucky. But the haze eventually cleared and I saw it for what it was: survival.

I could never resent my mother for that. I am grateful she did her best. But the accident that came after was something else entirely and the truth is I have blamed her for it; I told myself I didn't but under all the layers of hurt I held a simmering fury for her neglect. And I didn't set foot on a boat again until the day I stepped onto Yen's.

I stand, restless, and decide to see what's at the top of the stairs. I haven't climbed them all the way before, I haven't had the energy, but I've been dying to see the view. By the time I have climbed every step the world is spinning and what I am met with steals the breath I have left.

It is a huge, glimmering lens. I have never seen one so big or up so close. A dazzling pattern of glass cut into geometric angles, designed to project the light within it a long way out to sea. I don't know any more about it than that, I don't know how it functions, but its intricacy is a work of art and I long to see it lit from within.

Belatedly a punching bag swims into view, hanging off to the side, and behind it, Dom. He is red-faced and sweaty. Tape around his hands, some blood on his knuckles.

"It's a beauty, isn't it," he says, of the lens.

I have no words, can only nod.

He hands me his water bottle and I drink.

I take in the windows around us, slowly following their circumference so I can look at Shearwater. From the mountainous peaks to the inky beaches and the research base on its watery isthmus, I can see it all. It's obvious from this vantage that those buildings will be swallowed soon. An island made of the earth's crust and rising as those crusts push against each other, and still not quickly enough to escape the sea snapping at its heels.

"Do you know about Fresnel lenses?" Dom asks me.

"No."

"Come over here."

I go to his side, to the huge glass prism.

"For a long time, lighthouses didn't have these kinds of lenses around their flames," he tells me. "They used reflectors behind the light to beam it out. But then they realized they could get that light to travel a lot farther if they also used a lens in front. Now the lenses they first created for lighthouses had to be big enough to gather all this light and cast it an awfully long way, which made them heavy, so Fresnel came up with this new design. He cut out pieces of the glass like this." Here Dom runs his fingers over the angles in the glass and I watch them, mesmerized by their path as much as I am by the sound of his voice. "Which maintained the curve you need to focus the light, but it cut away the excess material and stopped the light from getting absorbed by the lens itself." He smiles. "I'm not the sharpest tool in the toolbox, so it took me a while to figure all that out, make it stick. But I was curious."

The idea of this lens excites me, the ingenuity of it. "And I guess the ripple of the lens means you can concentrate all these rays into one powerful beam."

"That's right." Our eyes meet.

I take a step away. "Do you spend a lot of time up here?"

"Yeah, the glass takes a bit to clean." He is nodding at the windows, but I can see from the state of the Fresnel lens that he also painstakingly cleans this glass, every tiny angle of it, despite it having no light to beam. "I do find myself up here," Dom adds. "Very often in those first years. I'd order books on lighthouse keeping and sit up here reading of an evening after the kids were asleep. Complete waste of time since I had no light to keep." He smiles ruefully, this man who believes anything that offers pleasure must be time wasted. "This lighthouse was shut down before it had a chance to become electric, so they had to keep the flame alive themselves all night. Most likely there would have been two blokes out here at a time, or a husband and wife, and they'd rotate through four-hour shifts. Four on, four off. Always keeping this light alive, no matter the weather or their own health. Trimming the wicks, keeping the flame clean and strong, making sure there was no smoke, lugging the oil up and down the steps all day and night."

"It sounds arduous. And lonely."

He nods. I can see he is swept away by the romance of it. He walks to the window, looking out at the ocean. "It was such a perilous bloody thing, getting aboard a ship back in those days," he murmurs. "Easiest thing in the world to get lost. Then you had bad weather to contend with. Not just storms but fog, too. Fog was a killer. But they knew they could rely on the two people up in this tower to be calling them in to safety. Their lives were in the hands of the lighthouse keepers."

Dom opens the door and steps out onto the small balcony that wraps the whole way around the tower, which I'm guessing was built so the keepers could clean the windows. I follow him and feel a battering blast of cold wind; my hands reach quickly for the railing, and then I feel Dom's on my back, steadying me, making sure I don't go anywhere.

To the west, the sun hangs heavy on the horizon, staining the sky gold.

"I managed to get hold of an old journal belonging to one of the keepers who was here in 1850." Dom is standing close so I can hear him over the wind. "What struck me was how often he'd hear from the wives of the sailors who'd set out here. They'd contact him—Morse code back then—and they'd ask if he'd seen this ship or that ship yet, and could he please tell them if William was still aboard and healthy, or John, or whoever. And I started to think about how so much of a keeper's job is to wait and watch, holding men's lives in their hands. And I'd dream, in those days, that my wife, that Claire was out on a ship at sea, and I was up here watching for her, and if I could just keep the light on I'd show her the way home."

My chest aches.

"Hell," I say softly, and he leans in to hear my voice. "Instead you got me, washing up on your shore."

Dom studies me. "That I did."

He guides me back inside and closes the door, shutting out the wind.

"A Fresnel lens and a punching bag," I comment.

The bag is swinging as though of its own accord, incongruous in the room.

"Helps Raff blow off a bit of steam," Dom says.

"And you," I point out.

Dom seems uncomfortable with this, that I have found him up here punching. He looks at his wrapped hands. "I don't usually . . ." Shakes his head. "I didn't ever want this for my boy, I wanted his life to be different. But he has such a temper. There's a *power* to it. I try to help him be equal to it."

"By punching?"

Dom looks at me.

I think of Raff's violin song, and of the pain in it. It's not my place to say anything, but we will be gone from here soon and we will never see each other again, and Dom already hates me.

So I say, "Instead of trying to make him as hard as his anger you could help him to be softer than it."

Dom's shoulders sag. He turns away from me. Walks to the window and slowly unwraps the tape from his bare knuckles. I watch him, unsure if I should leave, feeling a compulsion to speak again, to sweep the moment from the room, to undo any hurt I've caused him.

He beats me to it, taking us elsewhere and leaving my words behind.

"Have a look at this," Dom says, opening the Fresnel lens and showing me the lamp within. There is an elegant cylindrical flute of glass around the oil-wick burner. "This little glass chimney would have worked like a real chimney, drawing the hot air up through it, the oxygen feeding the flame and making it burn more brightly."

He takes such clear and simple joy from this feat of engineering, the clever details of invention, and I remember having this precise feeling years ago when I first wanted to understand how things work, and I feel it again now, but it is not this lens I find myself wanting to pick apart, to get to the insides of, to *know*. It is Dominic Salt.

Rowan

For long disorienting moments as I wake this morning I think I am in my bedroom in the Snowy Mountains. I wait to hear the song of the kookaburras, the magpies, I breathe in for the scent of eucalyptus and wattle. Decide I will go down the hill and feed the wallabies before the mist clears, will have my coffee down by the stream and greet the ducks, maybe catch sight of the platypus. And then I wake properly, I open my eyes and find myself a world away, and remember that those creatures are dead.

—

Orly crashes into my room and starts twirling around—trying to make himself dizzy? It works, and he dive-bombs onto the floor in a burst of giggles.

I stare at him. "You right?"

"Get up, come on."

"Why? What's so urgent?"

"Nothing, can't you just come and watch me do my school?"

I rub my eyes. "As riveting as that sounds, I've been given tasks."

"Ohhh. You're one of us now."

Raff stops by the door on his way downstairs. "Yeah, you'll never get another minute to yourself."

The boys do an imitation of their dad. "Hurry up! Hop to! Jobs, jobs, jobs!"

"What do you do around here for fun?"

Orly shrugs. "Watch movies I guess, but only at night when we've finished everything else. But there's no power now, so . . ."

"Jobs, jobs, jobs!" Raff booms.

"Hurry up, you lot!" comes the real voice of Dom from downstairs, which makes all three of us dissolve into laughter.

We spend the day doing chores. While Raff and Orly do school-work (they do an awful lot of schoolwork for kids who are meant to be on holidays), I'm asked to wash the clothes. It dawns on me only as I stare at the dead washing machine what washing the clothes means without electricity. I have to handwash every item, including all the stinky adolescent boy clothes and, worse, my bloodied bandages, which are stained beyond repair no matter how hard I scrub and beat. I rinse everything thoroughly (while also somehow making sure I don't use too much water, as instructed by Dom) and then hang it all out to dry. There's not a skerrick of sunlight so it's likely to hang there awhile. Next I chop vegetables to get the soup on the stove. Have some lunch. Spend the afternoon helping Dom repair a broken window, and then watch him and his boys do their daily exercises, body weights for strength, running up and down the steps for cardio, then boxing at the bag for both. I am dizzy just watching them. But honestly it's been a good day. I like having things to do, I like to feel useful instead of just being an extra mouth to feed. The simplicity of it reminds me of life on the houseboat, of a family apart from the world, toiling away together, and I wish Liv and Jay were here. Although they both hate chores with a passion, so would probably loathe life on Shearwater.

Finally we eat dinner and then Raff says he will take a plate down to Fen.

"We're going with him," I tell Orly. Because these kids haven't had a single moment all day to enjoy themselves.

"Dad too?" Orly asks.

I think about how much I want Dom to join us, and say, "He's not invited."

We pick up Fen on the way, giving her only a few minutes to eat her dinner and then tugging her along. We stop off at Dom's workshop to scavenge a few tools, which horrifies the kids—"We have to ask before we use any of this stuff!"—and then the three of them follow me around the coastline to the second bay, to the penguin barrels.

I hand out the shovels and hammers so each of us has a tool to hand. Then I look at the huge rusting barrels. "I think these have possessed this beach long enough." I swing my shovel hard into one of the old rivets, making an echoing clash of the metals. The penguins hovering around decide to move a little farther away but don't seem overly bothered by the noise.

"These are historical artifacts," Raff protests.

I hit the thing again. And again. There is a rush of power in my hands. An old familiar elation at the thought of building, of creating. I hit the metal until the rivet pops and the two sheets of steel are unhooked from each other. I start taking out each of the joins until I have them completely apart. "You guys get started on that one," I instruct of the second barrel. "I want the sheets separated."

"Why?" Orly asks.

"Quicker you do it, quicker you'll know."

They get to work.

"And while we're at it, let's curse the pricks who made them to begin with," I say, and hear them giggle.

It's hard work because the bolts and screws are so rusted, but I love it, I love the feel of the tools in my hands, I love the manipulation of the materials. When there's time, I have always made art, from little drawings of botanicals to metalwork sculptures and wood carvings; I've come to understand that it's good for my mental health but also, more than anything, I just find it fun. Once we have the metal in pieces, I stand back and look at each, taking in the lines and curves, letting it form itself. They take on a new space, they become. I move pieces to make this new shape. "As we do this part," I say, "we put all our gratitude into it. We put every good feeling into the metal, and we think about the creatures on this island and how much their lives matter."

They move forward, eager in a way I wasn't expecting, and I'm glad for the long bright evenings because soon we have built something new. Something to sit on this beach that doesn't hold death within it, that hasn't been used to commit atrocities.

It is a huge, rudimentary, metal penguin. It is cute and sort of funny, really, which I suppose is exactly what penguins are.

"They'll love it," Fen says proudly, and I know what she means: there is a call in this sculpture, a kind of reaching back for all the penguins who came before, for all the little creatures killed. A message to them.

"I don't think they're bothered by this barrel," Raff says. "You see them hanging about here. We're the ones bothered by it."

"Good," Fen says. "That they don't know. Kinder if they don't know."

I don't tell them I think trauma lives on in animals the same way it is shared through generations in people. I don't say I think everything on this island knows what these fucking barrels were for.

"It won't stay standing," Raff says as we walk home. "Not in Shearwater weather."

"Not unless we weld it," I agree.

"Dad has stuff for that. We could ask him."

"He'd just say it was a waste of time," Fen says. "And then we'd get in trouble for taking his tools."

"Well, he'd be right about the first part," Raff mutters. He has his father's work ethic. All work, no play. Which I guess is fine if you're a man in your forties or fifties or however old Dominic is. It's not fine if you're eighteen.

"What do you plan to do when you leave here?" I ask them.

Nobody answers. I wonder if it's because they don't know, or because they're scared to say their desires aloud.

Into the silence Orly says, "I'm going to visit Mum."

"She's in the cemetery at the top of the hill," Fen explains, which could be anywhere.

I reach for Orly's little hand. He holds on tight.

My intention is to return Dom's tools, carefully cleaned of any evidence of use. But as I near the entrance to his workshop I see movement and freeze.

The rolling door is open and Dom's bustling around in there. I'm about to hurry in the opposite direction, thinking to stash the shovels and hammers somewhere until he's gone. But something stalls me. He is bent over the floor. I glimpse a trapdoor. He's putting something in an underfloor cavity.

I wait around the back of the big building until I hear him walk away, then I wait a little longer to be safe—I have to roll open the door once more and I know he can hear the scrape of metal from quite a distance. I duck under a small gap and close it behind me. It's dark inside and it takes a few moments for my eyes to adjust. Shapes appear. The scent of woodwork, more familiar to me than any other smell. I can see he's pulled a trolley of tools over the trapdoor, which makes my heart thump a little more quickly. Why cover it like that unless you mean to hide it? I slide the trolley out of the way and open the hatch. It's difficult to see. A pile of things. Papers, I think. Books. And sitting on top is a phone. I'm fully expecting it to be dead, so this doesn't surprise me.

It's the phone case that stops my lungs.

Decorated with pressed and dried botanicals preserved between plastic. "Bit on the nose, Row," he said when I gave it to him, but I knew he liked it. I recognize his laptop, too, and there, among the pile of my husband's belongings, his passport.

Orly

Let's talk seed intelligence. Yeah, you heard me.

On the southwestern tip of Florida is a mangrove swamp, one of many. This swamp gets fed nutrients by the ebb and flow of the tide, which is one of the reasons it makes such a rich and diverse ecosystem. Its bacteria feed worms, oysters, barnacles, billions of them, and these feed fish and shrimp, which feed all kinds of water birds, as well as the odd crocodile.

The brilliance of this comes down to the intelligence of the mangrove seeds. Unlike most plants, which need soil to germinate, the mangroves have evolved a special way of helping their offspring survive. Instead of dropping the seeds like most plants do, they germinate while still attached to the parent tree (Dad would love this; if he could keep us attached forever I think he would), and then the seedling grows within the fruit, fed by photosynthesis, until it's ready to drop into the water.

This seed is more buoyant than other seeds. It knows where it's going and how it will get around: it's going to use the current. The seed travels along the Gulf Coast, looking for its new home. But something doesn't feel quite right to this seed, it detects some deficiency in the environment, some warning that the conditions aren't quite right. So it carries on, traveling around to Louisiana. The marshes here are healthy. The seed decides to stay. It physically changes its density—yep, you heard that right—so that it floats vertically instead of horizontally. This way it has a chance to lodge in the mud and send out roots.

But it doesn't lodge. It tries, it fails. It carries on. It changes its density back, so that it can float more easily and continue its search.

It has now altered its own form twice, by its own choice, in order to survive.

It travels on, carried by the ocean currents, down into Mexico and farther around the Gulf. At last it reaches the Yucatán Peninsula, so mangrove rich it's an oasis for the seed, a place to make a home. The seed changes itself yet again and this time it works! This time its long body is caught in the mud and able to take root. It can grow as part of this new mangrove swamp, which is so crucial to the health of the wetlands. And I think it must be relieved, I think it's earned its place in this ecosystem, this little seed; after all, it's been traveling and changing and searching for an entire year.

Is this how you feel after being swept in on a current? Will you change shape and put down roots? Or carry on in search of somewhere better?

Dominic

In some ways, in certain moods, it feels a little like Orly is my first child. I was there with Claire for the birth of Raff and then mind-blowingly soon after for Fen. I was there in the thick of it, for every feed, every nappy change, every illness. Of course I was. But I wasn't Claire, who knew what cracked and bleeding nipples felt like, who had to sit on a rolled-up towel to avoid putting pressure on the episiotomy stitches in her vagina. And before all that, who endured the morning sickness that lasted six months and made her vomit all day every day. Claire, who felt the postnatal depletion and depression, who was an alien in her own stretched and flabby body, who once shat herself because she couldn't get her pants off while also holding a baby to her breast, a baby that sucked and sucked and took all her vitality. Claire, who also had the hormones and the deep instinctive body connection and the bond that went deeper than her foundations, who had love like she invented it.

Parenting, for her, was in the body.

Problem is, I thought it was *only* in the body, and that's why she was better at it than I was.

What a mystery it was to me then: how she knew what temperature to keep the room overnight and what to dress the babies in so they'd be warm but not overly so, how she knew when to give paracetamol for a fever, and what times they needed to sleep depending on how old they were, and when to bring them into our beds for cuddles and when to be strict about sleep skills, and what the fuck sleep skills are, and not to use soap in their baths, and to try olive oil for the cradle cap, and which foods were safe for starting solids, and exactly how to serve them. How did she know all of this? It must have been built in, that's what I thought.

When Orly came along and it was just me, I realized how she'd known. She'd fucking learned. She'd had to, because somebody had to keep the babies alive, and so she bloody well got on with it. And now I was going to have to do the same, except without any backup, and the burden of this division of labor became astoundingly, mortifyingly clear to me. Oh, how I had coasted upon the back of this woman, deep in the trenches with her and also very happy to let her learn all the things and know all the things. How many times did I ask her which sleeping bag I should put the kids in? Or where the swaddles were? How many times did I pass over a crying baby, disappointed but also— come on, let's be honest—*relieved* to know that they just wanted Mum and that I would never truly be the last line of defense?

Then she went.

And here I remained, and it was just me and baby. I did not know how I could ever be enough for him. I thought seriously of finding another home for him. I told myself he would be better without me. That I would break him in some way. Because he had not come from my body, not in the same way he had come from Claire's, not in a meaningful way.

And then. There they were. Eight and nine years old. Having lost their mother and yet stepping forward to save me, teaching themselves what to do so that I wouldn't have to do it alone. I knew then that it was not me against the little fella; there were no lines of defense. It was the four of us together, always. Maybe Raff and Fen did more than kids ought to have to, or perhaps it is simply the nature of us, that deep in our cells we are nurturers. They changed nappies and fed bottles, they learned how to clean vomit out of car seats and scoop poo from bath-water, they rocked him burning with fever while I drove, maddened, for the midnight medicine. They figured out how to get him to sleep when he wouldn't go to sleep. But they also cuddled and played and laughed and sang, they read and told stories and they loved him. Purely and without resentment, and now he does the same for us, he nurtures and loves us. And within the sphere of my children's courage, of their generosity of spirit, I found a way to be more. To ask of myself more. We forged an unbreakable four.

For the first time in our life together, our life of four, I have started, against all my better judgment, to wonder what it might be like to add another, making five. Would the capacity of that love find its limit? Or would it soar?

Tonight, under the covers with Orly in my arms and his breath tickling my chin, I ask him what he hears in the wind.

"They're saying we tried to fix something that can't be fixed. Not without loss."

I pull away a little so I can look at his face. He is unbothered. This is why I don't usually ask him what the voices say—because his answers are terrifying.

"Are you frightened of them?" I ask.

He shakes his head. There is that, at least.

"What do they mean, tried to fix something?"

"With Rowan on the beach," he says, and I can hear the hesitation that means he wasn't supposed to tell me. "We pulled down the barrels and turned them into something else."

"What?"

"A big red penguin."

I find myself smiling, and it hurts, abruptly, that they would not want to tell me about doing that. That they wouldn't invite me to help them.

"Is Mum here?" Orly asks me.

Perhaps I should lie. Is this damaging him?

In the end it feels cruel to keep her from him. "She's on your other side. Her hand is in your hair."

He sighs, letting his eyes fall shut. The wind speaks again and this time I understand it. *You would have to let her go.*

———

Rowan is very quiet over breakfast. I catch her staring at me. The sensation of that gaze is a prickle. She has huge dark eyes and they remind me of the bottomless eyes of the seals. I find myself imagining again what her hair feels like, I imagine reaching out and running my hand over the short spiky ends of it, right now while sitting here at the brekky table.

"Dad?" Orly asks and I blink.

"Yeah?"

"I think I've decided on Tasmania."

"Huh?"

"For when we go back. It's the diversity of the vegetation," he explains. "The *Lomatia tasmanica* is a clone plant that only propagates by dropping branches and creating genetically identical plants, and it's been doing this for forty-three thousand and six hundred years."

I stare at him. "So?"

"Don't you want to live near that? It's incredible!"

I can't help laughing. "Yeah, sure. Wherever you want, mate."

"There's loads more interesting things, too. The mountain ash is one of the world's tallest trees. There are forests of seaweeds in the reefs. Heathlands and moors, ancient rainforests—"

"I believe you," I tell him. My eyes are on Rowan. She's not listening, she's worrying about something, and her face is cold like I've never seen it.

She stands abruptly. "Going for a walk."

"Where?" I ask.

She gives me this look like it's none of your damn business, which it's not, only it makes me nervous, her roaming around the island.

"Can I come?" Orly asks her.

She shrugs, heads off.

Orly looks at me for permission. I nod, because if he goes with her then he can report back later, and I do feel guilty about turning my child into a spy, but he's happy, he bounds off after her.

Raff and I sit quietly, finishing our breakfast. He is on his third bowl of cereal, a bottomless pit. I remember that feeling. An aching hole you could never fill no matter how much you ate.

He looks at me. "Are we really not gonna tell her?"

I don't know what to say. He has such a leveling gaze. A dismantling one.

"There's bad, and then there's bad," he says. "I think not telling her is *bad*."

"We don't know her," I say simply. "We don't know what she might do." Or what kind of threat she could become.

I run my fingers over the smooth finish of the tabletop. It feels like silk. The hours she must have spent to transform the rough, chipped timber into *this* . . . I am breathless anew, as I am each time I walk into this room and see this work of art sitting so casually in our old kitchen. I'm a handyman, I slap things together, bash in a few nails, hope they hold. Rowan is a craftswoman. And it's true, we don't know her, but there is surely a clue in this table to the truth of her.

Raff finishes his breakfast by drinking the remaining milk straight from the bowl. I should tell him it's bad manners but I don't have the energy.

He says, "Maybe we'd better get to know her then," and he is right; he is much cleverer than I am.

Rowan

I have an idea, based on the fact that there's a lab at the base. When you have watched a million hours of TV you know what luminol is. I *don't* know if there's likely to be any in this remote lab but I'm hoping the attitude to stocking it was the same as for the warehouse: prepare for anything.

Orly chats while we walk, babbling on about the plants in Tasmania, while I stay focused. Try to stay focused. I must be cold. Because if I am right, there can be no more of this chat, no more laughter. I can't enjoy his knowledge or his passion, his sweetness, his tiny hands, I can't enjoy him. I can't be warmed by Fen's open smile or her courage or her freckles. I can't feel worried about Raff's temper or moved by his violin. I can't think about the salt on Dom's neck or the way his beard might feel against my cheek or his secret gruff kindness or the way he loves lighthouses. I can't do any of that anyway—I have always prided myself on being loyal. But if I'm right about them having caused harm to my husband, then I really can't do any of it.

I feel quite sick as we walk, actually, and the pain seems to have returned to my body.

"Are you okay?" Orly asks on a rare break from his litany. I think maybe he is anxious about something and it's why he can't stop talking.

I nod, but my teeth are gritted.

"Are you gonna leave?" he asks me suddenly.

The question annoys me. "How am I meant to do that, Orly?"

"But would you, if you could?"

I look at him, wondering if he's lost his mind. "Yes. Of course."

"Oh." His eyes drop to the ground as he walks.

Don't console him, I tell myself. Don't explain it or make excuses. It will be easier on him in the end if he doesn't start to hope.

I try to figure out how to ask him something without scaring him. I shouldn't be asking him anything, he's nine years old and there's that common sense to be remembering, I ask anyway, I'm desperate. "Hey, you know how your dad and Hank didn't get along?"

"Yes they did."

"You told me they didn't. That Dom saw through him, remember?"

"Oh, well. Yeah. But Dad doesn't really make friends."

"Okay." I try to reframe my question. I get the feeling he's been told not to talk to me about any of this. "Do you think your dad might have been angry with Hank, for any reason?"

There is a look of genuine panic on his face. "No, why?"

"Is your dad an angry man?"

Orly stops walking. "Why are you asking that?"

"Sorry."

"He's not angry. You don't know him at all if you think that."

I meet his eyes. "I'm sorry, mate. I didn't mean anything by it."

I turn back to the grassy path, thinking that maybe Orly will go home now, but I hear his footsteps behind me.

"We're looking for something called luminol," I tell him as we go through the lab stores. There are three elephant seals *inside* the lab building—whether the door was left open or they *pushed* their way in, I don't know—but they barely glance at us as we pick our way around them.

"What's that?" Orly asks, reading the labels of jars and jugs in the dim light. Even during the day there's not much sun creeping through the small windows.

"It's a chemical you can use to detect other things."

"Like what?"

I shrug. "Copper or iron, I think. Cyanide."

"And why do we need it?"

Because it also detects blood.

"Less chitchat, more looking."

I find it eventually at the back of a cupboard, already in a spray bottle. I've got no clue if it will work, but I'm going to give it a try.

As we emerge into the sloshing seawater my eyes catch on something in the distance. Way out in the ocean is a splash, a kind of spray. "Look," I say, pointing.

He squints. It happens again. "Whales!" Orly cries. "Come on, we gotta tell Raff." He sprints off up the hill, vanishing into the tussock, and I am left to trudge after him.

Now that I have what I was looking for, I need a way back to that field hut. I will have to prepare myself to make the walk alone, but it's going to be hard to explain why I need to. Maybe I could just go. I certainly can't risk anyone finding out what I intend to do there.

It's the smell of bleach. It was so strong. It's been bothering me.

And I am trying to come up with a reasonable explanation for why Dominic has hoarded all of Hank's personal possessions, the things he would need, were he to have headed home as they told me. But I knew it the moment I met the guy: Dom's lying to me. And maybe it's not as bad as I have started to fear but either way I need to find out.

Raff is already pulling on a wetsuit when I finally stagger back to the lighthouse, luminol tucked away in my pack.

"What's happening?" I ask, hovering by the door to the boys' bedroom.

It's Orly who answers, as Raff is busy gathering what looks like audio equipment. "Raff records whale sounds."

"Did you see a dorsal?" Raff asks his brother.

"Too far away."

"How many blows?"

"Two? No, three."

"Was it tall or low and puffy?"

"Tall. But a bit puffy. Actually maybe it was low."

Raff laughs. "Thanks for your specificity."

"How do you get to them?" I ask as he thunders down the stairs.

"I'll take the Zodiac out." He glances back at me. "Want to come?"

God no. Going out on that little boat again is the last thing I want to do. But maybe I can convince him to take me back to the field hut. The trip's much faster by boat. "Okay."

"You'll be cold. We might be out there awhile."

I hurry to pull on every layer I can find, including the waterproof outer layers. "My clothes" are a cobbled-together wardrobe of extras from Dom, Raff, and Fen, which was generous of them, given they don't have a whole lot of clothing themselves, and I appreciate it immensely, but nothing fits me properly and I am only just starting to figure out what layers and items are required for which activities. For this one, I'll need just about everything. Dressed this way, it's boiling hot inside, so I head for the front door.

"Where are you going?"

I look back at Dom, who is peeling a mountain of potatoes at the kitchen table.

"There's whales!" Orly tells him.

Dom grunts in understanding. "And he's taking you?"

I nod. I think I am surprised there is no protest, no reminder of the chores Raff and I should be doing. Maybe whales trump the rest.

"Can I go too?" Orly asks.

"I need your help with the soup, mate."

Orly's shoulders sag but he doesn't complain, plodding over to lift a second peeler.

Dom glances at me again, maybe he can feel my frostiness. He says, "You watch out for my boy, alright?"

"I think he'll be watching out for me."

"All the same."

I swallow and nod. I will try.

Back down the hill we go. God I am over this hill. It's not just that it's a hill, and it's painful to go both up and down. It's also that it's so loud. It is a tunnel for the wind to shriek along and the more I traverse it—the more familiar my feet become with its lumps and grooves, its gullies and ditches—the louder it gets. I find myself dislodged, lifting my eyes to orient myself with the sea. I find myself hearing movement behind me and turning to see nothing but rustling tussock. I wonder if this is how it started for Hank. I wonder if everyone on this island is descending steadily into a shared psychosis.

Fen doesn't come—she is on seal pup duty—but she waves to us from the other end of the beach. Raff and I head out in the Zodiac. I sit at the back this time, where there is less spray and movement. Still, I feel a low queasiness at the thought of how close the ocean is, how flimsy this craft.

"What do you think it could be?" I ask Raff.

"I've learned not to trust Orly's clues," he says with a quick smile.

"But what are the options?" I press, wanting to get him talking.

"Plenty of things."

"*Oh*, I see, fascinating."

He relents. "Down here we get a mix of toothed and baleen whales. We'll look at where the dorsal fin is, that'll help identify it. Any markings on the skin, if it's smooth or wrinkly. What its blow is like. How many there are. Certain whales travel in large numbers, others like to be solitary." He adjusts his trajectory, eyes scanning. "Pilots for example are pack whales—they follow a single leader, and they're so loyal they'd even follow it to their deaths."

I think now that he's started, he's quite enjoying talking about them.

"Orcas are matriarchal—they hunt in packs and come up with intelligent ways of herding their prey into danger zones. It won't be a beaked whale, I don't think. They're very elusive, and most of what we know about them is from dead ones. Same with sperms. It could have been a fin or a minke. Or a sei, or a right. I dunno, there's loads."

"What are you hoping it'll be?" I ask.

He shakes his head as if refusing to jinx it. "They've changed their routes a bit in the last few years," he says. "I've noticed they come in closer than they used to."

"Less food for them, maybe."

I realize belatedly that we are heading straight out to sea, directly away from the island. Things inside me go to liquid. I grip the rope handles with white knuckles and force my mind away from the great expanse of ocean beneath me.

"There," Raff says, pointing, and I follow his finger to a smattering of dark, swift birds flying low over the water.

"What are they?" I ask.

"Sooty shearwaters," he explains. "They often follow whales to feed." Then he adds, "They breed in huge colonies, but they're smart— they don't visit their nests unless it's a moonless night, so they don't lead predators to the babies. Sometimes they're called moonbirds."

"You kids are all certainly full of interesting factoids," I point out. "You'll be good on trivia nights."

Raff thinks about this. "Yeah. I guess Dad's always tried to encourage us to be curious about the world."

I watch the moonbirds. They fly fast and low over the water, and their crisp, sharp wings dip from side to side, almost cutting through the waves. Beneath them I glimpse a number of fins emerging smoothly.

"Fin whales," Raff smiles. "They travel in huge numbers."

He is right, there seem to be dozens of them. The clear blue ocean is broken all over by sliding backs and dorsals and pectorals. Raff keeps steering closer to them and my excitement shifts to fear.

"Stop," I say. "Don't get too close."

"They won't hurt us," he says.

"Maybe not intentionally!"

Raff ignores me and my heart is lurching as he guides us into the pod. A fin rises up beside us, like a wave. I gasp, peering over the edge at the sight of thirty or forty enormous whales swimming beneath and around us; one of them glides directly below our boat, tilted so I can see that the underside of its mouth is pale and striped, and it's opening that mouth wider and wider to swallow what must be tons of water and krill. Raff gets his recording equipment and holds the microphone under the cold water. The terror does not leave me—any one of these creatures could breach a fraction too close and we will be capsized and I can see our tiny bodies down there among their enormous ones, I can see us battered and crushed into the depths. But they don't harm us, whether by luck or design, they swim on and away, and soon they have left us, and Raff doesn't chase after.

"You don't want to follow?" I ask.

"Sometimes I think it's better not to bother them too much."

In their absence he goes quiet. The joy seems sucked out of his face, leaving him tense.

"Are you okay?"

He starts the engine and steers back toward land.

I will only have minutes now. "Can you take me to the seed vault, Raff?"

"Why?"

"I want to see where my husband worked."

"Dad already took you, didn't he?" There is that shrewdness again, he is dissecting me with his eyes. Suspicious.

"I saw something I didn't like down there. Your dad ignored me, but I need to take another look."

"What was it?"

"I'll show you."

"We can't go south without letting them know," he says.

"Do you think he'll let you?"

Raff considers me for a good long while. Then without a word he changes course.

"It's called concrete cancer," I explain, pointing to the flaky patch on the vault wall. "It means water's getting in around the steel reinforcing, which is rusting and expanding and weakening the concrete. It'll be worse than what we can see. This entire wall is about to come down."

"This wall here?" Raff repeats, pointing at the eastern wall of the seed vault.

"That wall."

"But that'd cave in the whole place."

"Yes."

"You told this to Dad and he didn't care?"

"He's hoping the ship will arrive before that happens."

"But you don't think so."

"I dunno." I stretch my aching legs as we peer at the wall.

I can't imagine how Hank could have worked here every day and not have noticed this issue, and if he did, I can't imagine how he would just up and leave the seeds here to drown.

We stay the night in the field hut. Raff wanted to head home, but I convinced him it wouldn't be safe to travel at night and I guess I was right because he conceded. We didn't bring any food and the hut has been cleaned out of everything except a few muesli bars, so we sit, hungry and cold, watching the long twilight.

"Remind me why this was a good idea?" I ask through the chattering of my teeth.

He grunts.

I don't know when I'll get the chance to spray the luminol. I guess I am waiting for him to fall asleep, but he is upset about something. I can see the whites of his knuckles, the clenched jaw.

"Orly mentioned your friend," I say. "Alex."

Raff doesn't react.

"Do you miss him?" What a dumb question. Raff doesn't bother answering it, which is fair enough. "Is he your boyfriend?"

"We weren't together."

"Oh sorry. I got the wrong idea."

He shakes his head, frustrated. "It's just we never talked about that. It seemed too . . . small." Like an explosion he is up and pacing the tiny room.

"Talk to me," I say.

"I just need the bag," he mutters.

The punching bag. "Why do you need that?"

"For when the poison comes. You have to punch it out."

I frown, searching his face. "That's what your dad taught you?"

Raff nods.

"Okay. Well. We can just talk. It might even be better."

He is silent for what feels an eternity. Then he says, "Dad doesn't like to talk."

"About what?"

"About anything that matters." He thinks and then amends, "About anything that hurts."

I consider this. "Your dad's from a generation of men who were taught that speaking about their feelings was a weakness. Which means they didn't really learn the skill. And it is a skill, you know. Figuring out how you feel and then articulating it. It's not easy. But I think it's important to try or you just . . . there's too much to carry on your own, you know? Especially when you're bereaved."

"What's bereaved?"

"When you're grieving. When you've lost someone."

"When I think about her," he says, and I can hear his voice wavering, "when I see something amazing, I feel this rage. That she doesn't get to see it. She would have *loved* those whales. It isn't fucking fair." Without warning his fist slams into the glass of the window and leaves a snaking crack down its center. I watch him warily, but that seems to be the end of it. He rests his head on the glass and breathes deeply.

After a few minutes have passed, he dashes the tears off his face but can't look at me, mortified by the display. "Sorry. I didn't mean to . . . I don't want to frighten you."

"This isn't gonna work for you. You can't just punch things," I say. "You have to find something else."

It unsettles him, the thought that I could be giving him contradictory advice, and maybe Dom will be angry with me again but right now this kid needs help.

"I want you to know something," Raff says suddenly, and a hardness has come over him, and he is looking at me directly now, almost provocatively. "My family has been really lonely. My dad in particular. So you need to be careful with them."

"What do you mean?"

"I mean they might be inclined to trust you."

My heart picks up. "Why shouldn't they?"

"Because you're married."

I stare at him, confused. "Are you . . . Do you mean you're worried about us getting too close?"

"Orly's always wanted a mum."

"Oh Jesus." Something in me rears back in horror. "You don't have to worry about that. I'm not built to be a mother."

"And Dad?"

"What about him?" I know he's trying to piss me off, to push me away, that the intimacy of the last few minutes is more than he knows how to handle—I'm aware of this but it's still working because I think he's hit upon a genuine nerve.

"You're not planning on seducing him?" Raff asks me.

I burst out laughing. "Piss off, kid. You need to get off this island." I go into Hank's bedroom and close the door, and I am astonished to see that my hands are shaking.

—

I love my husband. I do. Trying to distinguish between loving him and being *in* love with him feels petty. I see his faults and I see what we lack. I can see that we fractured, and I know we both feel betrayed by the other. There is distance between us now and distance is like concrete cancer. With time it's fatal. I may not know what will become of us, but that does not mean I plan on "seducing" anyone else.

It does not mean I don't care if he's been murdered.

I wake in the night from another dream of the child's footsteps running away from me, disappearing between the floorboards where I can't reach him. The fact that I've dreamed the same thing twice in this room is as disturbing as the dream itself.

I take the spray bottle out of my pack and creep into the kitchen. Raff is asleep in the other room, but I don't make a sound in case he's a light sleeper. I look around at the space, not knowing where to start. The bleach smell is pretty much gone now. I spray the sink first but the luminol sits invisibly on the surface and then evaporates. I spray the bench tops, same again. But when I spray the floor, the liquid turns a bright, luminescent blue. I spray and spray, and the blue gets brighter and thicker and covers the entire kitchen floor and I realize I am wiping my tears with one hand and squeezing with the other, and I stop only when the chemical has run out.

"What's this?" a voice says, and I whirl in fright. Raff is standing in the dark, staring at the blue floor. "What is that?" he demands.

My mind races, trying to think what to tell him, but I can't come up with a lie fast enough and then I think fuck him and fuck Dom.

"It's blood," I say.

Fen

Under the surface it is almost pitch black. She is sitting on the ocean floor, counting the seconds. Her hair drifts around her in eerie tendrils. Shapes move, mostly kelp. And then something different slides into her eyeline. A large mass, drifting down from the surface. It's a sleeping elephant seal, its body relaxing into its deep dream state and moving into a gentle, downward spiral. Fen watches its passage until it bumps into the ground and settles there.

She wants to stay here with the sleeping seal, wants to know what it dreams of. But her lungs. She kicks off the seafloor and rises to the surface for air. It's too cold now, she shouldn't swim at night, but it is like entering a state of bliss she can't compare to anything else.

Fen emerges from the sea with a shake of her heavy, tangled hair. Unlike the elephant she saw, the furs are all up on the beach, draped over each other in huge mounds.

She scans the ocean, the horizon, looking for any sign of Raff and Rowan. She's been watching since they went out this afternoon, and she doesn't intend to give up the vigil, but she needs to get warm. She walks back to the boathouse. Peels off the wetsuit, towel dries herself, and draws on her thermals. On the windowsill are her mother's things, the items she's stolen from Dom. Something compels her to take the jewelry—the silver necklace, the earrings, and the three rings—and put them on. She feels the weight of them against her skin. They are warm, probably because she is so cold. Next she takes the silk scarf and drapes it around her neck. Then she draws her finger over her lips as though painting them with lipstick, paints imaginary eyeliner onto her eyelids. Is this what she will be expected to be when she gets back to the mainland? She feels like a child playing dress-up. She won't fit in, she knows this. Eight years is too long to expect a child's friendships to hold on, so she has no real friends waiting for her. She doesn't belong on the mainland, desires nothing about it, but she can't stay here. She's not a child but she isn't really an adult either; the last year has proven that. She is not her mother, not beautiful like Claire was when she wore these things.

She peers around the little shack, looking for any sign of her, any light or shadow, even a faint impression, but there's nothing. Even with the possessions to tether her, Fen's mother doesn't appear to her like she does to Dom.

Fen comes to her senses and takes off the scarf and the jewelry. She dresses and returns to huddle among the seals for their warmth, continuing her watch for the Zodiac. She isn't sure what time it is when she sees the shape of her father walking along the beach toward her. But it fills her with dread because he only comes down to her when things are really bad.

Dominic

When they don't come back in the night I start getting scared. I walk to the beach, force myself not to run. Fen is among the seals, a shape just like theirs in the dark. She rises, shadowy and almost monsterly with her insect-long limbs, and I think, not for the first time, what complete madness it is that she lives down here and that I let her.

"You're not supposed to sleep on the beach," I remind her, but I'm too distracted to press the point.

"They headed south hours ago," she says, pointing at the horizon. "I've been watching for them." She must see the terror in my face because she says, "It's okay. They went exploring. They'll be back."

Or they are both drowned.

I stay with her on the beach until morning. The sun never completely disappears; even in the deep dark of night there is still a band of warm light along the horizon. We sit on the sand and I think about how cold it is down here, how inhospitable, and as the sun rises I am distraught because this is how my daughter spends her nights, cold and alone among the animals, and how did it go so wrong. I am the monsterly thing. I don't know how to reach for her, how to hold on.

"Orly said he chose Tasmania," she says, the first words either of us have spoken in hours.

I nod.

"So is that it then? That's where we'll go?"

"What do you think?"

She shrugs. "I don't mind where."

"Raff said the same. Orly wants plants. Forests. Trees."

"What about you?" she asks. "Where do you want to be?"

I don't know how to explain that I can't leave, and must. That I can't be without my children, but that I don't know where we could possibly go that could ever be like it is here. So I say nothing and she doesn't understand my silence and the gap between us gets even wider.

"We can't stay here," she says.

I am surprised because I've never admitted to wanting to stay, but I guess my kids know me better than that.

"Even if the ocean wasn't rising, we still couldn't stay here."

"Why not?" I ask her. "You love it here."

"I know. But it's too easy for you to hang on to her."

I feel my face warm and look away.

"Dad. You've gotta let her go. I can't watch you like this anymore."

"It's got nothing to do with you," I tell my daughter, which is not true, it is cruel in its untruth, but it does what it needs to, it ends the conversation.

Orly makes his way toward us, greeting each of the penguins he passes with a polite, "Good morning, sir. Morning, madam."

He barrels into me and I hold him against me. His long white hair gets in my face and I absentmindedly start plaiting it for him.

"What did you and Rowan do in the base yesterday?" I ask him.

"Looked for a chemical."

"What chemical?"

"Can't remember."

The kid can remember the entire encyclopedia of botanical scientific names but can't recall the name of one chemical.

"Did she say what it was for?"

"She said biologists use it to detect copper and iron."

I have no idea what this could mean but it leaves me uneasy.

We climb the hill to walk along the headland. I am extremely aware of the minutes passing. We keep our eyes glued to the water, to the horizon, to the coastline. Raff knows not to do this. It doesn't make sense that they'd go exploring, not without telling me. If he goes out to record the whales, he has to be back within an hour or two. This is the only way we've been able to make a home here—by checking in with each other constantly, by never worrying each other.

"They're okay," Orly says. "They're coming home."

"How do you know?" Fen asks him.

"I would know if something had happened. They would have told me by now."

When at last we see Raff and Rowan appear in the distance my knees almost buckle. The little black Zodiac zooms up from the south, and I can see as they draw closer that Raff is at the helm and he looks fine. Rowan sits beside him. There is surprising relief in me at the sight of her.

They stop, though, before they get to the beach. It takes me only a moment to see why, another moment to watch what happens, and then my heart fails.

Rowan

We don't speak on the way home. A mantra ticks over in my head, a thought that drifted in early on, with no basis except a gut feeling, some terrible instinct rising to the surface. *They have killed him*, goes the mantra. *They have killed him.*

What follows that? Logically, what follows?

They're going to kill me too.

No. Don't be ridiculous.

Even the idea of them killing Hank is ridiculous. I can't wrap my head around a single reason why.

But then I suppose that's the way of all murders, isn't it, to seem a complete mystery until the motive is uncovered.

So let me lay it out for myself. Desperate emails, calling for help. *I am in danger*, they declared. Hank's possessions hoarded secretly under a floor. And now blood in the hut where he lived, a lot of blood.

What do I do?

I spot the research base in the distance, nestled between the two lumps of island. I am very cold, despite the layers. All I can think about is a hot shower, ten, fifteen, twenty minutes long. We speed around the isthmus to the northern side of the beach, to our beach, but something makes Raff slow to a stop.

"Look," he says.

It is another whale.

"A humpback," he says, and I can hear in his voice that this is the one he wanted above all others, and I want to snap at him that it doesn't matter, just get us to land, for god's sake, but I glance at his face and it stops me. He's just a kid, it's easy to forget he's still a kid, and he loves these whales, truly he loves them, and I don't think he sees them very often.

The creature crests the water, waving its pectoral fin at us, and we both wave back. We see a second, much smaller, fin do the same, and I don't think, I rocket to my feet because it's a baby, it's a mother and calf, and they are so lovely that both Raff and I are laughing, and I don't want to go back to shore anymore, I want to stay here with them.

I cannot, in this moment, fathom the men who came here on their boats to kill these creatures. I can't comprehend what could allow you to do that, what could drive you to it. They do not seem like they could belong to the same species, but maybe it is the animal in me that feels the love, the human that can detach from it.

I pull myself back to the moment and try to be within it. This will be over soon and I'll regret not savoring every second.

The whales disappear briefly and then we see the baby do a kind of awkward leap out of the water, barely lifting its body. We cheer for it. It is adorable. We can't see the mother anywhere, but we search for her.

"She might have dived?" I say after a while.

"Not without the calf," Raff says.

I look behind us to the three waiting smudges on the headland. What will I say to him? How will he explain the blood? Is there anything he could say that would satisfy me? Make this pain in my chest go away? How do we move forward from here? I don't know if I can climb that hill again, sleep in that lighthouse. I feel sickened by my thoughts about him, by the rising heat of my desire for him, by my lack of vigilance, by my distractions and my pleasure when I should have been pursuing Hank and nothing else.

That is the last coherent thought I have.

Because the mother whale, this mighty humpback, breaches the water right beside us, her body surging high into the air. Her arc is clear. She is so close I can see all the scratches on her skin, all the barnacles clinging on, every tiny detail. She blots out the sky. I know what will happen. We both do. I reach for Raff's hand and squeeze it tight, and I look into his knowing eyes with time only to say, "It's alright," before she comes down on top of us.

Raff

He thinks of his mother. Just her name. He doesn't have time to con-jure anything else. And then, as the enormous body of this creature he loves falls toward him, he thinks it's not a bad way to go. That actually, it is quite perfect.

Dominic

It isn't until afterward that I am able to make sense of it. I must be mad for thinking any of this, must be imagining things. But it looks like she twists at the last moment. It looks like she leaps, is falling, sees them beneath her, and then pulls herself to the side, angling that massive body away from them. It looks like she tries to save them.

Rowan

It is the storm again. The churn of the sea dragging me under. My body battered. My lungs exploding. I am tumbled head over tail and have no sense of up or down, it takes an eternity for me to grasp any stillness, any hint of calm among the maelstrom, enough to right myself and kick, reach, gasp the air of the roaring surface. My lungs shudder. I am somehow uninjured, somehow alive. It makes no sense. I look frantically for Raff but see nothing. I don't know where the whale is. Or the Zodiac. The ocean is trying to calm itself. I dive below but I can't see anything and it's happening again, this can't be happening again, I can't be searching for his body down here, reaching desperately—

We surface together. He gasps and coughs. He is alive, a few meters away.

I swim for him, grab for him.

He grunts, yells out. "My arm."

"It's okay, it's okay, you're alive."

"How?" he asks, all of him trembling.

"I don't know. I really don't know. Let's get to shore."

I try to support him as we swim. The weight of him in my arms is so much heavier than—

I wrench my thoughts away from that dark place, knowing I must be in shock if I am going somewhere I left behind so long ago. I don't want to think about it except I can feel him now. His little body weightless against me. Shearwater is a place of ghosts, after all, and it has found mine and delivered him back to me.

Raff and I lie on the black sand as they run to us. I lose time. We walk to the hospital, I think. We are both dazed and in shock. Raff's arm is broken, maybe. I am unhurt but the footsteps are pattering down the hallway of my mind. His laugh is in my ear.

All five of us sleep on the camp beds in the hospital. I sleep for a long time, I think, slipping in and out of dreams.

His name was River, my little brother.

Dominic

Raff's wrist is swollen to twice its size. He says he felt it twist when the humpback's body landed beside him and the force of its weight threw him hard. But, and here is the wonder of it all, it did not land *on* him. If it had, he'd be dead. I can't even approach how I feel about that, I can't go back in my mind to those moments, watching and powerless and so sure my son was gone. It's not about me, so I will leave that there. I have only very basic first aid knowledge with which to treat the break. I can't x-ray it without power, wouldn't know how to read an x-ray anyway. I bandage it and shovel pain meds down his throat. We don't have a freezer, which means we don't have ice.

He is awake and calm. I can't stop hugging him. I don't move off his bed, and he suffers me, as well as his little brother and his sister at his feet. He says he'll stay with Rowan until she wakes; I can only imagine what gets forged in the moments before a whale falls on top of you. I agree, wouldn't be leaving her anyway. We all stay. We sleep in the camp beds and sit talking in the camp beds and eat in the camp beds. It is the longest I have spent with all three of my children together in months.

Rowan sleeps. She looks different from how she looked when she arrived, when I watched her sleep and dream the first time. Perhaps it is not her, but my eyes, that are changed.

Rowan

When I wake it's to see his face and I am returned to the first time, to when my body was on fire. I am returned to the sea.

We are alone—the kids have gone to get supplies, he tells me, even Raff, who can't lie still despite a possibly broken wrist. I meet his eyes, this man who nearly lost his son, nearly watched his son die. I'm so sorry, I say, and he reaches to give me a hug, but it's awkward and we find ourselves moving so that we are in the same bed, facing each other, and I think how did we get here. I can feel his breath on my lips. I haven't seen his eyes this close before, today they are more gray than green, they are a storm.

"You've been sleeping again," he tells me. "And dreaming."

A prison of dreams.

I've never spoken of it. Not even to Hank. How telling that seems now. To share a life with someone but to never share the truth of that life, to never express how that life is damaged. Surely it was his right to know this wound in me, since it was bound, at some point, to become a wound in us? I'd simply worked so hard to leave it behind that I couldn't bear to bring it forward again, not even to speak it aloud.

But it is here now, and I am awake, and I don't feel so frightened of it. Shearwater is a place of ghosts, but mine does not haunt me, not anymore. I can name him, I can do that.

I tell Dominic, this stranger I do not know, this man who is lying in my bed and lying to my face, I tell him that there was a boat, once. That my mother and father had four children and raised us, for a time, on a houseboat. Three girls and one boy; I was the oldest, River the littlest. That we were all very good on the boat. When Mum and Dad went ashore to work, I looked after my sisters and brother. I cooked and bathed them, I brushed their tangled hair, read them stories, got them to sleep. We were wild, every one of us, often unclothed because it was easier to dive into the water and swim like fish, then swing on ropes to get back aboard. I held him in my arms most of the time, I swam with his face by my shoulder, his little hands curled against me. I made sure he didn't fall, but it was wild, I said it was wild, didn't I?

I loved him, and he drowned while I was meant to be watching him.

That's what I dream of.

His tiny bare feet on the deck, pitter-pattering toward me, and his laugh as I catch him.

Dominic is holding me and our lips touch. What a strange thing that grief can become need in moments, in breaths, in the strength of his hands. Maybe it's shelter. Maybe distraction. Or something else entirely. But there is old pain in me and we kiss as though we have kissed a thousand times before, as though in other lives we kissed every day, we kiss as though we have been waiting years to do so. He tastes of salt. I recognize his body against mine. And then I disentangle myself, saying, "I can't," and, "I'm sorry," and I walk outside to the black sand and the blood-red kelp and the bones, I walk among the bones to the sea's edge, this sea that brought me here.

If he has killed my husband.

What then. What will I be.

Dominic

I was taken to my knees by the fear alone. While she has endured the thing itself. Maybe it is not the same thing exactly because he was not her child, but then I think that is a very small way to look at love. He was hers, and beloved, and he's lost. I am sick with the terror of this thing, and I think that to survive it must take a fathomless kind of strength. It's this strength, her strength, that takes the edges of me. Those edges that crumble first into the sea.

Rowan

The kids are in the mess room eating two-minute noodles. They are vibrating, high on what happened. They tell me she saved us.

But I can't think about that, I can't go there, I have to be a different thing now, something with sharp edges and a solid center.

All five of us walk back up to the lighthouse. Dom and I don't look at each other or talk. It will be as if the kiss never happened. A fever dream. A betrayal, certainly, but more than that a softening. A weakening I can't afford.

He, Fen, and Orly carry armfuls of driftwood with which to make fire, and walk ahead to get stuck into the chores we've neglected over the last couple of days. Raff and I travel behind at a slower pace. Walking does not feel good—my body aches again, I am so sick of feeling like shit—but I'm more concerned about Raff's arm and how it will get fixed.

"Pain?" I ask him.

"Four," he replies, which has got to be a lie. How will he play the violin if his arm doesn't heal properly? He must see my concern because he says, "I don't think it's broken," showing me how he can wiggle his fingers. "Just a sprain." Then, "Are you gonna talk to Dad about . . . ?"

"The blood?" I say. "Yes. I have to, don't I? Unless you want to tell me about it."

He shakes his head quickly. "I don't know anything. Just talk to him." He pauses but I get the feeling he's not finished. "Sorry I was such a prick the other night. When I said you wanted to seduce Dad."

"Honestly that's the last thing on my mind." I try not to sound as guilty as I feel.

"Okay. Cool." He scratches the back of his neck. "I really do need to get off this island."

"We all do."

"I keep getting this feeling like Dad wants to stay. Even after they come to get the seeds. He hasn't said so, but . . ."

"What's there to stay for?"

Raff doesn't answer but he doesn't need to: we both know what would keep Dom here.

"You're an adult, Raff. It's your decision."

"I don't know if I could leave him here. And if Dad stays, Orly stays."

I shrug. "Look, at some point you have to choose your own life. We all separate from our parents."

That sounds cold even to me. I don't tell him it's not his job to carry his family. It *is* his job, because he has decided it is. I understand this maybe better than anyone. I think of the things I decided to carry, and how I had to make myself strong enough to do so, and then I think of my mum again. She was very loving in the beginning, but grief severs things.

Raff is working through his own stuff. "You know when she was coming down on us?" he asks slowly. "I had this thought. That I didn't mind." He grimaces. "Do you think that means I want to die?"

I shake my head. "No, mate. I think it just means you're brave."

"I thought of Mum, too," he says more softly. "And then it was funny, when I woke up and my arm was killing me, Dad was talking to me, and I wasn't really sure what he was saying but the sound of his voice was like . . . *home*, or something. And I had this other thought. That it should have been him I thought of. That it's not fair, is it. He's the one who's here, she hasn't been here in *years*, but we're all completely obsessed with her."

I think about how she is here among us, how even I, who have never met her, feel her presence.

"That's grief," I say simply.

Raff nods. Looks away. "Yeah. Anyway. I just want him to know."
We glance sideways at each other and he adds, "I won't leave him. I
won't leave any of them here."

The thought comes with simple clarity, and it is the last thing I need.
I won't be leaving any of them here either.

The old blocked-up fireplace hasn't worked in decades, but we are all
getting sick of feeling so constantly frozen; with reduced power for
heating we need fire. This means using brooms to try to clear out the
chimney. By the time Raff and I reach the lighthouse, Dom and Fen have
their heads poked up, giving directions, and I realize Orly is inside it.

"Get him out of there," I say, hurrying over.

"I'm good!" he shouts from within.

Dom looks at me like *see.*

"He'll be breathing in years' worth of soot and dust," I snap. "Completely stuff his lungs. Get him out now."

They pull him back down and the kid is covered head to toe in black
soot. He laughs to see himself in the bathroom mirror, before being
stood under the shower. The water runs black for a long while. When
the worst is sluiced away we fill the bath. I listen for any coughing, but
he seems okay.

Fen and Raff return to cleaning out the chimney while Dom and I
sit beside Orly in the tub. Dom doesn't look at me, and I think maybe
he's pissed off at me for telling him what to do, but then he rubs his
face and says, "I messed up. I think I mess up all the time, only there's
not usually anyone here to point out what an idiot I am."

I breathe out.

Orly reaches to stroke his dad's hair, getting it wet. "You're not an
idiot, Dad," he says cheerfully.

"You are," I say. "But the kids are alive. You can't have messed up
too badly."

I don't really want to sit here and make him feel better about himself, so I leave them to wash. I spend a little time alone in my room,

undressing and unraveling my bandages. They are filthy now and I've run out of fresh ones, but I don't need them anymore. I think I've become too used to them, maybe even a little scared of not having them. Scaffolding to keep me upright. Gently I run my fingers over the grazes and cuts, doing an inventory. Most have scabbed over and don't hurt anymore, but a couple of the deeper gashes are still red and tender. The one on my hip that Dom had to sew twice is particularly hard to look at, even since I cut the stitches out—it has always been the deepest wound. I don't think it will ever fully heal.

I swallow antibiotics and sit naked on the bed. It's cold, and I try to let that cold inside me.

I feel it then. Breath on the back of my neck. The sound of it in my ear.

"I can't protect them from what they've done," I tell her softly.

She grows and throbs and fills the room, faceless and breathing. But I'm too cold to let her frighten me. I dress as warmly as I can, pack my bag, and lift my walking stick.

We aren't going that way, I promise.

Orly

Plants, in a broad sense, are food. Not only for humans, but for animals, birds, insects. This is their main function on the planet, aside from creating oxygen. They feed life.

But there are some with a much subtler evolutionary design. Plants that wait patiently, taking no nutrients from the poor soil they exist within, their brightly colored and patterned leaves particularly delicious looking. Plants that draw the insects and the little rodents and the frogs to them—hungry creatures searching for food, tricked into thinking they have found a feast, before they themselves are consumed by the pitcher plants. The carnivores. These are plants that refuse to be prey. What possible need could we have to keep such defiance? The seeds of the deadly pitcher plants sit, gathering dust, in a far corner of the vault.

Rowan

The walk is slow in the dark, but I retrace the path we took, Dom, Orly, and me. The moon and the stars are bright. I pause by the crystal albatross lake, now a black sky pit to swallow me whole. I come to the grassy plateau where the baby petrels nest; it looks very different in this light, a sea of silver scales. I move swiftly as we did the first time, but I take a new route. He promised the wind he wouldn't come this way, and I don't know what I will find, but if I have to scour every last inch of this island to discover an answer I will do it. I will not sit still and wait.

⁓

Beneath the ash I see a glint. I unearth its source, brushing it off with a gloved hand. The glass has melted into a new form, it is curved and almost graceful. I don't know what this thing used to be—a vase, maybe, or a wine glass—but I am transfixed by the way the light is moving through its twists and arches.

"Oh god," I hear. I look up from the patch of debris I am standing within—once our kitchen—to the square Hank is sorting through—once our bedroom. I have the floorplan of the house marked out in a grid for us to work our way through methodically, sorting and removing and cleaning as if we are at an archaeological site. It is impossible to recognize any of these rooms now, so we have only the plan to help us understand where in the house we're standing, but even within these areas none of the possessions (if any are recognizable) are where we expect them to be. The fire has collapsed everything inward. We've only just begun, but I have a system: we carry rubbish and debris in buckets to the skip and then we sift through the remaining ash and charcoal with our sifting trays, and we will work our way thoroughly through one section at a time.

"My trophies," Hank says now, holding up a scorched and melted golden trophy he received as a child in some science fair. The fact that he had these items shipped from his childhood home in New York, over half the world and several oceans, goes a fair way to explain how much they mean to him. And yet Hank has been reacting this way, with vivid despair, at every recognizable item he has come across, from old CDs to beard trimmers.

I suppose, woodenly, that my lack of sentimentality has turned out to be a good thing, that it was right, in the end, not to keep anything of my mother's, and to tell myself it was because I wanted nothing from her or of her.

"Put your mask back on," I say to Hank.

He slumps onto his overturned bucket, holding the trophy to his chest and gazing around at the house. I pick my way over to him and gently move his mask into position. I stroke his hair, once. Then I return to my work, knowing that it will be me who clears and sorts through this house, room by room, while my husband grieves his losses.

"I'm going to take the job on Shearwater," he tells me without warning.

I straighten and look at him over the wreckage. I am so hot under this protective gear.

"I've been saying no because I needed to be here if we were going to have kids," he adds. "But you're never going to give me those, are you?"

My mouth opens but no sound comes. That he is doing this now, in this moment, is astounding to me.

"There's nothing here for me anymore," Hank says.

I turn and walk out of the ruins. I walk past where the eucalypts stood tall and proud and so very old. Then into the forest of alpine ash. They are dead now. Everything seems to be. It is an eerie place of white and black. There is no birdsong. No rustle of tiny feet under brush. I sink onto an overturned piece of roofing tin that has flown a long way to land here. I don't cry for my husband, who wishes to leave me. I cry for the forest. For the trees and the shrubs and for all who lived within it. So many species. So many creatures I'd come down here to look for each day, and delight in the glimpses I caught. I cry for my life here, in this little patch of paradise. For the safety I felt. For the woman I was while living here. I fed the magpies each evening in this spot. I waited for the passage of mother wombat and her baby, ambling slowly by. Her burrow was here somewhere.

I stop crying and stand to look, unsure why I would do this to myself. Any remains I might find will only make it worse. But I lift the sheet of tin and rest it against the burned husk of a tree. I can see the opening of the burrow in the earth. I get down on my knees, then onto my stomach, pressing my whole body flat into the ash. And I look.

I think my husband loved me as a vessel. Not consciously, I don't think so little of him that I believe he could be conscious of this. But somewhere deep within. A buried truth in the darkness. He never took the time to discover my body, he never explored it for what it could offer aside from the obvious, he never found in me, in my essence, a purpose other than to carry children, and when I admitted I couldn't do this for him he turned away from me. He had no more use for my limbs or my skin, my muscles or tongue or fingertips. He couldn't even *see* me anymore, my flesh. I'm not sure that such a turning away could exist in the same body as love. I'm not sure it's possible to make so small a thing of love. I think love expands when it needs to, it adapts, it embraces.

But then, mine didn't do that either, did it?

Hank and I carried on, pretending it was alright. He video called me from the island once a week. There was comfort in the familiarity of him. Still married, after all. Maybe I would follow him to Shearwater one day. Maybe we could salvage a life together. But every day I did not come.

And now there is this day. Here on a windswept, starlit hill, and I think I have found something, and the broken years fall away. I think only of him as he was in the beginning, when he taught me how things could grow, how they could entangle. I think of how I loved him when that love was simple. Because I am quite certain I have found his grave.

Dominic

She disappears. She doesn't tell us where she's going, and she doesn't let the kids go with her. I spend every minute waiting for her to come back, forcing myself not to go out in search of her. She is not mine. Still, I wait for her.

I thought she would ask me about the blood in the hut, but she didn't. It's disorienting. All I have is Raff's explanation for their trip south, how she presented as worried about the concrete, but he suspects she was using it as an excuse to get back to the hut, where she used her chemicals to prove blood was spilled. He swears to me they spoke no more about it, that he told her nothing except to talk to me.

She did not talk to me.

She must suspect violence. She must think I'm lying to her.

Why did she come here.

I lie awake, obsessing over these questions. Thinking of her. I have an urgent need to fix this, but I don't know how. I feel lost at the thought that she will not come back to us. To me.

When Rowan returns, I am expecting a confrontation. But instead she gathers more supplies in her pack and sets out again without a word. This time I follow. Because strapped to her back is a shovel. I think of what's buried in this island and know I can't let her dig it up.

I lose her for a while; I've been leaving a huge gap between us. I think she has walked all the way down to the southern beach and the seed vault, and my heart lurches, but I can't find her at either place. I retrace my steps and by following the shoreline back around I eventually see her in the distance. How did she know to come here? Did one of my children tell her? Or has she been out searching, roaming. Hunting.

She is crouched on a sloping hill, overlooking the ocean. The view is spectacular, it's why we chose this spot. The shovel is moving. She's already dug out the raised mound that sits beneath the rudimentary, nameless headstone.

My dread explodes into horror and I run to her. "Don't," I say. But when she looks up at me I see a different woman, a creature of certainty, I see that she will never stop digging, not until she's found him.

With a shaking hand I reach for the shovel. I say, even though it's the last thing I want to do, "Let me." Because I can see the pain in her exhausted, hollow face, I have seen the damage done to her body, and this hole will take many hours, it is deceptively difficult to dig a grave, I know it is because I dug this one. I dug it with my son, who wept as he shoveled earth long into the night.

I do the same now. I have spent countless hours digging holes in this hillside. I did not think I'd be spending more.

What will you tell her? my wife asks. I didn't hear her come but she's here now. I wish she wasn't. I don't speak to her, I dig.

When we reach him, I lower the shovel and we both slide into the hole. Our hands gently pull the last dirt away from him. There's no coffin; he is simply wrapped in a sheet. I have been very careful with my shovel.

"This will be bad," I tell her. "It's been a few weeks."

She nods. I can see the muscles of her jaw clench. She is readying herself. Folds back the covering from his face, and looks.

I didn't know if we would be able to tell, but we can.

Rowan starts crying. She covers her face and weeps, and then she reaches for his face, which still looks like his face, and she smooths her fingers tenderly over his cheeks, brushing the hair back off his forehead, and through her tears she asks, "Who is he?"

Alex

Alex came eight years after Tom did, and that's how his life has been since. Trailing behind his older brother, who is everything to him. He never probes too deeply into why Tom means everything to him, for fear of uncovering hidden pain about their father having left. He prefers to just let it be fact: all Alex really wants is to be close to his brother. Tom did swimming in school, so Alex had to do swimming too. Tom learned the guitar, so Alex learned the guitar. Tom developed a passion for mathematics and science, so Alex decided he would be passionate about the same. When Tom left university in Chicago and went chasing the worst storms to hit the country, Alex had all his fears realized: he was being left behind. It was this damn eight years between them: What had possessed his parents to leave it so long? Why couldn't they be two years apart like every other pair of siblings he knew? Tom didn't stay put anywhere, he followed weather events, studying the extremes endured around the world—at one point he found himself in Siberia, of all places—while Alex was still trying to get through high school. When Tom moved for a time to Svalbard, Alex was limping through his biology degree. Alex only caught up to him, at long last, on his most recent venture into the wilds of the world: a stint at the research base on Shearwater Island, which was dealing with extreme weather shifts, enough to garner Tom's interest. So much farther away than Tom had ever gone before. All the way down near Antarctica. By this stage Tom was very good at remote, at cold and exposed, at quiet. Alex had never been away from the bustle of the city. But he was determined. He had chosen to study, in a somewhat calculated way, pinnipeds and ceta-ceans, creatures that traversed the world, that could be found in many pockets of many seas, and thus hedged his bets. A bizarre choice, for someone who had never seen either a whale or a seal. The closest he'd come to an ocean was Lake Michigan. But he knew Tom would choose a rough-edged coastline somewhere. And this time Alex was going with his brother.

The research base on Shearwater is full of interesting people from all over the world. Many of the scientists are from Australia or New Zealand, because of the proximity, but there are quite a few Americans to make Alex and Tom feel more at home, including Hank, their team leader. None of the researchers can make much sense of Alex, who has extremely limited field experience, almost no publications, and who chose to study sea creatures without knowing the sea. It's quite clear that he has attached himself to his older brother and been pulled along to this outcrop of the world. As a result, Alex never feels very comfortable among the inhabitants of the base. But then he meets Raff.

⁓

"Do you know someone hanged themselves off those?"

There is sun, and they are lying in it, letting it warm their faces.

"Off what?" Alex sits up, shields his eyes, follows Raff's pointed finger to the fuel tanks in the distance. "No."

Raff nods. "I heard talk about it, a few years back."

"When did this happen?"

"I dunno. Before I came here."

"Why?"

"I have no idea."

Alex stares at the big round barrels, at the metal walkway near the tops of them. "Very sad," he says, letting the image go.

Raff shrugs. "I tried to look it up online, but I couldn't find anything. It's probably an urban legend, like the Shearwater Carver."

Alex shudders, he hates that story. A man so overcome by the spirits of the dead that he took a knife to all the researchers in their beds, killing them one by one. It can't be true, surely, but it is disturbing enough that the story exists at all, that there is such a presence here that anyone who comes tries to make sense of it.

He thinks of the weekly psych sessions they're each required to complete, check-ins to make sure they aren't suffering any mental health problems due to the nature of their isolation.

"Why does everyone here love saying the place is haunted?" he asks. Halloween is always celebrated with more gusto than Christmas or New Year's.

Raff's mouth quirks. "To laugh, instead of being disturbed."

He supposes that makes sense. Hates thinking about any of it, so turns his mind ahead.

"There's a botanic garden just outside Chicago," Alex says.

Raff looks at him and grins, knowing exactly what he's doing. "And I'm sure he'd love it. But it's a long way from the sea."

"Alright, where, then?"

"Vancouver Island," Raff says without hesitation. "The most whale sightings of any place in the world."

Alex smiles and thinks about this. "Loads of orcas and humpbacks there."

"And seals and sea lions."

"Vancouver Island it is then."

They laugh, but the laughter trickles away, both aware of how unlikely this plan is to happen. Still. It is nice to lie here in the grass and the sun and daydream.

"A few years ago," he tells Raff, because Raff loves whale stories more than anything and Alex is always searching his mind for things to tell him, "researchers watched as several orcas attacked a gray whale and its calf. The orcas killed the calf. But then something happened that nobody had expected. Humpbacks arrived on the scene, more than a dozen of them. They ignored the krill-rich feeding waters around them and instead put all their energy into fighting off the pod of orcas, stopping them from eating the dead calf. The humpbacks spent over six hours protecting that baby and it wasn't even their own kind."

Raff looks at him.

"There've been hundreds of accounts of humpbacks helping other species," Alex says. "Some of them even include humans. It defies reason. Some scientists say it's because they're attuned specifically to the sound of orcas as a threat to their babies. But that doesn't explain all the stories."

"Then why?" Raff asks.

"They feel empathy," Alex says.

—

When Hank makes the announcement to all the researchers gathered in the mess, it's like a lifeline for Alex. Three extra months here on Shearwater. Three extra months with Raff. And during these months Raff will turn eighteen and then maybe Alex will not feel so guilty for the things he imagines doing with him.

Despite the excitement that blooms at the thought, Alex waits to see what Tom thinks about staying on another season to help Hank categorize the seeds in the vault. Their team leader has asked for three extra sets of hands.

He is lucky, then, that Tom has fallen in love with Naija, the base doctor, who wants to stay and help.

—

On the morning of Raff's eighteenth birthday, there is a storm brewing.

Things have started to get very bad on Shearwater, but Alex wants to give Raff one good day to forget all the rest, all the shit with his family and with Hank, just one.

Alex, Tom, and Naija are living in the red field hut and spending most of their time in the vault. It is a strange experience, and at first Hank made them take a lot of breaks, insisting that so much time underground, specifically under this ground, with this particular task and all its complicated tragedy, could very well make them loopy. So he was on them all the time, checking they'd eaten, checking they'd slept well, checking they'd been up and out for fresh air. This task was asking a lot of them.

All of that stopped when Hank began to change.

But in any case, for Raff's birthday, Alex has a plan.

They've never spent a night together. With Raff sharing a lighthouse with his family, and Alex sharing a tiny field hut with two other scientists, and their whereabouts always needing to be accounted for, there's no privacy. But there is an empty field hut, with a green door.

On this stormy morning, Tom is drinking instant coffee in the kitchen. Alex makes himself a cup and silently rehearses what he will say.

"You and me on first shift this morning, Al."

Alex nods. "It's Raff's birthday."

"I don't want to know. I don't want to know anything about any of it."

"Nothing's happened," he assures his brother quickly. "But I won't be sleeping here tonight. I'm gonna stay in the green hut."

"Shit." Tom rubs his eyes. "That's dumb. It's not safe."

Alex rolls his eyes. Gives his brother a look. "We're leaving in a couple of months. And then that'll be it. And everything here is nuts and I just want him to have a nice birthday. That's all."

Tom shakes his head. "I really don't want to know."

Later, once they've finished another monotonous day underground, Raff waits outside in the Zodiac for Alex to stuff things into an overnight bag. Naija is teasing him mercilessly and laughing that booming belly laugh of hers and Tom is ignoring the whole thing.

But as Alex goes to leave, he says, "I don't like the storm, Al." And coming from Tom, who is an expert on storms, that actually means something. But Alex is already on the train tracks, barreling out of the station. He shoves Tom as he dashes past him.

"See you in the morning."

Raff drives the Zodiac through raging winds and rain and swell that drenches them, mooring it to the metal steps of the green cabin. They climb up and into the shelter, but before Alex closes the door he looks back to the red, where he can see his brother in the doorway, lifting a hand. Alex waves back.

The storm grows. They both spend some time watching it through the windows, noting the rise of the sea, acknowledging with wonder how high it's come, how it smashes against the walls of the huts. They can recognize that the waves perhaps should not be so high or so violent, but they are distracted.

Alex wakes in the middle of the night to a mighty crash. The rain and wind are both so loud he is deafened. Tom is in their room, looming over them, and behind him is Naija.

"Come on, it's not safe." His voice is barely audible over the sounds of the storm and the creaking of the cabin pylons.

They don't need to be told twice. Alex and Raff grab their things and head for the door. They climb down the steps into the Zodiac, battered by the weather. Raff doesn't wait—Tom and Naija's Zodiac is here too, they'll be right behind—he takes off into the waves, headed for the shore.

But in Raff's Zodiac, Alex turns to look behind, to check his brother is following. Instead what he sees where the green cabin sat only moments before is something different, shapes he can't make sense of in the dark and the swell. He blinks, squinting, desperately trying to understand, and then the whole shape moves and he realizes what he is looking at: the cabin has come off its pylons and is on its side in the water. A wave dumps onto it, disappearing the entire hut. Alex screams and Raff grabs for him but Alex is swift, he is plunging into the rough ocean, mad with terror and with grief for he already knows, deep down. The waves batter him and he realizes he may have drowned himself, too, but while there is blind hope he will still try to find him, he will kick and struggle against this violent sea, reaching in the dark for Tom's body.

He loses consciousness for a second or two but revives quickly as he's pulled back into the Zodiac. Raff's strong arms have plucked Alex from this maelstrom and the engine is gunning them away from the hut.

What madness possessed him to bring them out here? To this flimsy matchbox house on its toothpick legs? It's been said for years the green cabin isn't to be occupied, not since the sea got so high. His brother told him this morning it wasn't safe.

His brother, whom he has killed.

⁓

They do manage to recover the bodies. Dominic and Raff do. They go without telling Alex, and they don't ever show him what they've found, they simply invite him to help bury the sheet-wrapped figures. Alex is distressed—he and Tom have been raised firmly secular and yet he feels a need to wash his brother's body properly, to give him some sort of ceremonial burial. Instead he shovels dirt onto Tom. A grave down here at the bottom of the world, an unmarked, anonymous grave in the middle of nowhere, without any way to call for help or tell his mom. As he shovels the dirt he thinks of how he has always been trying to catch up to Tom, has spent his whole life chasing after, and how he might actually be able to do it now: in eight years Alex will have closed that gap at last. It is a disaster. It is unbearable.

He finds himself walking north to the isthmus and sitting in that same spot, in the grass overlooking the base, he does this often, no matter the weather. He finds himself looking down at the fuel tanks.

Rowan

His name is Alex, Dom tells me. Raff's Alex. His voice is soft and aching as he tells me a story of field huts and the sea, and of Alex's guilt.

"There are two more," Dom says, pointing farther along the hill. "One for Naija, another for Tom."

I look at the handsome young face in his seaside grave and what I think is that I have had enough digging. I will disturb no more resting places.

I don't know what's happened to my husband but if he is in a fourth grave somewhere here I decide I do not need to find it, or see his face, or know one way or the other. It is possible he has done what Alex did when presented with an impossible life, an impossible choice. Some part of me suspects this and will start building protections against it, but maybe not, this may not be right either, and so I give up, I give over to the tide, to the story I've been told that he has left Shearwater and that I will see him again someday. It's all I have the capacity to deal with.

There's just one thing I can't square. One thing stopping me from surrendering to the story.

"Why do you have his passport?" I ask.

Dom and I stare at each other.

He lets out a long breath. "Shit," he says. "You must have been thinking something really bad."

I wait.

"I don't have a good answer," he warns me. "You won't feel comforted by it."

"Just tell me the truth."

"He left it."

"Bullshit."

"I told you it wasn't a good answer." Dom rubs his face. "He was struggling. I said that, right? He started talking about letting all the seeds drown. He said we should all just drown. The whole lot of us. Humans, animals, plants." Dom shakes his head. "I've been trying to spare you, but I think he was having a psychotic episode. When he hopped on that ship it was like he was fleeing for his life. He left everything. We went to clean out his room the next day, and it was like he still lived in it."

"How would he have got through customs without his passport?"

"Fucked if I know. But a navy ship's not gonna turn around and sail all the way back down here just to get one idiot's documents, I'm damn sure about that."

"Why are they hidden under your workshop then? Why not just tell me all of this?"

"I did tell you. But I could see you didn't believe me, and I knew if you found the passport you'd think something terrible."

"Why should it matter?" I demand. "What I thought? If it wasn't true?"

Dom lets out a breath. "It matters to me."

We stare at each other. I try to read him. His face seems open, regretful.

Maybe it's because I want to, but I think I do believe him.

It is a gray afternoon by the time we have buried Alex once more. I tell him how sorry I am with every shovel of dirt I heap back over him. This poor boy.

Dom and I make our way to the red field hut—I find that I don't want to sleep in the blue hut, Hank's hut—and we collapse exhausted into beds in separate rooms. I expect to sleep for days but I can't. It is too bright, maybe, even with the blinds drawn. I think of cabins swallowed by waves, I think of a young man in that rough water down there, trying to save his brother. I think of earth, of shovelfuls falling over that wrapped figure, and of his face. I think of the blood Alex must have spilled in the field hut, his own blood, and what it must have done to Raff to see it lit up in blue. Of Yen's eaten body in the sun. I think of the whale, of the barnacles on her body.

I think of what my life will become if I ever make it off this island. Of how, by the sound of it, I will be caring for a husband with serious mental health problems, a husband who did not spend a single moment taking care of me when I lost everything.

I must sleep because some time later I am woken and I think I have woken to someplace new.

A few days after the house burned and we were still sorting through the wreckage, Liv came to help, and as she and I surveyed the wasteland before us, she said, "Maybe this could be freeing. Do you feel freed?"

I looked at her in bewilderment, not sure how it was possible for someone to get something so utterly wrong. I felt the opposite. I felt a prisoner of the loss, and of the memories, and of so much time wasted.

But this evening. This evening I have woken to the sensation of having shed a skin. In my sleep I have let something go. An entire life.

I go into the small living area to find Dominic taking off his shirt.

Which is the last thing I need.

"Sorry—"

He doesn't look at me, doesn't seem embarrassed, just continues to take off his clothes. "Dirt's driving me crazy," he grunts. It's true, we are filthy from the digging, and the coarseness of it against my skin has been awful between the bed sheets. It looks good on him though.

"Going for a swim," he adds, unbuckling his belt. I stare at him, stripping down to his long johns. His chest is covered in dark hair but I can see the lines of the muscle beneath the skin, his broad chest and shoulders and strong arms, and I want to touch him with a hot kind of want.

"A swim?" I repeat. "Where?"

He looks at me like I'm a moron. "In the ocean."

I turn to peer through the window. I'm not sure what time it is, but the sun is setting slowly, the evening sky streaked orange to violet to navy. Here, that could mean anywhere from 10 p.m. to 1 a.m. "In that ocean, which is so rough it drowned two people and sank a building?"

Dominic shrugs. "I can't stand it."

He walks for the door and the metal stairs, climbing his way barefoot down the rungs and onto the rocks. Aside from the violence of the waves, there is also the cold to contend with, and I watch him flinch as the water reaches his toes, his feet, his ankles.

He glances back at me once. "You coming?"

My feet curl over the edge of a metal rung, and below me is a drop onto slippery rocks, and before me an icy, drowning ocean. A man who is not childless, or safe in any way, a man not mine. But he is wading into that freezing water and he's shouting in pain, and he's laughing, it is uninhibited, and some part of me can perceive a threshold laid out before me.

I take off my clothes, all of them—he has seen me naked anyway, he has picked over my prostrate body, what does it matter, a body seems a meaningless thing now—and I walk down to the water's edge. This water I have feared for so long.

I sink into it. The cold is sharp enough to steal air and thought. I am battered and for a brief second I am filled with the terror of it, of being back underneath, and then I release it, I let the water batter me and I survive this battering, I surge to the surface with a scream, and Dom is laughing and using a towel he's brought to wrap me up, and he's saying, "You're a mad woman, you are."

Our bodies are close. I stand almost within the sphere of his. If I look up, and he looks down, I think we might fit together, the lines of us. But we are too cold, we go inside, and the tension of it will kill me, the unfulfilled want. I don't know where to put it, it doesn't fit within me.

We dry ourselves with trembling hands. My teeth chatter. The saltwater stings. I watch him. Neither of us has put clothes on yet, we are huddled in towels.

"I want . . ." I try to say it, say anything, but the words fail and I am aching, I am so needful I can't speak.

He looks at me, takes me in. Then he crosses to push me against the wall. His hand goes to my jaw, tilting it, to my throat. "This?" he says against my mouth and I nod. The kiss burns.

He pushes my towel to the floor and he looks at me as though he's never seen me before, and he touches me and he is reverent, and I feel strong. I feel alive. He drops to his knees and runs his tongue from my naval to my breast, tasting the salt on my skin, and mere minutes ago I thought a body was meaningless. His tongue drops lower, tasting me, and I am already so wet I could come in seconds, but he stops and rises, leaving me ready to burst, and as I am throbbing with need he lifts one of my legs around his hip and he fucks me deeply and I lose my breath and my sight and I dissolve around him until he is holding me up, holding me so I don't slip to the floor. "Oh god," I breathe, dizzy, and he kisses me again, lifting me and carrying me to a bed while our mouths are still pressed together and then he makes love to me more slowly, letting the orgasm build again until I can feel it everywhere, every edge and tip. When he has come too, we lie together, entangled, and I taste his neck, his collar, where I have imagined tasting a thousand times before.

We sleep, I don't know for how long, but when we wake it's because our tummies are rumbling with hunger. I feel a powerful surge of guilt. I long to be able to call Hank and tell him what I've done and how I feel, but this is not something he will forgive, and so maybe the need to tell him is really a need to end us.

Dom and I rise and dress, and we don't speak much except to mention the food and how we'll cook it. I brought rice and frozen curry in my pack, but only enough for one, we will share it and still be hungry, but I am always hungry on this island.

We get a couple of pots going on the camp stove. We stand on opposite sides of the small kitchen, pressed as far from each other as we can be. He stirs the curry slowly, helping it defrost.

"Should we not have done that?" he asks softly.

I shake my head. "No, I don't think so."

"I'm sorry."

"Me too."

He looks at me. "It's just—I thought I could have died from wanting you so badly."

I close my eyes. My heart will explode, it is beating so frantically out of my chest. I hear him move but I don't open my eyes, I squeeze them more tightly shut. I feel his breath on the back of my neck. Then his lips. A sound leaves me. He takes my clothes off and his mouth moves down my spine, over my bum, his tongue finding me again. I turn and press him to the floor so I can straddle his lap. I hold his chin and look into his eyes and when he tries to kiss me I don't let him, I fuck him slowly, watching him, his eyes and his mouth, and it isn't until we are both coming that I kiss him, taste him, breathe him in.

The curry is bubbling over the pot and we break away to rescue it. After a moment of battling the stove we look at each other and we can't help it, we laugh, both a little in shock.

We eat the curry beside each other on the couch. We talk. We agree we won't let it happen again, that it's best if it doesn't but it does, several more times in the night. I feel lost within it, within a sea I have never swum. I thought I knew the texture of desire.

"How will you live here if no one comes to bring you supplies?" I ask softly in bed.

"Did I say I planned on staying?"

I leave the question where it is. I don't think Dom genuinely believes they will stay, but I think he is struggling enormously with the idea of leaving, and those are two different things.

He sighs. He is tracing my lips with his finger. "I've had fantasies about buying a boat. So I could come and go more easily."

"Would you be allowed to just . . . stay?"

"No. But I'm not sure anyone would bother to stop me."

"And the kids?"

"My kids stay with me," he says, absolute.

"And when the sea gets too high?"

He doesn't answer. Pulls his hand from me.

"Dom," I say, "it's dangerous here."

"It's dangerous everywhere. Right? I won't let anything happen to them."

"But you're asking them to have that same vigilance and that's not fair on kids."

"Rowan," he says calmly, and his tone warns of a blow. "I won't make decisions motivated by your trauma. You're not their mother."

I turn away, embarrassed. But he pulls me back. "Sorry," he is saying. "I didn't mean for that to hurt."

"I don't want them to be mine," I tell him. "They *can't* be," and he nods, and he is kissing me, and we both pretend what I've said is true.

A storm comes. Shuddering claps of thunder, streaks of lightning. Crashing waves and shrieking wind and it feels like this cabin will be taken, it feels like we are within the story he told me, and I can't believe, suddenly, that we are sleeping in such a hazardous place. The sky has fallen dark, finally, the storm has swallowed even the band of sunlight on the horizon. Dom snores lightly beside me, but it is too cramped in this bed and I can't make my mind stop whirling. I give up on sleep and go sit in the living room so I can watch the lightning through the window. I take the blankets from another bed and huddle beneath them. Imagine the sound of the pylons creaking, the waves smashing through the windows and into this room, filling it so quickly that I don't have time to swim for the door.

"How long you and Hank been together?"

I am startled out of my daydream. Dom doesn't sit on the couch beside me; instead he sinks into the armchair, wrapping a quilt around his shoulders.

"Do you want to go there?" I ask him.

"Think we'd better, don't you?"

"We can leave this in the cabin, when we go."

"Can we?"

We can fucking try, I think. *We have to try.*

"Nearly ten years," I say.

"How come you never had kids?"

"We didn't want any," I reply bluntly, and why is it that I feel this need to be defiant about it, even with him? There is unfathomable pressure on women to have babies—it is our only purpose—and when we don't, we baffle people.

I take a breath, come down off the ledge. "I didn't want any. Hank did."

"Ah." Dom's eyes are on the streaky sky. "Because of River, do you think?"

My immediate reaction is to say no, of course not, why should it need to be about that? But with him not looking at me I am able to breathe instead. My eyelids fall shut and I sit with it. Poke around in the dark for the truth. It is tender and aching, like the wound on my hip. "It's just . . . too dangerous. And I am a coward."

"No," he murmurs. "You're not that."

"I can't have children that I may not be able to keep safe."

I open my eyes. Dominic nods once, accepting that.

"He's never forgiven me for it," I say. "For not wanting them. They asked him to come to Shearwater years ago, asked him a few times, but he always said no. I think he thought he could change my mind. Then the property burned, and he gave up. He was on the next ship out." It sounds bad, when I say it like that, and Dom's expression agrees. I try to explain. "I think he just felt like there was no use staying anymore. He didn't have anything left."

"He had you."

I smile humorlessly. "Cold comfort, I guess." Having me didn't turn out to be enough for Hank. "We didn't break up," I clarify.

"And then you came all the way here for him on a flimsy private boat." Dom sounds perplexed, almost angry.

"He asked for my help," I admit. "He said he was in danger."

Dominic frowns. I can see his mind working this through. Then he says, "I think he was. Inside him, I think he was."

"Why didn't anyone help him?"

"We tried. We gathered around, I promise we did. But there was no way to call for help and we were in over our heads and he didn't want our help. He was furious. He wanted to destroy things."

"But he only ever wanted to plant things," I say. It is so broad, the distance between the man I know and the man he became while he was here. It is so sad.

But that's not the full truth, is it? He plants things but sometimes I glimpse that tiny seed of nastiness within. It appears only in brief flashes, the lightning outside and then gone, hidden behind the charm, the friendliness, the laughter—but it is there. His selfishness. An ego so fragile, he takes hits to it poorly. Which is why I don't think we'll survive what I've done.

"Did you and Hank have a plan for after Shearwater?" Dom asks me.

I shake my head. "He couldn't talk about after."

"But in your mind, there is an after, for the two of you?"

A flash of his face in lightning. I say, "I don't need to explain to you what a marriage means."

"No," Dom concedes. Then he says, "But they do end. I can tell you with great certainty that they do end."

"Do they?" I ask. "Yours hasn't."

He is startled, I think.

"Let's not pretend," I say, "that I'm the only one here being pulled in another direction."

Dominic and I fall asleep where we are, curled in our blankets. I listen to his breathing. As I drift off, I am locking doors, building firmer barricades. But he wakes me in the early morning with a soft question, the sound of which could almost be a dream.

"Could there be an after for the five of us?"

Dominic

There is a bad day ahead. No avoiding it. When the ship comes for us, she is going to know the truth. I don't know what it will do to her or make of us, but I understand what it means to lose someone suddenly, I know how words unspoken can be a poison within, so if I am to lose someone slowly I will make sure there is nothing unsaid.

I do not want to leave this place, but I would do it for you, I would do it with you, if that is something you might want.

She has her own words that must be said.

"I don't want children, Dom."

And I come with three and so that is that.

⁓

I remember a morning, one of many that all bleed together in my mind. A morning I rose, shattered by grief and weariness, stumbling into our living room in the city. I remember wondering why I could hear no crying, no morning calls for a bottle, and then seeing my son on his back in a shaft of sunlight, with the small lean bodies of my older children laid around him, I remember their fingers tickling his belly and his smile, his first smile. They looked up at me with such awe, such delight. A smile, Dad! He's smiling! And I thought, this is why we survive.

Dominic

Before we return north, we visit the seed vault to check the temperature. It's sitting at minus ten, and the water from the tunnel has started seeping under the seal on the door. On top of which, the concrete cancer Rowan identified has spread substantially.

"Four weeks until the boat?" she asks.

I nod.

"I don't think it'll make it. Not without some repairs."

"I thought this vault wasn't your problem."

She faces me, impatient. "Well since I'm the only one here who seems to be taking this issue seriously, I guess I'd better get to work on it. I'm gonna need tools. And another laborer."

On the walk home I think a lot about what she said in the field hut. *I'm not the only one pulled in another direction.* What disturbs me is not the truth of this statement, but that Rowan knows it. For the last few nights I have been telling myself that if there is a reason she and I could never . . . *become*, that reason is Hank. Honestly I've been telling myself that since the day we replaced the roof and she told me of her house. Then I told myself it was my kids, it was Rowan not wanting kids. Two problems beyond my power to solve. But as we walk across Shearwater, headed north to our lighthouse, I wonder if those things have simply been excuses.

If they were not problems, would I be free to love her? Truly, and with all of myself?

My wife moves at my side. Just the warm rustle of her. A light touch of her fingers on mine.

Fen

It is only by chance that she sees. With their father having followed Rowan south, Fen has come up to the lighthouse to check on her brothers and help with the chores. It's through the laundry window that she sees them approaching together from the south. She wonders what's happened, if Rowan knows anything, and if everything will change now.

She watches them for a few moments but can't decipher any clues from this silent walk. She's about to turn back to the washing when she sees them stop. They are still a short distance from the lighthouse, and in discussion about something. Are they arguing, standing like that face-to-face? There is no anger in their postures. Instead there is something soft. Their outlines seem a little smudged. Fen watches, stunned, as her dad reaches for Rowan's face, his hand at her jaw, tilting it up so they are gazing at each other, and they are standing closer now, and he is speaking again, something murmured, and Fen feels an explosion in her chest. It takes the space between heartbeats for her to identify this sensation as relief.

She watches them all afternoon, but they don't look at each other or touch in the same way. And when she follows her dad up to his room, her heart already sinking with the knowing, she hears him talking to his dead wife and all her relief sputters out.

Fen knows what she has to do. To give Dom and Rowan a chance. To give them all a chance for something new.

She waits until her dad is in the shower and then she moves quickly; there will be only a few minutes now. She fills a bag with the last of her mother's belongings—more books, trinkets, jewelry, clothes—and then she bounds down the stairs to pull on her coat.

"Hey," her brother says, and she whirls.

Raff is in the doorway, watching her.

"You don't need that stuff," he says.

"I know," she says. "Don't worry."

"Whatever you're doing, it'll make things worse," he warns.

"It won't," she promises, although maybe it will, at first. But she is thinking long game here. She's doing this for all of them.

On the beach she has a small campfire that she tries to keep lit. To this she adds driftwood and the kelp she has been drying to make a bonfire. She gathers the items from her boathouse and lays them all out on the black sand, looking at each. She has a moment of uncertainty. The memories she has of her mother wearing these things are precious to her, and undoubtedly Dom has more of them, memories tied to every single thing here, and without the items will those memories disappear? Is that what Fen wants?

All she knows is that her dad must be freed of his ghost. So, one by one, she starts placing her mother's belongings on the fire.

Dominic

I notice the absence immediately as I reach for clean clothes after my shower. All of Claire's things are gone from the cupboard. I wind my way downstairs to where Raff and Orly are starting dinner. Raff's chopping with his bandaged wrist, which is a good sign.

"How is it?" I ask him.

He holds it up. "Swelling's almost gone. Definitely not broken."

I nod, relieved. "Good man. You guys know what's happened to . . ." I falter, unsure how to put it. "The stuff in my cupboard?"

"What stuff?" Orly asks.

"Mum's stuff," Raff says.

"What stuff?" Orly says more loudly. "I didn't know we had Mum's stuff."

It hits me. How wrong this is. Hiding away her belongings like a greedy dragon hoarding treasure, instead of sharing them with her children. What the fuck is wrong with me.

"Fen's been taking it," Raff says. "For a while. You didn't notice?"

There are a lot of things I haven't noticed about my daughter; that is becoming crystal clear.

I need to see her. Make sure she's okay. I will tell her I'm sorry for not checking in sooner, and for not having shared her mother's things with her. All that stuff, the jewelry and the clothes, that should be Fen's now, it should belong to her, she shouldn't have to steal it. I feel a bit queasy.

"What's going on?" Rowan asks, appearing in the doorway.

Nobody says anything; it feels awkward.

I meet her eyes and say, "I think we should take our dinner down to the beach this evening and eat with Fen."

The boys make sounds of excitement and a smile splits Rowan's face. "That's the best idea you've ever had."

Raff

The fire is too big. That's the thought he has as they approach. He knows before anyone else does. He's always been able to read his sister's mind, just a little. He knows, too, why she would do such a thing, but he doesn't have the same hope she does. Just a sick question: Is this what will break them?

He moves into the front of the group carrying their foil-wrapped food. He isn't sure what to do but he thinks he should get ahead of it somehow.

"Dad," he says, as they reach the sand.

"Yeah?" Dom seems lighter, and it leaves an even deeper pit in Raff's stomach.

"It's not to hurt you," he says.

Dom frowns, confused, and then a wariness fills his eyes, and then, as they reach the bonfire and he sees what Fen is putting onto it, something like disbelief.

"Dad," Fen says. Pleading. Apologetic. But she carries on, she throws a book onto the flames and a strangled sound comes from Dom. He lurches forward to rescue it, and his sleeve is alight, and before Raff can even think what to do, as he watches on in shock, Rowan is removing her own jacket and using it to smother the flames on Dom's arm.

Belatedly Raff grabs his little brother and lifts him into his arms. He can feel Orly's heart racing against his chest.

Dom is staring at the burned edges of the book, and at the fire, at all the things he can make out among the flames. Nothing remains unburned.

"Why?" he asks Fen.

"To free you," she answers.

Raff isn't sure his dad will reply. He doesn't for a long time. Then Dom says, "I had no idea you had such cruelty in you."

Fen's face falls, tears flooding.

Dom sinks to the ground and rests his head between his raised knees, and he weeps. He didn't do this when Claire died. Not that Raff ever saw. He never broke, not once. Now he is asunder and Raff doesn't know what to do.

"Go back to the boathouse," Rowan tells Fen. "All three of you. Stay there until I come find you."

Then she goes to Dom and she crouches behind him and puts her arms around his shoulders, and she holds him with her lips pressed to his neck, his cheek, and what's more, Dom lets her. The sight is so shocking to Raff—and, he thinks, to his brother and sister too—that they are wordless as they walk to the boathouse. He carries Orly, and Fen cries silently beside them.

Within the little shack, Raff settles his brother and sister on the mattress under the blankets and sets their plates of dinner beside them. Fen has composed herself for the sake of her brother and reads to Orly from whatever she's partway through. Raff waits to make sure they're okay before he succumbs to the thing building within. "I'll be back," he says, can barely say, and then he walks from the boathouse and back up the hill, not looking at his dad on the sand or the flames beside him, not looking back at the fuel tanks to where the swinging body will be waiting for him. He walks all the way up past the lighthouse, and he keeps on. Up a different peak. To the communications building at the very top. It is astounding, actually, that the rage survives this long, with this much exertion to wear it out. He is expecting it to be gone by the time he gets here but it isn't, it is as vivid as ever. Because he can't stop thinking how utterly wrong this is. This wasn't supposed to be their life. He doesn't know how to save them from it, how to hold them together, and he's furious with Fen for doing this, and with his dad for letting it get so bad that she felt she had to. Dom is just letting her drift away, drift right out to sea, and he isn't doing a thing to stop it. And Raff is livid with himself, too, for never being able to save anyone.

He takes his hydrophone, this precious thing his dad saved up and gifted him, this thing that brought him so much joy, that he shared with Alex, and he smashes it to pieces.

It is only later, when he has emerged, that he thanks fate or the universe or luck that his violin was not here too.

Rowan is right. He can't go on like this. He needs to find something else.

Rowan

This family is falling apart.

I sit with Dom on the sand for a long time, until the fire has burned itself out. There's no way to douse it—it's quite the blaze. So we watch. He's still holding the partially burned book. I can see enough of the cover to know that it's *Jane Eyre*. I take it from him gently and brush the burned edges away, open the pages to see they're mostly intact. Claire's writing fills the margins. "I think this was the best one," I murmur. "She put herself into this one. It'll be enough."

"There was so much that she loved in there," he says, of the bonfire.

"I know about things burning," I tell him, and he looks at me for the first time. "I know about sifting through ash to try and find anything that survived. They're just things, and you don't need them, but it's okay to grieve for them."

I hand him the book and he gazes at it.

"I'll go check on your kids, and then we'll walk up home, get some sleep. In the morning we'll start work on the vault." I know him well enough to know he's going to need something to work on, something important.

—

There is no rust converter, so we will have to manually scrape the rust from the steel. We set up two ladders with a scaffolding tray between them so Dom and I can both climb up and halve the time of the job. First he uses a rotary drill with a chisel attachment to chip away all the flaking concrete—it turns out to be a huge area, much larger than it first looked, and we don't say aloud that we don't think we can patch up this problem; instead we silently go about trying. Once the steel rods are exposed, we start scraping off the rust. It takes a few days of neck-craning, arm-straining work. It's not difficult, just tiring, especially dressed in the bulky cold suits. We don't talk much while we work, but the silence feels prickly and full of noise. The monotony makes way for thought and my thoughts are out of control. Once a minute I think of his question, his offering, and I think of my response and how blunt it was, blunt like a sledgehammer. I think of his kids and how much I want to be around them. I think of the way he broke when his wife's belongings were gone from him. I don't know how he feels about that fire now, or about me. I don't know if he is freed, as Fen intended, or more tightly bound than ever. But I know there is something different in the space between our bodies, there is heat now, and *knowledge*. An intimacy so blazing it is very difficult to ignore, to undo. That is what we're attempting: to pretend it never existed. Even as I imagine his hands on me and then his mouth, the weight of his body on mine.

We take breaks from the vault often, though they slow us down. There is no other option—we can't let ourselves get too cold, must always be climbing out of this freezer and warming thoroughly under blankets by a fire before we head back down.

Once the rods are clean, we refill the open area with mortar and leave it to dry. While up on the ladders we've spotted more patches of concrete cancer, so we work on these next. There is simply too much moisture in these walls, trickling down from above. The permafrost is melting fast, and permafrost is not meant to melt. This place was never prepared for it, for a thing that couldn't be conceived of. The storms grow more violent. The pump works hard to siphon out the water, but I feel like every time my feet touch the ground they are a little more submerged. We carry buckets of water each time we go. And the kids are on round-the-clock seed-sorting duty. They do this with gusto, for there are just so damn many—thousands and thousands of containers that need finding and moving. It is an incredible feat, the list Hank has made. No wonder he became consumed by it.

"I think we need to get them out of here," I say after a week has passed. "All the seeds that need saving."

The kids have finished sorting the containers, but Dom's and my efforts to repair the vault have amounted to very little. The wall should hold out for a while longer—if we are lucky, until the ship comes in three weeks—but new cracks appear by the day and water trickles in from every angle and the temperature has reached minus eight and continues to rise.

"They all do," Orly says, and there is an uncomfortable pause.

I look at Dom. "Is there anywhere dry we could put them?"

"Gotta be dry and very cold," he says.

"Has the freezer on the base started flooding yet?" Raff asks.

Fen nods. I haven't heard her speak aloud since the bonfire. She has gone painfully silent. Dom is the same toward her; he doesn't look at her, doesn't address her. The tension between them is unbearable. And I don't think it's anger, exactly. Neither of them seems to have any kind of temper. It's just . . . distance. I can see how this divide could grow until it swallows even the memories of their closeness. I can see how distressed it's making Raff, who looks between them constantly, too silent himself to come out and say anything that could bridge the gap.

"Could we move it?" I ask.

"Move what?"

"The freezer? To higher ground."

Dom scratches his chin, looking skeptical. "Dunno how we'd manage that. It's a room, not a box."

"What about the freezer back up in the lighthouse?"

"It's too small," Orly points out. "We'd only fit a fraction of what's here."

There is silence.

I look the kid in the face. "We might need to make some tough choices."

"No," he says. "Hank already halved them. It can't be less."

"I don't know what to tell you. This place is going under fast."

"Then fix it!" he demands.

"Hey," Dom says softly, and Orly bites off whatever he was about to yell at me. He turns on his heel and disappears into an aisle of seeds. The rest of us look at each other helplessly.

We keep going, keep patching, keep pumping. It is, as Dom put it, pushing shit up a hill. And as we work we are all probably thinking the same thing: Orly is the only one who knows enough about the seeds to know which to save, and this is a terrible thing to have to ask him.

I tell myself he'll be alright. That he has to be. Because he's a kid, and kids are resilient.

But as night falls and we all slide wearily into bed, I hear the patter of small feet and there is a boy climbing in with me, and he tells me the story of the dinosaur trees. And I can understand why he might not, in fact, be alright. Why maybe none of us will be, because we have, all of us humans, decided what to save, and that is ourselves.

Orly

There is a tree that once grew, long ago in the time of dinosaurs. Everyone thought this tree had gone extinct two million years ago. Which means that in all human history, not a soul had ever seen this tree. It was gone like the dinosaurs.

And then one spring afternoon in 1994, a park ranger was exploring the rough terrain of a national park in Australia's New South Wales. This stretch of rugged forest was mostly unexplored, and on this day he saw something no human had seen: the bright-green fernlike foliage and bubbly black bark of the long-extinct dinosaur trees, the Wollemi pines. It was the greatest botanical discovery of the twentieth century. They had been here, secretly, for two million years.

How had they survived so long? Surely only by staying hidden from us, everyone agreed on that. The scientists who were taken to confirm their identity were blindfolded so they'd never know the exact location of the trees and the information couldn't spread.

Only 10 percent of the Wollemi's seeds have a viable embryo, and most of these are eaten by cockatoos, so the researchers needed to act quickly, harvesting the seeds they could salvage, studying, preserving, and keeping them safe. The seeds can be found only at the very top of its branches, hidden within cones, and accessed by descending, harnessed, from a helicopter. A kind of extreme sport, a spy mission. Extract the seeds. Save a species.

Fast-forward a few decades. There's a much bigger danger approaching. A fire, an inferno, destroying everything in its path, plants and animals alike. They're calling it a "megafire," they're saying no fire has ever been as bad. It's burned twenty-four million hectares and three billion animals, and it's headed straight for the last remnants of the dinosaur trees.

Firefighters pull on their helmets and protective gear and they descend from their choppers into the dense burning forest. They make a barrier, they take up positions, and they fight this fire with everything they have. They save one of the world's oldest and rarest plants.

The Wollemi's location is never revealed to the public, even throughout this incredible mission and the worldwide joy of the rescue.

Now the seeds we have of the *Wollemia nobilis* sit in aisle G, row 12, and they are not on Hank's list.

Rowan

The ship may not arrive on the exact day it is due, but apparently it's usually only a day or so off on either side. Which means we have about a fortnight remaining on this island, and though we should all be joyful at the thought of escape, at the thought of this exhausting, stressful work coming to an end, we trudge through our days and hours like we are marching to our funerals. Dom and Fen *still* haven't spoken, and I don't know what will become of this family once we leave the island. Nor if I will ever see them again.

Which is exactly why I'm throwing a dinner party.

I send them all upstairs to their rooms while I do the cooking; they will hopefully take the opportunity for a nap. It takes me a few hours to get the last items in the oven and then I duck into the bathroom with the clippers. I haven't touched my hair since coming to Shearwater; this is well overdue. I set the blades and start shaving, working from front to back.

Fen appears in the open doorway, watching silently.

"Dinner won't be long," I tell her.

She doesn't speak until I've finished and am cleaning up the fallen hair. "I want to feel lighter," she says softly.

I straighten, meeting her eyes in the mirror. I smile.

The thick, salty hair falls to the ground in heavy chunks. It is much more satisfying than shaving my own short hair. Fen's perched on a stool before me, studiously not looking at her reflection, but down at her hands.

"I think it's time for you to move back to the lighthouse," I tell her.

She shakes her head. "He doesn't want me here."

"He's grieving, but he'll get over it."

"We were broken even before the bonfire."

"No you weren't," I say. "There's shit to grapple with, I'm sure."

"You don't understand," she says. "He won't talk to me. When he looks at me he sees something damaged."

I don't ask what happened. If either of them wanted me to know they would have told me. Instead I find her eyes in the mirror. "No, kid. That's what you're frightened he'll see."

When all her long hair lies in tendrils on the floor, I use the clippers to tidy the edges, but I don't linger too long. I can touch anything up tomorrow; it's getting late, and we need to eat.

"Okay," I say.

Fen takes a breath, and looks at herself. She gasps. Hands fly to cover her mouth. She looks every bit as wild as she used to, only now she looks fierce, too, and sleek. I wait, unsure if this reaction is good or bad. But she turns and hugs me tightly.

I hurry back to the kitchen to light a dozen candles. It's really late now, and full dark.

"Okay," I call up the stairs. "Dinner's ready!"

They all but trip over themselves coming down.

"Oh my god," Fen breathes.

Laid out on the kitchen table is our feast. I have cooked a roast chicken (which took days to defrost) and all the trimmings: platters of roast vegetables, stuffing and gravy, fresh bread, as well as a fettuccini dish with lemons and butter and capers for anyone who doesn't want to eat meat. There is a cheesecake and mud brownies (favorites in my family, both of which I have made for Liv and Jay on every birthday since we were kids), and a bottle of wine, and a weird homemade lemonade I tried to make for Orly which is basically just a sugar syrup with frozen lemon cubes in it. Within the light of the sea of candles it seems almost mythic, this feast.

The family are dazed. I am not sure how Dom will feel about it, but we look at each other and there is something hungry in him.

"Your hair!" Orly points an accusing finger at his sister, staring wide-eyed at her skull.

"The bald twins look like they're in a cult," Raff agrees.

Fen and I share a glance and laugh.

"First we drink," I say.

Instead of pouring the wine into cups, I take a swig right from the bottle and pass it around. "Let it stain your mouths and dribble down your throats," I say.

Dom doesn't say anything as Raff takes a gulp, but when Fen reaches for the bottle I feel him stiffen beside me, and I touch his arm to stay him. She is nearly eighteen and she deserves to be a teenager for a night. Fen takes a gulp and then passes it to her dad, who does the same, and Orly has his lemonade, which he says is the best thing he's ever tasted, probably because he's never tasted so much sugar. We keep passing the bottle until it's gone, until it has stained our teeth and lips and chins.

Dom can't help himself, he says with an ache, "The rations, Row." Not just the food and drink but the candles, too, and the gas it took to cook all of this.

I say, "Fuck the rations," and we eat, every last morsel of it, savoring our mouthfuls and moaning with delight. We eat until our bellies can't take another skerrick, until we are, at long last, full. Then we sit back in our chairs and Dom and I drink sherry and we talk, and while Dom and Fen don't speak directly to each other, there is an undeniable easing of the tension. As the kids chat I watch their dad's eyes, I watch how that gaze moves between each of his children's faces, I see the pride there, the swelling of his chest, the tiny quirks of his lips, the joy they give him. I think how lucky they are to have him, that it was into his care they were born. What a gift to be so well loved.

We decide we will take it in turns to each have one really long hot shower. There is a risk, of course, that the hot water will run out, so we spend time discussing who most deserves to go first and who should be last, and when we can't agree on that we decide to draw straws.

"Is this what it's like on the mainland?" Orly asks. "You can stay in the shower as long as you want?"

"Not really," Dom says.

"Oh." Orly looks sad.

"I dunno why you're complaining," I tell him. "The battle it takes to get you in a bath, my god."

He giggles, then turns serious. "So. I was thinking about your snow gums." He is looking at me.

"Were you now," I murmur.

"I was thinking you're gonna need help to replant them."

Fen nods eagerly.

"And to rebuild your home," Raff says.

I stare at the three kids.

My eyes and throat prickle. It's the openness of them, and their generosity. It's the thought of them entering my other life, my real life. Of meeting my sisters and their children. Of setting foot on my land, which is ash now but still mine, and so much a part of who I was. I feel impossibly moved by the three of them, I feel a thrill at the thought of offering this land to them, a place to keep them, to provide for them, but I am simultaneously overcome with the reality of the promises I've made, the obligations I am bound to. Dom is looking into his glass. He says nothing, maybe wishing as I do that things could be so simple.

We don't clean up straight away, which is tantamount to a crime in this household. We leave the mess, leave carnage behind us, and I hand Raff his violin. He looks hesitant, but I say, "Something to call the ghosts," and he understands, and nods.

I guide them all outside, into the windy night. It is dark still, but the nights here are so short that the early morning light is already starting to creep its way in.

"It's cold!" Orly shouts.

"Then you'd better dance," I say, and we do. All of us, even Dom. As Raff plays a riotous, endless song, we lift our arms and we spin and twist and twirl and jump, we make shapes of our bodies, we make languages of them. I see Orly on Dom's shoulders, his hands lifted to the stars, giving great whoops of excitement as his dad runs in wide arcs. I see Raff stamping his feet as he plays with abandon, and Fen making him laugh so hard the music skips but only for a beat. I see a moment—a moment to make my heart falter—in which father and daughter stumble face-to-face and look at each other, I see them each trying to decide what to do, how to move through this moment, and then I see Dom reach for his daughter's hand and spin her, I see him dip her low and I see her laugh. I close my eyes, drinking it all in, knowing it is a place in time that I will never forget. The world is dangerous and we will not survive it. But there is this. Impermanent as it may be.

I am certain I'm not the only one who feels the presences on the wind. All the hungry ghosts of Shearwater Island, come to dance with us on the hill.

Dominic

To live for your children seems a normal thing, a respectable one; to live because of your children is something else. Mine are the blood of me, and the oxygen in that blood, the airflow and the neurons firing and the stretch and release of muscles in limbs, they are the foundations that make up my skeleton, all the collagen and calcium upon which I stand and fall, and the pulse and the flow and the beat. But I think maybe this is too much for them to be. The breath of a man. The life of him. I think it is too heavy a thing for children to carry.

We dance on the hill and I watch them, and I think that I have been holding them hostage. So we will leave this place and I will let them go, I will let them become. Not Orly yet, but one day. And for the first time I realize that this will not lessen the profundity or fervency of how I love them. It will not mean I stop protecting them, would not lay down my life for them, will not be there every second that they need me. It just means that I can't let them worry about me anymore. Whatever that takes.

I look at the woman who has made all of this clear to me. Who has given us this gift. She is so beautiful in the glow of the rising sun, as she tilts her head back to laugh with my children. How did I not see this beauty the first moment I set eyes on her?

Later, we huddle in front of the fireplace to get warm. Rowan rises for bed before the rest of us. I take her hand, wanting to stay her, but she looks at me and tells me to enjoy the moment with my kids, and I know what all of this has been about. She has done this for us.

When it is just me and my children, Fen moves to sit beside me. I feel no hurt or betrayal—all of that has trickled out of me. Instead all I see now is how terrible it must have been for her, to do such a thing, to think she *had* to do it, for me. I reach out and run my hand over her short spiky hair. In her eyes is a question.

"Impossible to tell from the seals now," I say, and she smiles.

Fen takes something out of her pocket. "I saved these."

In her hand are Claire's three wedding rings. The first engagement band I saved up for in our early twenties, the wedding band, and the ring I got her on our tenth anniversary, not long before she died. An immense wave of emotion rises up in me at the sight of them. Something like love and loss and pain and relief. For a second the desire to take them and close my palm around them is so strong I can hardly breathe. But I only need to look at my children and it passes.

"Those are yours," I say. "One for each of you. That's what she'd want."

Rowan

Morning is bad. We have barely slept. I knew we would be punished for this and we are, we are a chorus of moans and groans as we drag ourselves up to start another day. It's been raining on and off but any larger storms have not yet reached us. Nobody talks much as we travel down the coast and then splash our way through the tunnel to the vault. But it is a different kind of silence than the depressed trudging we have taken to lately: this is a silence that holds purpose. A great crack has opened in the concrete of the back wall and water is gushing from the schism. The decision is made for us: there will be no more futile patching, no more scrambling to remove water. We are surrendering this vault to the sea, and we are going to save as many packets of seeds as we can by ferrying them up to our lighthouse freezer. And maybe there are too many, and maybe there isn't enough time, but we will just . . . keep going. We will run, for every second of the time we have left.

We speed like mad up the coast of Shearwater to our beach, where we pile the first load onto a pallet. The pallet is attached to the back of the quad bike and then dragged up to the lighthouse freezer. And then we run back down the hill for another load. It is grueling, and the rain is harder and more lashing than we'd like, but we keep on. The vault floor is underwater, the empty bottom shelf submerged. The pump does next to nothing. The crack gushes.

I have felt this kind of frenzied focus before.

But the end of all that effort came to nothing. No matter how hard I tried I couldn't save my home. We were forced to flee, *Hank* forced me to flee. And I saw, in my effort—and Hank's lack of effort—a simple truth I did not want to acknowledge. He did not love our home like I loved it. Not even the garden we grew together. He did not love it like it was his body back up on the hill, burning.

We went to sleep that night on the ground of a crowded evacuation point, a showground filled with displaced people. We lay under a sky of falling ash, drifting and dreamy like snow. I imagined it falling to cover my body, to embalm me.

But tonight sleep comes easily, knowing the people around me care the same way I do, they care more, they are willing to fight.

***

The next morning, there is a throng of seabirds not far off the coastline. They dive and squawk and wheel through the air.

"There'll be a big school of fish out there," Raff tells me. He and I are in the front Zodiac, returning from the vault with our first load for the day. Fen is in the boat behind us, and following up at the rear are Dominic and Orly in the Frog.

The rain has paused, but the charcoal sky remains full and poised. I hear a clap of thunder off in the distance. Huge waves look white on the horizon.

"There's rips all through here," Raff tells me as he steers out of them. "Sea's not happy today."

The birds don't seem it either; there is something tense about the sound of them, though they should be joyful at such a buffet. I can see the school shimmering at the surface of the water, a broiling pot.

And then for the second time in a short span, Raff and I round the rocks of the headland and come in toward our beach, and we see our two humpbacks. Only this time it's not their tails arching gracefully out of the water or the sprays of their blowholes. It's their bodies on the black sand.

Raff lets go of the throttle and the boat comes to a stop, lifted by the waves. He has gone bone white.

"What are you doing?" I ask over the crash of surf.

"They're dead."

"Maybe not."

"Even if they're not, we can't refloat them."

"Let's at least investigate," I say, though I know he's right.

He steers the Zodiac onto the shore. The rest of his family have seen the whales now, they're nearing the sand too. I don't wait for them but run to the mother whale. She doesn't seem as big as she did when she was falling on top of me; nonetheless she is a very large creature. The curve of her back is about as high as my head, her length many times mine. I can't tell if she's alive. There is no breathing happening, no movement. Raff goes to her closed eye, which is as big as a grapefruit. He very gently touches the eyelid, and it opens.

We both gasp. The whale's eye swivels to us. "It's okay," I say, needing to comfort her.

A burst of air leaves her blowhole.

"Pull something over your nose and mouth," Raff tells me. "They carry heaps of bacteria."

Dominic, Fen, and Orly are joining us now and we all pull our neck gators or scarves over our faces. Dom moves past us to check on the baby, and his kids are following, but I find I can't go over there, I can't even look at it.

"It's alive!" Orly shouts at me and I could dissolve with relief, although maybe this is worse because all it means is witnessing a slow death.

We convene a little way up the beach.

"What do we do?" Fen asks. "We have to keep them wet, I know that much."

"Raff?"

"There's no use," he says.

"Mate," Dom says softly, pulling his son's gaze to him. "Let's just talk it through, get it straight. What are the main concerns?"

Raff rubs his eyes, maybe searching his memory for what he knows about strandings.

"Their own weight is crushing them," he says. "And they're overheating. We have to stabilize them before we can think about trying to get them back into the water."

"Good," Dom says. "How do we do that?"

"Like Fen said, keep their skin wet and covered so it doesn't get damaged by the sun."

"Okay, so we'll set up tarps," Dom says calmly. "And we can cover them in wet sheets, and we'll use buckets. What else."

"I think we have to help their fins from getting fractured," Raff says. "You dig holes for them."

The mother whale's fins do look at an awkward angle on the sand.

"When's high tide?" I ask.

"It's falling now," Fen says, "lowest around four this arv, then it'll be back in tonight around eleven."

"That's our timeline, then," Dom says. "We'll need high tide to get them out."

But Orly is shaking his head. "What about the seeds?" he asks. "We're not even close to finished."

It is a disaster, there is no doubt about that. We don't have enough bodies, enough hands.

"How do you eat an elephant?" Dom asks him.

"Dad!"

"How?"

Orly sighs. "One bite at a time. Okay—but we're not forgetting about them."

"We're not," his dad agrees.

The kids hurry into action but I take Dom's arm and pull him aside.

"We shouldn't do this," I say.

"Do what?"

"We should take the kids away from this beach and put them back on the seeds. That might actually be achievable."

Dom frowns, searching my face.

"This is not. This is cruel," I say. "It will be backbreaking work for hours, purely to watch the animals die."

Dom looks at the whales, and then his kids, considering my words.

I will him silently to listen to me. To not put them through this. He meets my eyes. "You're probably right," he says. "But I think not trying would haunt them more."

On the crest of the hill I look down at the creatures on the sand. They are close to the waterline; at high tide that water will come up and over them, but I don't think it will be enough to wash them free. We are doing this, Dom has decided. So we may as well do it properly. My mind starts thinking about angles and equipment. I don't think we have a crane at our disposal, but I definitely saw a tractor with a bucket attachment, so that will have to do. The baby will be easier to refloat but I don't need Raff to tell me it won't survive without its mother. I'm not sure she would survive either, without her baby. There is no point saving one without the other.

We have the weather on our side. There is no sun to harm the whales' skin, and there is a light drizzle to help keep them wet and cool. We wet the sheets and blankets and drape them over the huge bodies, covering as much area as we can, and we move quickly to dig the holes for their fins, so they can lie comfortably. These holes we fill with seawater to help keep them cool, and then we are running up and down from the water with buckets.

I signal to Dom. "You and I will need to think about how to move them. We've got about eleven hours until high tide."

"No crane," he says.

"No, so it's trenches, and that's best done while tide's low."

We leave the kids to keep filling buckets while we jog over to the storage unit at the base. The tractor, as well as having a forklift, has a long-armed bucket excavator we can use in the sand. Dom fills the tractor with diesel. I drag things out of the way so it has a clear exit through the roller door, and he drives the old yellow vehicle onto the beach. The wheels are so enormous that they aren't bothered by the seawater lapping at them; I am hoping like hell it doesn't get bogged, and Dom manages to steer it up onto the sand and back over to the whales. He works the controls so the bucket takes huge mouthfuls of sand and dumps them to the side, slowly gouging the beginnings of a trench. I worry about the noise freaking the whales out.

I take the moment to remind the kids to have some water. Raff is running himself into the ground. Hours pass. Fen, who has taken to timing the whales' breaths, says their breathing has slowed and become more regular. Hopefully this means they are less stressed. On a five-minute break somewhere in the afternoon, I move so I can see the mother's right eye, trained always to rest on her calf where it lies beside her.

I look at this whale's skin, all the scratches and barnacles I can recall so clearly in my mind. I place a flat hand on her body and I try to feel the beat of her heart.

"I washed up on this beach," I tell her softly. "My body was brought here by the sea and lived. Yours will too."

Her eyelid falls closed and in this moment she seems so weary. But it opens again and she looks at me, and I know why.

"What do you want me to tell it?" I ask her, but I already know.

I don't want to go to the baby. I can't bear the thought of it, have been trying to pretend it's not even here. But I think this mother needs me to and I think I would do anything for her. So I walk over to this smaller whale and I place my hand gently on its head, near its open eye that is looking at me. "Little one," I say softly. "You're not alone."

The tide is coming back in now. We still have a few hours until it's at its highest, and Dom is making great progress. The trench for the adult whale is done—he has dug a long pathway as far into the water as he can move the tractor, and he is now working on the same kind of pathway for the baby.

Fen and I start getting a tarp beneath the smaller creature. We stand on either side and work the material slowly and carefully down into the sand, sliding it inch by inch under the weight of the huge body. It's slow, difficult work, tiring on our hands and backs and necks, but soon it's done. There's no point trying to do the same for the mother—even if we could get one underneath her, she's far too heavy for a tarp to make any difference. Instead we work on digging the trench up around her body.

All day I have been readying myself for this not to work. I think of how we will console the kids. But here is the nature of life. That we must love things with our whole selves, knowing they will die.

It's raining hard when the tide reaches us, too soon. The ocean will need to do its work for the mother whale; there's nothing more we can do for her now, so we set to dragging the baby out into the waves. I think it probably weighs about a ton. We aren't making much difference. Too few bodies, one of them a child. Though he is straining as hard as the rest of us, using everything he has. I can see tears streaming down Raff's cheeks and I don't know if it's the effort or the knowledge that this won't work. The baby isn't moving. But we keep pulling, all of us. I have spent many years working my body hard, but I have never asked it for this much, I have never demanded anything of the sort, and I think we will all, at least, know we left nothing behind. We gave it everything. We tried for them. And as we pull and pull and pull, with waves smashing into us and Dom pulling the greatest load of all, I start to feel a little give. As the water flows over the smaller body, as it sucks powerfully back out and we drag in time with it, the tarp moves. Water gets in under it and with every wave the baby whale is lifted a touch more, is inched farther out until finally the water is deep enough that the creature can float. We see its fins lift, we see its small knobby dorsal, we see its body move from side to side, finding its balance, and then we see it start to swim, and we are all of us cheering, our throats raw, our bodies spent.

As one we turn to the mother, who has not moved.

Rowan

My mother and I have not spoken much in the time we've spent here on her couches. We haven't spoken much in many years, really, but today I am determined to cover a little ground with her, to make sense of some things because it is clear to me that she does not have a lot of time. I don't make the mistake of pausing the film she's put on, I just talk over the top of it.

"Why did we live on the boat?" I ask.

She doesn't look at me. "What?"

"Why did you want to live on a boat with four little kids?"

"What do you mean? We all loved the boat."

"Yeah, I know, but what made you choose it in the first place?"

Maybe I am expecting some story of wanting a life of adventure, but she says, irritated, "A flood destroyed our home, and we didn't have a cent between us or anywhere to go."

I stare at her.

I have never in my life heard her speak of such a thing. I can't wrap my head around it, and my first instinct is mistrust, but there is no reason for her to lie. My mind darts back, touching upon memories, trying to reshape them. What had my parents gone through and why was it a secret? Why was I responsible enough to look after my brother and sisters but not to know the reason I had to work so hard to keep them safe?

"Why didn't you tell us that?" I ask.

"We spared you from it. You were little."

"Okay," I say, keeping my voice level. "Then did it not seem irresponsible to leave babies alone on a boat?"

"We didn't leave him alone," she says. "He was with you."

"I was thirteen. And watching three kids."

"That's right."

I stare at her. The cancer has stolen any youth from her face; it has made her ancient and barely recognizable. I can't remember what she looked like before this. There is a hot thing growing in my abdomen, in the middle of me, it is expanding and making it hard to breathe. I think I was going to reach for forgiveness, here at the end. I won't get it, I can see now. She hates me for losing River. Will blame me until her last breath. If I want sense from what happened I will need to make it myself.

"I've been so angry with you for putting me in that position," I tell her. My voice breaks. "Why did you have kids if you weren't going to bother keeping them safe?"

She says nothing. She's just watching her movie.

Mum passes away not long after this. It feels protracted and agonizing but in reality it is not so long. Liv and Jay come so that I'm not alone when it happens, though they haven't been here for the last months of deterioration. In the ten years since River, Mum has not made herself easy to love. They barely know her. *I* am more of a mother to them. Dad doesn't come back to say goodbye. His means of survival was to get away, get as far away as possible and pretend none of it, and none of us, ever existed. To be honest, I understand that. He cut himself free so he would not be dragged under.

With three of Mum's four children sitting around her bed as she takes her last breaths, I let go of blame. It was not my fault River died and it was not my mum's. I thought she chose that boat and that life of danger, but really the flood chose it for her, it was this crumbling world. And there will be more floods. More children swept under. But they will not be my children.

I am so sure. I am thinking of words to make sense of this, to offer some comfort. I knew this ending, I have known it all along, and we should have walked away at the start.

And then. The pathways we have carved begin to work. I watch in stunned disbelief. The sea is wild and powerful and it is not done with her, it is hungry to have her back. It surges. This is what saves the whale: this impossibly high tide.

We watch as her massive body is dragged back out along with half the sand of the beach. We see her float, tilt, and then swim. She swims. Straight for her baby, who is waiting for her. Mother and calf come together, slide over and around each other, we can hear their calls, see their fins lift. It's dark; they are gone quickly, their skin as inky as the waterworld embracing them.

But I can't move. I can't leave this as easily as they can. I watch where they disappeared for a long time. It doesn't make sense that they should have lived. An impossibility, to shake some foundation of me. Something I have learned to rely on.

I see Dom holding his children. Raff and Orly first, and then his daughter moves to be tucked into his embrace, which is big enough for the three of them.

He sees me watching and moves a hand, gesturing for me to come. He seems to think his arms wide enough to hold me, too.

I don't know if I can cross to them.

But a mother and her baby have survived tonight. On a night I thought bound for death we've witnessed life instead. They didn't surrender, they held on, they fought, and my god, so did we. These kids fought, they pushed themselves past every threshold. Knowing all the while that it would probably be for nothing, they pushed on anyway.

If they can do that, then I can cross this beach to them. I can put my arms around them, I can help him to hold them. What kind of idiot would choose only a quarter of the love they are offered?

———

Dom delivers us home, one at a time, on the back of the quad bike. Orly first, then Raff, Fen, and me last. I try to make the walk myself, thinking to save him a trip, but my legs are gone—I take a few steps and end up on the ground. So I sit in the rain and I make silent apologies to Hank for the choice I've made. It is a betrayal but it's done, I can't turn back. Perhaps I will be as our home was for him: a simple enough task to cut himself free of. I feel delirious. I can hear the wind, as Orly does. It warns me to be careful, it doesn't know I have had enough of careful.

Dom is white with exhaustion by the time he returns for me. I am sitting in the grass and for a disorienting moment, in the blast of the engine and the headlights, I think he will run me over. I see my body collided with, dragged along.

But he stops.

In the dark, on the ground, in the grass.

I say, "Before I came here, I didn't care about anything. I didn't want anything. It's really . . . desolate, not wanting anything."

Dom meets my eyes. His expression, it could kill me.

"Now," I say, "what I want is for your beach house to have a workshop that's big enough for both of us, and all our tools."

I am not the only one with a choice to make, and I don't know what his will be. But he smiles and I have never seen this smile before. "You'd hate being near the ocean," he says. "In a place that could wash away."

"I'll go anywhere with you," I tell him simply.

"And I you," he murmurs, and we are kissing and I feel it again, that sense of time folding over on itself, of a thousand lifetimes spent together. If it is our bodies that should one day be washed up onshore then I hope they will do so together.

He helps me onto the quad behind him. I snake my arms around his middle, rest my head on his back. The blood rushes in my ears and every bump hurts my teeth. At the lighthouse we are too tired to climb any steps so we both sink onto the floor of the living room, beside the fire that has burned down to coals but is still warm. There are no pillows or blankets but our fingers are touching as we slip out of consciousness. Deranged with exhaustion.

"Goodnight, darlin'," I hear him murmur. "Love you."

But something about the ring of it makes me unsure if he is talking to me or his dead wife.

———

Wake up.

Wake up!

I drag my eyes open. The world is blurry and spinning. There is a face over mine. I adore this face. But I would very much like it to stop talking.

"Come on," Orly is saying. "Hurry up. We have to go back for more seeds."

"Oh my god," I manage to utter. "Couldn't I just . . . die? Instead?"

"No, get up, come on." He turns to his dad who has flung an arm over his eyes in protest. "Dad, you promised. Get up."

Dom groans. "What time is it?"

"It's 7:30. I've let you sleep in."

"Wow thanks," I mutter. I get myself upright, stumble to the kitchen for coffee. Fen is already there, making a pot. She looks about as bad as I feel, pale and very slow moving.

"Raff's had a bad night," she tells her dad, who disappears to check on his son. Orly, Fen, and I eat toast with jam and honey because we are all desperate for the sugar hit.

When Dom gets back, he looks worried. "His arm's swelled up. I think he's sprained it again. He's gonna stay here and rest."

"Oh no," Orly moans, more I think for being a man down on our mission than out of concern for his brother.

We get back to it. Everything is terrible but I look at Dom and feel woozy with love, I am limerent. I look at his kids and for the first time in a long while I see a future. As we carry our containers out through the chamber doors and into the long tunnel, though, I hear a faint, echoing scream in my ears and a chill moves down my spine. I look ahead to see if Orly heard, but he's facing forward and I can't tell. It's as if the island is reminding me not to forget, for a single moment, that this is a place of death.

When we return for the next load, I catch sight of Orly talking to himself. He is standing oddly in a corner, and his hands are moving as though he's explaining something, and then I hear the lifted note of his voice, a kind of plea.

It frightens me.

He sees me and his hands drop.

"Who were you talking to?" I ask him.

"No one." He walks past me, getting back to work.

Later I catch a snippet of a whispered conversation between father and daughter.

". . . it's a violation. And we are all going down for it."

"Don't you worry about that. It's for me to reckon with." And then Dom adds, more forcefully, "This is not on you, darlin'."

Later still I see Fen resting her forehead against a wall. I cross to her, worried.

"Are you okay?"

My voice startles her and she whirls as though caught in the act of something. "I'm fine." She hurries back to her task, not looking at me.

Outside, I catch Dom's arm as he is about to climb into the Frog.

"What's up?" he asks.

"Is something going on?"

"With what?"

"I don't know."

He searches my face. I don't know how to explain the unease or what to ask him. All I know is that it's starting to feel distinctly like they are keeping something from me again.

I wake in the night with words playing over in my head and a racing heart. Dom is wrapped around me, his mouth pressed to the line of my collarbone, my hand in his hair, his words in my ear.

We tried. We gathered around, I promise we did. But there was no way to call for help and we were in over our heads and he didn't want our help.

I stare at the ceiling.

There was no way to call for help.

I sit up.

"You okay," he mumbles.

"Toilet," I say, and stumble for the door.

My feet are very cold on the stone steps as I move down to the bathroom and lock the door behind me. Why didn't I get socks. I sit on the closed lid of the toilet. I don't look in the mirror. I close my eyes and I will my slow dumb fucking mind to do some proper work.

Dominic told me when I first got here that the communications had all been sabotaged by someone right before leaving with the other researchers on the ship.

He told me Hank left on this boat. Distressed enough to forget his passport. Okay.

He then told me a story about three scientists who did not in fact leave on that boat, but stayed behind to help sort seeds, and who then all died. Because there was no way to contact the mainland, all three have been buried on the island.

Firstly. Why would Hank not have stayed on as part of this exercise? To finish his own work?

Maybe because he was unwell. That stands to reason.

But then.

Dominic said *there was no way to call for help.* Which means that when Hank was here, losing his mind, the comms had already been sabotaged.

Which means, if I have this timeline smoothed out correctly in my head, Hank couldn't have left on the ship with the majority of the researchers. It means he did stay on, with Naija, Tom, and Alex. Somebody broke the radios and then several people died, and Dom is lying to me about it.

I climb the stairs to the boys' room and creep in quietly. I sit on the side of Raff's bed and gently touch his shoulder. His eyes open and he looks at me, without any other movement.

"How did Alex die?" I ask him.

Disbelief clouds his face. "What?"

"I'm sorry, kid. But how did he die?"

"Have you lost it, Row?"

"Raff."

"He hanged himself, alright? What—"

I reach forward and hold him tightly, and he hugs me back, but I am thinking about how that blood in the cabin didn't belong to Alex after all, it belonged to someone else.

———

I keep my eyes glued to them. They're acting sketchy, something has them spooked. Orly keeps going to stand in that same corner. Fen is anxious. She argues with her dad, and they're being careful not to let me overhear.

I notice what I should have seen weeks ago. That often, when we have carried our last containers out through the tunnel and are loading them onto the boats, Dominic goes back to do a last check of the temperature. I've never once questioned it, but today I think it is weird. Why not just check it all before we leave?

So I give him a few minutes to get ahead of me, I wait until the kids are occupied, and then I slip back into the tunnel to follow him. I don't turn on any lights but walk in darkness. I try to be silent but there is a lot of water in this tunnel now.

Inside, I can't see him.

I slip into a far aisle and make my way slowly toward the back of the vault. My heart is beating very quickly. In the corner where I keep finding Orly, there is nothing but an air vent. I'd assumed it was a cooling vent but it doesn't look like the others, and if it's not, where does it go?

On the back wall is a door. Dom said this was the door to the air shaft. As I get closer I can see it's not properly closed. Which is odd, because he specifically said they don't open it in order to keep the temperature from plummeting.

Everything in me is a frozen kind of calm as I reach for the handle and pull it open.

It is indeed an air shaft, long and narrow, with a ladder that stretches right up to the sky; there is a tiny dot of light, way up there—a glass panel in the hatch covering. I turn my neck and follow the shaft down. The ladder reaches to a floor deeper in the earth; I can barely see it in the dark but I can hear a voice floating up to me. Dominic's voice. I don't know what he's saying, but he is returning to the ladder.

I recoil, darting to hide in an aisle. Between boxes on shelves, I can see Dom emerge. He closes and locks the door behind him, and I hear him splash his way out of the vault.

After a few breaths I return to the door. It locks from this side, so I am able to open it and climb into the secret shaft, and down the secret ladder, rung by rung to the bottom. The air is much warmer here; it has never been refrigerated like the vault has.

It would have been a simple storage room, once. A concrete square. Now it has rows of water bottles, boxes of the same food supplies I've seen in our pantry, a heater, and one of the camp beds from the research base.

Sitting on which, staring at me in complete disbelief, is Hank Jones.

Fen

Fen is sixteen when she first sees Hank. He's shouting at someone driving the Frog onto land, signaling that they need to wait for a pair of gentoos who are waddling across their path. He is the new team leader of the base, here to spend a few weeks in handover with Carol. Fen is sad to see Carol go—Carol taught her how to cut open the giant kelp and cook fish inside. None of them know what to expect from the new guy, but Fen likes that he is concerned for the penguins.

She doesn't have anything to do with Hank until a few months later. He has offered to give the three kids a lesson on the island's botanicals, which Dom thinks is a great idea—they can use it as part of their coursework. Fen and her brothers head down the hill to meet Hank the next time he's going south to the vault, and as they speed along in the Zodiac he tells them in his New York accent (so he says, she wouldn't have a clue) about the seeds he has been tasked to look after. He explains about the importance of the vault, he talks about the dangers in the world that may give these seeds value, he says that some have already been used. He speaks of seed banks back on land and how so many have been lost over the years, he tells them how some plants don't have seeds or seeds that don't survive the freezing process, so scientists have taken to culturing their tissues and cloning them as a method of reproduction. He talks of biodiversity and the interconnectedness of all living things. He says his favorite seeds are from a type of orchid, and then he shows them these seeds, which are so small they are practically invisible, and says that the only way to collect them is to let them fall onto a type of fungus and collect this instead.

Fen is aware, after a few lessons like this, that she is developing a crush on him. She has been raised by a man so reticent his silences can last days. So all of Hank's talking, all of these conversations—they are a revelation to her. It is actually possible to know what someone is thinking, it is actually possible for them to tell you! It makes her feel grown-up, to *know* someone like this. He's smart and passionate, and he's funny too. Plus there aren't many choices on this island for people to fantasize about, and the fantasies come without her permission, anyway. One day he is just an adult she doesn't know, like any other, the next he is filling her thoughts.

Time passes and Fen enjoys these fantasies. They give her something to do. She would be bored without them. Never, in any of her wildest imaginings, does she think anything will happen between them. And, if she is honest with herself, never has she *wanted* anything to happen. The fun of the crush is that it exists in her mind. That it is her secret. And that she is safe from it.

Fen is seventeen by the time Hank's new orders are given. They will both be staying on for another three months and then heading off island for good. Something in him shifts at this point. She can feel the nature of his interest in her changing. Everything about him takes on an urgent quality, a sort of frenzied abandon.

When he says he's noticed her watching him, she flushes, she feels caught. When he says he knows she likes him, that he can feel her attraction, she realizes she has done this to herself, that it's her fault. She tells herself it's what she wants. She's old enough, it's legal, he says, and anyway they're leaving soon. Actually, his exact words are "It will all be over soon."

It's not at all like how she imagined it. Still, she is flattered he wants her. She can't believe her luck, to have been chosen.

She's not aware of a wife.

It is crucial that her dad never know.

Each month Fen dreads her period; she marks its impending arrival on the calendar so she can be prepared for the pain of it. Which means she is aware of this day passing her by. At only one day late, she becomes convinced. She spirals. Panicking, thinking through every implication. The worst part of this is that her dad will have to be told, because he will need to take her off island so she can get an abortion.

Fen spends a couple of hours wallowing in the misery of it, in the fear of what will happen to her body if she doesn't get this dealt with immediately. There is an immense urgency in her. (And deeper, a sadness that could swallow her whole, if she allows it to.)

What if . . . Could she keep it? Children shouldn't have children and she has no mum to show her how to do it, but she has the best dad in the world, and she has pretty much raised a baby already herself . . . Her family would help her, she knows they would. But Fen doesn't think the question is whether she'd be capable, but whether it's what she wants, if it's what she's ready for, and it's not, not yet. One day, but not this day, and not with this man.

As the hours pass, she pulls herself together. She is very good at calm. She comes up with a plan. Hank will help her, he has to, he loves her.

When Fen arrives at the vault to tell him, he seems weird. He's been pretty weird for weeks now, but today he is opening containers and pulling out seed packets and dumping them in a pile on the floor. All his meticulous categorizing out the window.

Where are the others? Tom and Naija and Alex? Why aren't they stopping him from doing whatever this is?

"What are you doing?" she asks.

He doesn't look at her, just carries on with his work. "It's the end of it all."

"What is?"

"They don't get to tell me to drown half. That is not something any bureaucracy gets to decide on."

"So then don't," Fen says. "Just tell them you won't do it."

"If I refuse, they'll send someone else down here."

"Okay, so what . . . ?"

"Don't worry about it, kid."

He is enraged, she realizes. This is not a good time to tell him what she suspects. But he turns to her and levels that look on her, and it seems to say *why have you bothered me*, and she gets flustered, wanting something important to justify her presence here. So she blurts it out. *I think I'm pregnant.*

At first he doesn't react. Hank is calm as he leads her out of the vault. They walk in silence to the blue field hut.

"Where are the others?" she asks.

"Up at the base."

Her stomach sinks. Something feels so off. He's not looking at her. He is watching the ocean. "You know what's hilarious?" he asks. "My wife was right."

It takes a moment for that word to sink in. Wife. And now she can hardly concentrate on what he's saying.

"I've always wanted children but she kept saying it was wrong. Bad for the world, bad for the kids. I thought it was just an excuse but she was so fucking right. This world is a dumpster fire."

Fen is dissolving. He has a wife. This is bad. This is way worse than she realized. She is a party to something cruel.

"I've figured out how to solve the problem," Hank rambles on (he is always rambling on, how has she abided this?). "You know Orly's wind voices?" he asks her. "I thought he was really screwed up." Hank laughs bitterly. "I was the one who didn't have a clue. This place is full of them."

"Of who?"

"Of the dead."

She is staring at him and her skin is crawling. He's always joked about how stupid her superstition is.

"I think this is where things come to die," Hank says.

"I'm gonna walk home. I'll see you later."

"Fen."

She pauses, though she very much doesn't want to.

"I figured out what has to happen. It's impossible to choose. Do you understand that?"

"Yes."

"So I won't. Nobody will. They will all drown. Every one of them, and every one of us, and then everything will start again."

She doesn't know what he's talking about and she doesn't care, she just wants to get back to her family. But he pulls her in for a hug. As he holds her he says, "I'm so sorry this happened. It's my fault and I'll pay for it in the end, I'll pay for it all." Then he pulls her down into the seawater and shoves her head under the surface.

First there is shock. There is disbelief. But she is strong, and she has very good lungs. Her brothers and father like to say she was born for the water and maybe that's true, she is certainly at home beneath its surface. So if he thinks this is how to kill her? He is mistaken.

The secret is simple: you have to know how to stay calm. Panic—even a slightly raised pulse—is your enemy. Even when the pressure comes, even with the pain. Fen lets her mind go blank and her body go limp. She plays dead. The seconds tick past but she doesn't move, doesn't panic. Finally his grip on her head loosens a fraction and she uses the moment to twist out of his hold. Instead of surging up beside him she kicks out underwater, swimming as far into the sea as she can. She is not frightened of the burn in her lungs, she knows it well because she is always pushing to its edge, always wanting just that little longer beneath. Even so, she is all too human.

Her head bobs out of the water like one of the seals. She sees him in the shallows, waves crashing against his knees.

"Fen!" he shouts.

He won't come after her, not while she's in the ocean—he's got no chance of outswimming her, and anyway there are people running down the hill toward them. It's Raff and Alex. She wonders how much they saw.

Fen watches her brother, who is a lot bigger than Hank, tackle the older man to the ground. Together, he and Alex drag Hank into the field hut. She watches that door; she isn't coming out of the sea until she knows it's safe. Alex returns and waves her in, but she doesn't move, she treads water, watching him. He comes down to the shoreline and shouts to her. "Are you okay?"

She says nothing.

"Your dad's on his way, okay?" he calls. "And Raff's watching Hank. You can come out."

But she can't. She won't. She starts to shiver, her teeth chattering. She will have to move soon, she doesn't have her wetsuit, she might be in shock.

"Fen, baby," Alex calls. "Please come out. It's too cold."

In the end it's Raff who wades into the water and pulls her bodily to shore. "Why did he do that to you?" he is asking. "Why was he doing that, Fen?" But she can't talk.

That was a man who said he loved her. She does not understand.

Alex has blankets and they wrap them around her, and Raff keeps holding her, but she is staring fixedly at the door to the hut in case he comes back out, someone has to watch that door, she can't even blink, don't they understand he could come back out.

Eventually her dad speeds down the coast to the rocks. There is no beach here, but he doesn't care, he turns off the Zodiac and jumps into the water, climbing to where they sit.

"What's going on?" he asks, and he is looking at her and it feels like he is seeing everything. She is so ashamed.

"Hank was trying to drown her," Raff says, and he sounds bewildered. He sounds like he too is in shock.

Dominic looks at her but still she can't talk, her jaw is locked, and she can't take her eyes from the door.

"We were coming down the hill and they were talking by the water," Alex is explaining, "and we saw them hug, and then he was just, I don't know, holding her head under water."

It is so bizarre, so unbelievable, that they all stare at each other.

When Fen nods, confirming it, something falls over Dominic, a cold, mechanical kind of certainty that is utterly unlike the ranting anger Hank displayed, no, this is something other, and Fen should be terrified, but instead she is glad. She watches her father go into that field hut, and she knows something bad is about to happen, but what she discovers is that she hates Hank with purity and completeness, and she is grateful for her dad's size and his fists, which she has never understood until now. She knows what the fists are for now, she knows why someone might need to punch a bag over and over.

She is able to look away from the door at last.

Fen won't ever ask what happened inside, but it is obvious that Dominic has nearly killed Hank in that little kitchen. It is only Raff, with strength that almost rivals his father's, who manages to wrestle Dom away before it's too late.

Tom, Alex, and Raff get Hank to the hospital on the base. Naija will treat him. Dom takes Fen home to the lighthouse, where they sit at the kitchen table and talk.

When she explains that she and Hank have been in a relationship of sorts for about a month, she sees the horror that falls over him and she will never be able to unsee it. She knows exactly what he perceives her as now. Damaged. Broken.

He asks, "Has he ever forced you?"

"No."

"Has he ever hurt you, before this?"

"No. He's not himself," she tells him. "He wants to drown all the seeds. So that no one can ever make the choice. I saw it in his eyes—he won't stop until he's drowned them all."

She gets her period two days later.

Dominic

Something at the heart of me fractures when I see the fear in my daughter's eyes. I can't fathom how I let this happen, how I let her stray into such danger without noticing. I am astounded at the unlikelihood of bringing my children to a place so remote and *still* having something so terrible happen to her. Maybe it is not unlikely at all. Where men go there is harm. I have failed her, and I have to do better. I have to *be* better.

I wish I had killed Hank, but I didn't, and now there's a problem to be dealt with. I'll need to radio the mainland, get some authorities down here to pick up the bastard. But when I walk up to the comms tower, I find every piece of equipment dead, as if it has been gone at by some kind of rabid animal. Wires have been cut, instruments have been cracked, holes have been punched. I try a few buttons but there's nothing, no response from any of it, and I can already see that this is well beyond my capacity to fix. If there is any part of this job I'm not great at, it's the electricals.

It's not difficult to piece together what's happened. Hank didn't want anyone to be able to call for help before he'd finished destroying what's in the vault. Or murdering my daughter.

I go back to the lighthouse and gently try to explain it to Fen. I consider not, but I think she deserves to know.

She flinches. "So we're trapped here with him? We're just going to be stuck on this island with him for two more months?"

"I'm not letting him anywhere near you," I promise her. "You're safe."

But she is shaking her head and I can see she doesn't believe me. Why would she?

I go to the hospital. Raff, Alex, Tom, and Naija are all sitting outside in frantic discussion. When they see me approaching, they stand up. Raff comes to head me off, and I realize they are worried I am here to make another attack. I raise my hands, show them I mean no harm.

"How is he?" I ask. Not because I give a fuck how the asshole is, but because I need to ascertain when he'll be well enough to be on his feet, at which point I will need to contain him.

"Not good," Naija snaps. She is looking at me like I am a monster, and maybe I am.

"Right, so he's sabotaged the satellite and radio equipment."

"*What?*"

"It's out. I'll start trying to repair it, but it's not gonna be working for a while, okay. So when he starts to come good you let me know."

"Why?"

"Because we'll need to move him somewhere he can't escape from."

"I beg your pardon?" she says.

"Okay, hang on," Tom says. "Let's talk about this."

"Of course," I say calmly. "Let's talk."

They are all still reeling from the news of the radios—it is a spine-tingling feeling to know you have no way to call for help, to know you are truly stranded. It will take a while for that to sink in, but right now, we have a more urgent problem.

When nobody says anything, I lay it out for them. "We have a man here. He's had some kind of breakdown. He's decided he has to drown all the seeds in that bank, and he's also decided he has to drown my seventeen-year-old daughter. We don't have any way to contact the police. We've got eight weeks until a ship comes for us. So what would you like to do with him?"

⁓

Hank gets out of the hospital twice, and twice he makes his way down to the vault and starts throwing packets of seeds into the ocean. No amount of reasoning will get through to him, and it takes it happening a third time before the others agree he needs to be contained.

It's Orly who tells us about the storage room.

All he knows is that something is wrong with Hank, that he's sick and a threat to the seeds, which Orly cares about more than anything. He tells us of a room Hank showed him when they were down here together (I live in a state of rolling nausea at the thought of how much time I let that man spend alone with my children). There is a lot of arguing. Talk of it being inhumane. Worse than a prison cell. Not to mention right beneath the seeds he's trying to destroy. There is also talk of it being the only place we can be sure is secure. I don't bother getting involved, I wait it out, knowing he's going down in that cement hole whether the others agree to it or not. My mind is made up the moment I explain the idea to Fen and see relief in her eyes.

So we come up with a regimen. He needs to be toileted and fed, he needs to be able to wash, he needs company, he needs his health and well-being checked on, he needs books and things to do. Naija is very clear on this: we will try to make him as comfortable as we can. But we will not be letting him out. Not until the ship comes.

Soon they are dead. Naija and Tom first, and then Alex. And my children and I are digging graves and keeping our prisoner alive, and we are barely holding our heads above water and that's when a woman washes ashore, seeking to find this man and set him free.

Rowan

"Rowan?"

My husband and I stare at each other. We are both in shock. He looks pale and tired enough to shrivel into a husk. His hair is brushed and tidy, but long. His clothes are clean. He doesn't look underweight or starved. There are books strewn everywhere and notepads he's been scribbling in. There is a terrible smell coming from a bucket in the corner. I take all of this in, and I take in what it means, and I am raging, my heart is raging, but I don't have much time.

"What are you doing here?" he demands. Thinks better of it. "Get me out, you have to get me out, please help me."

I am nodding, peering around, trying to think. "He'll be back any second."

The fear that fills Hank's face is telling enough. "Don't let him know you've found me. Don't let him know, and then sneak back and let me out." He crosses the small space to me, grabbing my arms, and his grip is rough, tight, it frightens me. "They've been keeping me down here for weeks, they're fucking crazy, he nearly *killed* me, Rowan, you have to help me."

"I will," I promise, trying to free myself from him. His eyes are frantic, darting, my god, what has he been through? He seems so small. "It's okay," I tell him. "I promise I'll get you out of here. It's why I came."

"Go, quick," he hisses. "Don't let him know, and *don't trust him.*"

I climb the ladder as fast as I can, lock the door, and run.

The tunnel seems darker than it has before. The splashing of my feet echoes in my ears.

What the fuck is going on? Why is he being held down there, what possible reason could there be to do that to someone, it doesn't make sense, I can't make it make sense.

There is movement ahead. My pulse stutters. Will Dom know what I've done? What I've seen? What will happen if he does? Will I end up in that room too?

Calm down. The shock of what I've seen is making my thoughts pinball, but I need to keep hold of reason. I must remain perfectly even-keeled as though I have seen nothing, and I need to buy myself time to think.

His footsteps arrive and we nearly collide in the dark. His hands are on my arms, my shoulders, there is tenderness there. *Don't trust him.* "You okay?" Dom asks me, and the earth shifts off its axis. Everything he has ever said to me will need to be reevaluated in this new, ugly context. There are lies within him, and malice, and violence. At the very least he has kept a terrible thing from me, he has worked hard and elaborately to keep it from me.

"Forgot my scarf," I say, and there is, I think, a survival instinct that is keeping my voice normal.

He puts his arm around my shoulder and we walk the rest of the way together. Outside, when the others are occupied, I vomit behind some rocks. The sky spins above. It happens again over the edge of the Zodiac.

Fen slows her boat and calls out to me. "Are you okay?"

"Seasick, I guess," I call back.

At the lighthouse I tell them I need to lie down, I must have a bug. Dom makes me a cup of tea, gets me water and Advil, tucks me under the covers and kisses my forehead, it's all very sweet and the whole time I am screaming at him silently to get away from me. They leave for another trip and I stare at the ceiling. I meant to think and plan. Instead I am blank. I can't conjure a single thought that makes any sense, that has any true form.

I am so cold, I can't stop shivering. I am only a body. A body that loves his. A body revolting against me now, because it wants his, wants never to be parted from his. It doesn't care what he has done. I did not feel this way when Hank left. I did not feel an absence I could die from.

At some point Raff knocks on the door and pokes his head in. I am calmer now, so I gesture and he comes to sit on the bed. His heavily bandaged arm is back in the sling. He looks pale and in pain. Am I to fear these kids, too? They must know about Hank—Dom would need their help keeping him alive, which means they are complicit. The performance of it all is staggering, all that time I spent in the vault, so close to where my husband sat, and them pretending nothing was wrong. I find I can't access any feelings to go with this knowledge. Just disbelief. These kids, who are so kind and warm, all three of them, locking a man in what amounts to a dungeon. Can you blame kids for the decision of a parent? Not Orly, surely. But Raff and Fen are pretty much adults themselves.

I can't escape some of the blame either. I asked Dom straight why he had Hank's passport and he said he just *forgot to take it,* and I believed him. The insanity of that is mind-blowing. My own stupidity, unbearable.

"You're sick?" Raff asks me.

I nod. "Your arm's bad."

He shrugs. "I made it worse. Easy trade for their lives."

The whales. They seem a lifetime ago.

I study his face as he peers out the window. "Are you scared?"

Raff doesn't look at me. Just nods once. There will be no violin without a properly working hand.

"I need to ask you some things," I say.

"Okay."

I lick my lips, my whole mouth feels dry. "Your dad said Hank started to become unwell, at the end."

Raff nods.

"Did Dom ever have to be violent with him?"

The boy goes very still.

"You can tell me," I say. "Whatever it is, I'll try to understand."

Raff's head tilts and he is studying me the way I am studying him. "You love my dad," he says suddenly, like it is fact.

"No," I croak. Because I can't. Not now.

"So you know," Raff goes on as though I have said nothing, "deep down, you know as well as we do, that everything Dom does is for his kids."

—

The storm arrives. Mighty claps of thunder and a dazzling light show. The wind is wailing and as though swept in by it, Orly appears in my room. I pull back the covers for him and he scurries under. His warm little body is like a hot water bottle in the cold. "Where will all the animals go?" he asks me. "When the island's gone?"

I think of Ari and Nikau and their egg. I think of King Brown and his harem of mother seals and their babies. I think of the thousands and thousands of penguins.

"They'll find another," I tell him. But we both know there is no island like this one.

As I hold Orly I think of how he stood at the air vent, talking to Hank. He knew. He has known all along that my husband is beneath the ground.

Still, I can't bring myself to let him go.

Dominic

I make the last trip of the day alone. The storm has begun and Orly needs no convincing to stay home. Fen hates being anywhere near the vault so she too is happy to remain at the lighthouse. But there's time in the day for another load, and in truth I can't shake the bad feeling I am getting from Rowan. I can't shake the image of her emerging, alone, from the vault.

I climb down into the bowels of the world.

He is sitting on the floor with papers on his lap. He is drawing something. I don't care to know what.

"You're back," Hank says, without looking at me.

I had thought maybe I'd be able to tell. That if I looked at him, I could read on his face whether he'd seen his wife for the first time in many months. But I can't see anything.

"Toilet bucket needs emptying," he commands. "I need more toothpaste and another notepad."

Naija used to sit with him and talk to him. She said it was important for his mental health. She also said she needed to try to make sense of what he did, and what he wanted. For herself, she needed to understand what his own internal logic was, assured me that no one was "just crazy." I don't know if she worked it out, before she died. I never cared to know.

But it occurs to me now that Rowan will need the same answers. That she will expect me to know them, to have at least tried to know them.

"What gets me," I say, instead of asking him anything, "is that in your psychosis you had to drag my seventeen-year-old daughter down with you."

Hank looks up at me. Smiles a smile of infinite wisdom. "I know it's easier to tell yourself I'm crazy, but I'm not," he says. "And none of that matters. It's so small. Don't you get it? Of course you don't, you're a dumb thug. Let me spell it out: we're all fucked. We're dead. Everything is dead. All life: drowned, burned, or starved."

I feel a chill run down my spine at the recognition of these words. I don't understand how Rowan could have loved this piece of pond scum, of animal shit. I wish she didn't see the world the same way he does, with such bleakness. But I do know how to answer his proclamation.

"Maybe we will drown or burn or starve one day, but until then we get to choose if we'll add to that destruction or if we will care for each other."

He isn't listening to me, but I don't expect him to. He never did.

I get home, drenched and dripping. I remove my outer layers in the mudroom and then climb the stairs to Fen's room, which is now Rowan's room. I don't know where my kids are. I am shivering with the cold. I find Orly and Rowan sleeping beside each other. I crouch quietly by her face. She wakes with a start, and for a moment in the dark it's like she's expecting someone else or doesn't recognize me.

"You're wet," she murmurs.

I nod. I can feel the drops sliding from my hair onto my face. I can feel them trickling icily down my spine.

"How are you feeling?" I ask her.

She shrugs.

I want to run my hands over her hair, but something stops me. It is possible she knows her husband is beneath the vault. It is possible she thinks I am the beast who keeps him locked up. It's possible she knows nothing at all, that she's just feeling unwell. Either way, there is a boat traveling toward us, it will be here any day now and it will carry us away from here, and if she's right, if Rowan—and Hank—are right that the world we are returning to is a hostile place intent on our ends, then there are things that need to be said.

"If we don't have a lot of time left," I say. "If there's nowhere safe to go back to—"

She doesn't let me say it. "I feel sick. I feel so, so sick, Dom."

"What can I do?"

"Leave. I want to be alone."

"Okay. I'll tell you in the morning."

She looks at me and very clearly says, "This was a mistake. Me and you. Me and your family. And what's worse, I knew better."

I swallow. The world is spinning a little. "You're wrong," I say. "You're only with him because it feels safer to be with someone you don't love, but that's not smart, it's cowardly."

She rolls away, muttering, "I told you I was a coward, didn't I?" and I can feel that this is the end. She means this to be the end.

I reach for Orly, but she shakes her head, laying a hand on his back. "He can stay."

Perhaps he is the only one she felt a true love for.

My wife is waiting for me in my room.

"Fuck," I say, on a breath.

She is at my elbow, reaching for me, but I don't want this.

"You're not real. This isn't real."

If you could have me back, flesh and blood, would you want me?

"Don't ask me that."

I can smell her and it fills me with an old longing.

Am I so easily replaced? Was it just a mother for your kids that you wanted?

"Don't. I loved you long before we had children and I have loved you after."

Still?

"Always. But I want something real."

It will never be real. It will kill her, when she knows what you've done. You will have killed us both.

She has been in labor for thirty-two hours when I am told that the baby is in distress. She can keep laboring and do this vaginally but it's likely the baby won't survive. It is not, however, as simple as giving the go-ahead for an emergency C-section. With a surgery like that the surgeons are in danger of rupturing the tumors inside her, the ones we have known about for a few months. The existence of these tumors, these cancers, required a swift decision at twenty weeks to terminate the pregnancy so she could be operated on before the tumors got any bigger. But my wife. Oh, my wife. She is too brave for her own good. Too naive, too ruled by optimism. She wouldn't terminate, and she wouldn't die, either. She decided they were both going to make it through. She promised me it wouldn't come to this decision. But it has. And it has fallen to me, because my poor wife is so exhausted she is in no state to make a lucid choice.

My immediate instinct is to tell them to save Claire. That we can make another baby, but we can't make another her. We already have two children to think about, and they need their mother.

But I know, I can't pretend not to know, that this isn't what she wants.

She told me what she wants, she has been telling me for months. She's even made a declaration to that effect, and signed it, and I could supersede that document if I wanted to. It's not possible to articulate how much I want to, and the doctors are looking at me to decide, they know what she wants but they're giving me the choice, and it is this more than anything that makes it clear to me. She deserves to have her wishes respected. She deserves to have the person who loves her most in the world listen to her. So I tell them to save the baby, to cut him out, and I tell them not to kill her in the process, I warn them that I will come after them if they rupture a single tumor, if she does not wake up tomorrow, but of course that isn't within their power to promise. I kiss her, I say her name and I tell her it will be okay, I kiss her more, on her mouth and her eyelids and her cheeks, her eyes are rolling back in her head and this feels so wrong, she is reaching for me and I am holding her face in my hands but they are removing me now, making me put on a gown and cap and scrubbing my hands sterile and by the time I get into the operating room she has gone. They have tried and they have failed, and she does not wake up.

But.

There is something else drawing breath. Bravely swimming his way to the surface to find her. She will not be there to meet him, but I can be.

I can be.

Orly

I have been saving this one up ever since you told me about your nature corridor. You seem sad now, so here it is, to cheer you up.

The banksia plant has many different species, but they are all found only in Australia. It's famous to us Aussies, it's very well loved and a particular favorite of many, probably because the banksia is a symbol of the burned, parched land we live upon, and of how our precious, diverse botanicals are able to survive such a harsh and rugged environment.

The banksia's flower is large and cone-like, with thousands of tiny florets in bright vibrant colors, shaped into spikes and spirals. I can't describe them, I'll stop trying, just look at a picture when you get a chance. They take months to develop, weeks to open.

Wildfires are common things in our bushland. Indigenous peoples have known for millennia that fire brings with it life. Rebirth.

The banksia's seeds, which take a long time to mature, are held within a hard, woody capsule that has two valves. These valves will open to release the seeds only in extremely high temperatures, like those you get in a bushfire.

The banksia will wait, and wait, and wait for this fire to come. Only with flames and smoke licking at everything around it will it open its valves and let its seeds be taken on this hot, burning wind. Only to black ground, only to ash, will the banksia give its seed. And only within this scorched wasteland can it survive and find a way to thrive. From beneath the carpet of ash—which the untrained eye would look at and see death—comes life, bursting free.

Rowan

I am going to miss waking to the sound of his voice more than, perhaps, anything.

"That's a good one," I say when he is finished.

"Right?"

"Is it on the list?"

"No."

The water in the vault was knee-high when we last left—it will be higher again now. Several of the lower shelves are submerged, there are containers floating listlessly. I wonder what this family intends to do with my husband. If they have decided his cell shall become his grave, too.

"The lower storage area will start to fill up soon," I say.

Orly frowns. What do I mean?

"Down the air shaft. Water will start getting in there. It'll fill up. So if there's anything down there, you and your dad should think about moving it now."

He flushes a little, then nods. He is bound to be confused by my pointedness, but I don't think he will read the subtext behind the words; he is far too trusting to think I wouldn't be up-front about what I know. Orly jumps off my bed and I hear his feet slapping down the stairs.

I rise and stand by the window. Though it's morning, it's almost dark enough to be night. Birds whoosh by, pinwheeled by the wind. There comes a rolling grumble of thunder. The storm has not abated, instead it seems to be gathering steam. It might be as violent as the night I washed up here. It might be worse.

I dress warmly, protectively. Mentally I am arming myself. I don't know what I am going to do today, but I am going to do something.

There is a kind of mewling coming from the walls. An animal whimper. It is not the first time I have heard strange noises drifting to me on eddies but it is the most substantial. I press my hands to the stone and follow the grooves with my fingers. The sound comes again, a little louder: there is a creature in pain. I am able to trace it down the staircase to the bathroom.

I knock on the door. "Fen?"

"Who's with you?"

"No one, it's just me."

I hear a scuffle and the door opens. She's already moving back to the empty bathtub, where she sits hunched over, in bra and undies.

"What's going on?" I ask, closing the door behind me.

"Lock it."

I do. "Fen. What's—are you okay?" I sink down beside her. Her face is puffy, she's been crying. There is some blood in the tub.

"Don't be nice to me," she says.

"Does your period always hurt like this?"

She nods.

"Have you taken painkillers?"

Another nod. "We don't have any pads left and I keep bleeding through tampons so I have to stay here."

"Okay. Do you want the shower on? Might help with the cramps."

"I've already had my shower minutes."

I turn on the shower, getting the water nice and warm for her. We both watch as the smears of blood trickle away down the drain. Her underwear gets wet but she doesn't mind.

Someone knocks on the door. "Piss off," I yell, and they do, I guess.

"Does yours hurt like this?" she asks me.

"It did at your age. I remember feeling crippled by it. It gets less painful with time."

"Thank god. Having a baby is not worth this."

I smile. "Most women would say it is."

"But not you." She says this like a statement but when she looks at me, I can see it's a question.

I shrug, can't bring myself to meet her eyes. I am starting to realize my answer isn't as simple as it once was and there is a hidden world of pain here for me.

"I thought I was pregnant," Fen says abruptly and now I do look at her, I stare at her in shock.

"When?"

"Before you came. I wasn't. It was just late."

The question is very loud between us, but I don't ask it. It's not my business.

She asks it for me. "Don't you want to know who?"

I don't reply.

Fen starts to cry again and I get a bad feeling in my guts.

"Let's just get you sorted," I say briskly. "We can get some cloth for you to use instead of a pad. And I'll get you some more painkillers."

"I need to tell you who."

I meet her dark-brown eyes. "No you don't, darling," I say.

Because she is seventeen and he is forty-seven. Whatever happened, she is not responsible for it.

Fen lets her head drop onto her knees and she cries hard and long. I stroke her shaved hair gently, letting her get it out. There is trauma here, I can hear it, and I can hear relief, too, maybe that it's over, maybe also that I finally know.

When she is spent, when all the tangles within her have unspooled into the porcelain tub beneath her, she rests her head wearily against the wall. I sit crammed in between the sink and the bath, watching her. She says, "I'm so sorry."

I just shake my head. "You don't need to be."

He is the one who will be sorry. I could kill him for it. For hurting her. For the affair too, I suppose, but far more for choosing to have it with a child. I could watch him drown. Maybe I will. It is clear, now, why he's in a cell.

"Have I ever told you about my husband?" I ask her.

Fen frowns, searching my face, unsure what I'm doing.

"Hank is a narcissist," I tell her. "He is very good at convincing people he cares about them. But in reality his whole world is just—himself. He can't think beyond that. He can't *feel* beyond that. He's charismatic and clever and this allows him to collect people. A lot of people have fallen under his spell and there's no shame in it."

"Is that why you married him?" Fen asks. There is recognition in her eyes, as though this is all making sense to her.

"Yeah, I suppose so."

"Why didn't you leave, when you realized it?"

I think about this. "I think it suited me to be with someone I knew would never look directly at me."

She breathes out. Then says, "But you're so nice to look at."

It makes us both smile. I lean over the bath to hug her. All I can hope is that having some understanding of who Hank is will help her process this.

I tell Dom and Orly that Fen has bad period pain and won't be joining us today. Dom says she can just take some Advil and be right, I tell him to shut up. Orly moans about us being down *another* set of hands— three is not nearly enough—but his dad replies that three is what we are, so we'd better get moving.

Dom drives the Frog, while Orly and I follow behind in a Zodiac. The rain is heavy and fat, it falls hard, and from the look of the black sky it doesn't plan on going anywhere soon.

From the mouth of the tunnel we can see water rushing like white water rapids. Dom says simply, "This is our last trip. And you're waiting out here."

Orly doesn't argue. "Better make it count then, guys."

As Dom and I wade down through the freezing water I think of Hank. I wonder if Dom means to drown my husband; I wonder if I might let him. I have never been so angry.

All the ice on the walls of the vault has melted away. It takes a lot of effort for Dom and me to move through the freezing water; we are slow, and it feels pointless if you stop to think, so we don't think, we keep on. We carry our containers to the floating pallet we've tied with a rope to the chamber door so it doesn't float away. We don't look at labels, we just take from the pile Orly instructed us to focus on. With every container I carry, I contemplate a plant species that may survive because I forced myself to keep going, to keep moving through this freezing water. I can't feel my feet. We don't think about what's getting left behind; there will be time for that later, a lifetime for it.

When a second crack opens in the wall, letting a deluge pour free, Dominic shouts that it's time to go. That entire wall is about to give way and the cave we are in will crumble.

We steer the floating pallet out through the chamber doors and up the tunnel. The water is around our waists now, already higher than when we entered this morning.

"Dom," I say as we wade through the dark. Because maybe there won't be many more chances.

"Yeah?"

"You need to talk to Raff and Fen."

"About what?"

"Whatever it is that they want to talk about."

He looks at me, understanding. This is a very weird time to have this conversation and I think he understands the why of that too. "I don't know what to say to them," he admits.

"Then just listen." I let go of the barge for a moment so I can reach for him, reach for his cheek. "Okay?"

Dominic nods. "Okay."

At the mouth of the tunnel I think of the man we've left behind, waiting and alone. I make a decision, I make several. I can't let my husband drown. No matter what he's done, that's not a thing I can do. I will come back for him.

We load the boats, heads ducked against the battering rain and wind. Orly hunkers down in the back of the Frog, trying to take shelter, while his dad and I run back and forth like mad things. "Get going!" I shout to Dom when we've finished.

He nods. And then he pulls me against him and kisses me.

I can feel in it a farewell. He knows something. He might be planning something. He has done bad things. It doesn't matter. I put all of myself into this kiss, I cling to him. If this is our last, I hope he feels within it the days, hours, minutes left in my life, I hope he knows I am giving them to him, every one of them.

He says, "Get in the boat. Please."

I pull back from his lips. My heart is a wild thing.

"I can't leave him to die," I say.

There is no surprise in his face. He has already worked it out. "You don't have to," he says, so calm. "You just have to get in the boat."

"Why did you do it?" I ask. "He and Fen—"

"He tried to kill her," Dominic says. "He held her head under the water."

I stare at him.

"He is dangerous, Rowan. I couldn't tell you where he was because I could never be sure you wouldn't let him out. Or that Fen would be safe from him if he was free."

The cold is working its way up from my numb feet to my guts, my chest, my mind. I have rage in my heart for what Hank has done, at the thought of the ways he has hurt Fen and broken apart this family. But somehow I also have pity for his sickness, which has transformed him. He needs help. He needs treatment and medicine. He needs to get away from this island.

"We still can't let him die," I say.

"You don't have to," Dom says. "But I can."

"Dom," I say, squeezing his hands.

"I've thought a lot about what I'd do if the vault flooded before the ship came. I was going to hand him over to the authorities, but nature's decided for me."

"If you do this," I say clearly, "if you make me part of it, there will be nothing left for you and me. Do you understand? We won't come back from it."

His eyes close as though he is in great pain. "Row," he says. He looks at me. "I'm sorry. Truly. But I have to protect my daughter."

Dominic

About halfway home I decide I'd better not let the fucker drown. Rowan's right. I don't want her to bear the same loss I have. I don't want to carry his death or meet his ghost. Most of all, I do not want the violence of it to scare my daughter any more than it already has.

The only way back in, now that the vault is too dangerous, is down the shaft, which has been rusted shut for many years and will require an angle grinder to open. I look through the curtain of rain and can barely make out the black inflatable boat up ahead. They'll be drenched in that thing; I should have made Orly ride with me but he loves being with Rowan—he senses an ending the way we all do. At some point very soon our lives together on Shearwater will be over.

I have been preparing myself for the day she'd find Hank. I don't know if it will be the ruthlessness of the captivity or all the lies I told her, but one of them will end us. I saw the horror in her eyes, felt the retreat within her. I knew it was coming and yet I did not realize it would feel so bad, so ruinous, I did not realize there could be no preparation for this kind of pain. It is really fucking sad that it should take loss to know the precise quality of love.

As I reach our beach and drive the Frog up onto the sand, I can make out the reflective red lights on the back of the quad bike, already halfway up the hill. I will let them come back for the seeds in my boat, while I go straight for the tools to get the son of a bitch out.

Rowan

There is a ship on the horizon. I can see it from the kitchen window, even through the storm. It has arrived one day too late to save a great many of the species in that vault. But it may have come in time to save a man's life. It will be full of naval officers. I can tell them where he is and they can retrieve him, and I won't have to go back down there. I am shaking with the relief of it.

I need to take the quad back for Dom and Orly, but first I unpack my load of containers. Our freezer is just about full. Both Raff and Fen are there, making space for this last lot. The only way we've been able to pack them in tightly enough is to follow Fen's idea of removing them from their containers and storing the little plastic bags of seeds. They help me open my last containers and take the precious bags out, placing them gently on the piles. I look at these seeds, pausing to note that the bag I have just placed on top contains something rather extraordinary looking, and not what I was expecting. The wrinkly seed seems to sit within a hood, a great draping hood that curves around like a papery moth wing, and then at its base is a long needlelike point. The shape of the whole thing is that of a sickle, and this hood is so fine—parchment thin—that light travels through it, illuminating the delicate filaments and giving the illusion of movement. I stare at it, taken aback by its loveliness, and then I look at the label. *Pterocymbium tinctorium* (Malvaceae)—or the melembu, from Indonesia. I don't know what this name means; it could be any kind of plant.

I look at another packet, also strange. A walnut-shaped seed is covered in long, thick, blond hairs that stand on end, a child's drawing of a golden sun. The *Aulax pallasia* (Proteaceae)—or the needle-leaf feather-bush from South Africa. Again, no idea what this is; I have read Hank's list a few dozen times, scanning my eyes over the seemingly endless and incomprehensible Latin names in search of containers to collect and move, and neither of these is remotely familiar. Doesn't mean much really, there were too many names for me to memorize of course, but a thought starts tugging at the back of my mind.

I look at more of the seeds, now exposed.

There are the Wollemi pine seeds, and the common dandelion seeds. I know those two and I'm not surprised by them, but the next looks like a weapon. It is covered in sharp tusks or antlers, and it's called a *Cullenia ceylanica* from Sri Lanka. There is a seed that looks like a jellyfish, with a hood and several long tentacles. There is one with two chambers, both an impossibly vibrant and deep inky-blue color. One that is long and curling and snakelike. One that looks like a pineapple. Another like a wiry bird's nest. They are strange and otherworldly and I was not expecting their beauty. They don't look anything like seeds as I know them. When I reach a packet containing the *Banksia grandis*, from Australia, I know what this is—it is a giant banksia—and I know what he's done.

"What's wrong?" Raff asks me, because I am standing in the freezer, staring at the sea of seeds around me.

"Nothing," I say.

As I approach the beach, I can see my hope was in vain—that ship is too far out. It will take time for them to prepare and load their Zodiacs, to reach us, to understand. The weather might even be too rough to disembark at all. The air shaft will be starting to fill.

Dom is loading the Frog with tools. I kill the bike's engine and jump off. Shout through the rain. "What are you doing?"

"I'm going back," he yells, with a shake of his head like he can't believe he's doing it.

"Where's Orly?"

Dominic straightens. He frowns, and meets my eyes, and in the space of a moment I see a universe pass through him. "He was with you," he says. "He told me he was going on your boat."

He sees the answer in my face. Orly told me the same thing.

Orly

If you have anything down in that storage room, it's time to move it.

That's what she said, and it has been ringing in his ears since.

The thing is, this is all his fault.

On an unusually sunny afternoon, Orly took a couple of his dad's tools into the communications building and smashed everything to pieces. He broke things and he opened them up and he even cut wires for good measure. He wanted to be sure.

Because Orly, alone of anyone else on the island, could see that Hank Jones, his mentor, the leader of this place, was going mad. Orly was there as Hank talked through every element of every decision he was having to make. He explained how he went about choosing the seeds, he was doing it by nation and by cultural necessity, he was saving food staples and then widening out to more unusual tastes, but he would argue with himself, he would say that if he didn't save this seed then he might as well not save that one, because those two plants fed each other and one death would lead to two, and how could he waste a single spot on the ship? Things like that. He was tormenting himself, Orly could see that much. He tried to help, but Hank didn't want his help, even though he'd said Orly was very clever and that he was Hank's only true friend in the world.

Orly knew that if anyone else started to notice how unwell Hank was becoming, they would definitely want to call a doctor. And if they did that, then Hank would never finish his task and the seeds would be left to drown, all of them.

So he simply removed the problem. He made it so that Hank—along with Orly and the others—had to stay and finish. That nobody could be called. That he couldn't be taken away.

But that was before Hank started throwing the packets into the ocean. It was before Tom and Naija and then Alex all died, before they needed to be buried.

It was before Hank needed to be contained so he didn't do any more damage than he'd already done, before the vault started flooding for real, before a woman showed up, stranded, wanting to get home. All things you might want to contact someone about, really.

The whole thing, he can reflect now, every bad thing that led to another bad thing, would have been avoided if they'd had a radio to call for help.

So now the very least Orly can do is save the poor man, once his friend, from drowning.

He has to swim down the tunnel and through the vault. The power is out so it is dark and cold, and it is very, very scary. He thinks he will drown down here. But he knows that at least he will not be alone. His friends are always here to keep him company.

You're doing so well, they say, their voices in harmony with the rushing water, their voices *are* the water, as they are the island, every blade of grass and shard of rock and the wind, always the wind. *Just a little farther now, not long to go. Mind the container there, move to your left, that's it, straight ahead now, keep going.*

"It's so cold," he tells them.

There is a colder place than this. Don't let it find you. Keep swimming.

So he does. They make him brave.

He reaches the door to the shaft. There is so much water that he isn't sure he'll be able to pull it open against the pressure, but the second he tries, the second he unlocks it, the door explodes into him and a body launches free.

Orly is thrown backward. The water catches him, slows him, but his head still hits the ground and things go dark for a moment. He is pulled out of the water by rough hands. There is a face crouching before him.

"Thanks, kid," his old friend Hank says. "I need you to climb down that ladder now. Wait there. Someone'll come for you but I need a head start before you tell anyone I'm out."

Orly is confused. He doesn't understand what's happening, knows only that he is being shepherded onto the ladder.

"Good boy," Hank says. "You'll be okay. Climb down there and wait. Your dad'll come."

And then the door is closed and locked, and he is alone in the long thin shaft, clutching onto the ladder. He thinks, too late, what he should have said, what he might have explained if his head wasn't spinning. The vault is flooding. It's very difficult to get through the tunnel. Soon it will be impossible to reach this room. They don't know I'm here, they won't get to me in time. I was trying to save you.

Rowan

Dom drives the boat like a madman. It is a miracle we don't wreck. The waves are enormous.

South Beach is gone now. The sea has swallowed it. No more red kelp or black sand. No more seals or penguins. I hope desperately that they have found somewhere safe. As we speed down toward the mouth of the tunnel, I see a great chunk of earth crumbling into the ocean. The cliffs are changing shape. If the seed vault hasn't caved in yet, it will not be long.

Dom goes straight for the hatch on top of the hill, running like a rumbling great bear with tools slung over shoulders and around hips. I watch him for less than a second, but the impression of him, of how he looks in the rain as he tries to save his son, will stay with me always.

I take a different path: I go in through the tunnel. I don't know what I will find, but it is a place of terror now, this watery grave. I shout Orly's name over the rushing water. I am half wading, half swimming. It feels awkward and too slow. The water is an old enemy and my mind turns dark, it turns bad, it tells me the water will move within and fill me to bursting. It tells me I am going to die down here, with all these lost species of plants. It takes deep, profound stubbornness to keep moving past these thoughts, to forbid them from taking hold.

He's not in the vault. My heart is galloping. The weight against the door to the shaft is so heavy I can hardly get it open. Which means that if I go down there, I don't think I am returning this way. I won't be able to push this door back open.

Orly might not even be here. It's possible he and Hank got away. But if he is, if he is trapped down there, if there's even a *chance*, I can't leave him. I step through the door and let it close behind me.

"I'm here," says his little voice in the dark.

I feel my way to his side. He is sitting on Hank's camper bed, and my arms go around him. We hold each other so tightly, his little cheek to my lips.

"You found me," Orly says.

"Course I did," I say.

"I let Hank go."

"Okay." It takes me a minute to work that through. "And he just left you here?"

I feel Orly nod and that's it. I am done with that man, a man I do not know. Maybe I never knew him, if he is capable of this. Maybe I have never known myself.

"I can't believe you came down here on your own." I think better of it and add, "Well, I actually can. Same insanity that might urge a boy to completely ignore every seed on that list and choose whichever ones he wanted."

There is water getting in from somewhere, I can hear it, can feel it around my feet. And I don't know how much air there will be in here, without power or vents.

"You figured it out then?" he asks me. "The seeds?"

"Yeah. I guess I know you too well."

"Do you understand?" he asks me. "People find a way to survive no matter what, we'll figure out the food, we always do, but the plants won't, they will go, and so will the animals that need those plants, so we have to help them."

I nod, I can't speak. Because I should have guessed. That the seeds he would choose to save are the strange and the unlikely. The species we don't need, the ones we don't want, cannot eat. That Orly would choose these because no one else would.

"I did grab some rice and wheat though," he adds, and I laugh, and pull myself together.

"We'll deal with it later," I say. "Right now we're gonna climb the ladder and go out the hatch."

"The hatch is sealed. I already tried it."

"Your dad's up there opening it."

We feel our way along the walls to the shaft, manage to find the rungs of the ladder. There is hardly any light coming in from the glass in the hatch as the sky above is almost black with the storm. Just as I am thinking about that glass we hear it crack.

"Cover your face," I tell Orly quickly, and we both shield ourselves from the falling shards. "You okay?"

"Yeah."

We climb, with him above me, rung by rung. It's a long way, and we are moving slowly in the dark, forced to feel our way, and it's slippery. I don't know where the water is coming in, but halfway up, a crack opens in the wall and it's like a wave is dumping onto us.

Orly screams. I press him hard to the ladder so he doesn't slip in the downpour. It doesn't slow, we have to keep climbing through it. Once we are above this crack I look down to see the deluge; the shaft is going to fill more quickly now.

"Dad!" Orly shouts frantically for the last several meters until we reach the hatch.

"I'm here!" Dom bellows. We can see him through the small opening. "You guys okay?"

"We're okay!" Orly tells him. "Get us out!"

"Working on it, mate. Hang in there."

So we hang in. Orly keeps his eyes on his dad. I keep mine on the rising water.

Fen

As she makes her way back down to the beach, Fen is distraught by how little attention she has given the colony in the last few days. She can hardly see them through the rain, has to run the whole length of the beach before they appear, huddled together in an effort to protect the little ones. Though really it is not a beach anymore. Just a thin line of rocky coastline. The black sand has been eaten. There is no sign of any penguins, and the birds she can see in the sky are less flying than being thrown. Fen could almost be taken off her feet, too—she feels as though if she let herself she could be carried away—but she loves these creatures, so she will be solid and heavy, she will keep her feet anchored to the ground.

King Brown sees her first, he lifts his head and barks *where have you been?* She strokes his back as she steps past him into the huddle, watching for babies though they are much bigger now, almost ready for the water seeking them. Some of the mothers are barking at her too, Silver and Tiny, but they quiet when she sits down among them. The rain is smashing them all and the larger seals are doing their best to protect the pups. A storm like this could kill all the juveniles not yet ready to go to sea, and any of the adults who stay with them. Fen moves some of the babies into more sheltered spots behind the big males, but she can hardly see—even with her hood raised there is a steady stream of water in her eyes. Some of the seals abandon the colony, flopping into the water and disappearing beneath the waves to where they are safer. But those with pups stay, they will stay as long as they can. Fen thinks she will too but the wind and the rain are pummeling her and the waves are sweeping under her, threatening to wash her out. She is gripping at the rocks with frozen fingers. She doesn't know what to do, how to help them. She loves them but she doesn't think she ought to die here because of that love. Once, not so long ago when she was a child, she might have thought that the noble thing to do. Now she feels very far from a child, and if nearly being murdered has taught her anything it's that she wants to live long enough to get off this island. The salt of it lives in her veins; it is such a part of her that it is slowly killing her.

"You'll have to swim," she says aloud, though they've never spoken each other's languages and the seals can't hear her over the storm anyway. She looks at the pups and says it again. "You're ready. Make yourselves ready. Let your bodies do what they were born to do and swim."

All she can do is urge them. She can put all the years they have spent together into her urging, and hope that whatever connection they have goes beyond their species. Or, if she is nothing among them, at most an oddity—if they hardly notice her, as she most often suspects—then she will hope it's their own nature they listen to, that ancient call to the waves. It is too soon, they are too young, but sometimes the world asks more of us.

She wishes them courage, profoundly and with her whole self, and then Fen runs.

She is slammed by the wind into the rocks and feels her shoulder jar. It hurts but she doesn't think it's dislocated. Fen steadies herself and keeps going. She is aiming for the boathouse, though god knows if that will hold up in this weather. The closest building after that is the sleeping quarters, but it doesn't have a roof anymore. Beyond that is the hospital, which feels very far away right now.

She risks the boathouse, keen to get within some walls, and closes the door behind her. Inside it's much quieter, but she can see the remaining Zodiac bobbing wildly and water is spilling onto the floor with each surge of the waves. The roof creaks loudly, threatening to be taken.

And then she hears something else. Something distinctly human. Fen peers around in the dim light. She can't see anything. There are goosebumps on her skin.

A figure moves. Rising from behind a fuel drum.

"Hey, kid," says Hank.

Raff was back at the lighthouse but Fen has no idea where the rest of her family are. She doesn't know where her dad is. She is alone with a man she has been so frightened of that she has been driven out of her home to live by the sea, a sea into which she always thought she'd have a better chance of escaping him. But today that sea is as violent as this man is.

Fen reaches for something she can use as a weapon, and her hand finds a torch on the bench.

"Don't call me that," she says, and she hears a fierceness in her voice that hasn't been there before.

"My god," Hank says. "It's got you too."

She swallows. "What has?"

"You're all mad," he says. And she wonders for a moment if that could be true. If Hank is the one sane soul among them, the rest lost in a shared spiral. They've kept him imprisoned in a basement, after all. That's a pretty crazy thing to do. Half of them talk to ghosts, and she chooses to live with seals, for god's sake.

Fen decides it doesn't matter. This man tried to kill her.

"What's the plan, Hank?" she asks him. "What are you gonna do?"

"I don't know," he says. "I don't think I can go back. Not now. But I'm too much of a coward to die."

"You're fine with killing, though?" She is so angry with him. She hates him, hates how small he has made her.

"What do you mean?" he asks.

"You've been drowning things."

"The ocean's been drowning them."

"You put my head under the water."

He frowns. "Did I? I don't remember that."

Fen stares at him and is surprised to feel the hatred trickle away. Instead all she can see is how unwell he is.

She knows what she will do now. She will get him safely onto that ship and then she will leave him in the hands of people who will know what to do with him, and she won't think about him ever again, not for a single second of the rest of her life, and that will be her revenge. And she and her dad will talk about all of this, she'll explain to Dom that he did not fail her, that she's powerful, and expanding, and she will tell him she loves him and that she's going to carve a life for herself now, but that she won't be far from them, from her family, not ever.

"I think you need to get off this island, Hank," Fen says, lowering the torch.

That's when he lunges at her.

Raff

Raff is alone in the lighthouse when he feels the pull of his sister. Not a pull, exactly, but she pops into his mind with such clarity that he is immediately compelled to know where she is. He takes the stairs two at a time. Looks through every room of the building, just to be sure, before he heads out into the storm. Each step hurts his arm. He is exhausted, body and soul, and he just wants to lie down. But not only has he lost Fen, he is also realizing that he doesn't know where the rest of them are. They were all meant to be home hours ago.

Raff starts to run.

Dominic

The calm inside me is like nothing I have known. The focus is precise. Because when I see them climbing the ladder of the shaft I know they can't get out through the vault, which means if I can't get this hatch open then the woman I love and my boy, my baby boy, are both going to die. So I will get the hatch open.

I always thought it had just rusted over, but I see now that it's been intentionally welded shut, no doubt when the fur-trade storage facility got turned into a giant freezer and they needed to make sure it was properly sealed. This is a problem, because what I thought would be a quick job with the angle grinder is actually turning into a very difficult task with a tool that might not be sufficient for it.

There is no way I'd have enough time to go back for different tools. Not even close. I have to use what I've got.

I make the decision to break the glass while they're down near the bottom, rather than waiting for them to get any closer. They'll need air, and we'll need to communicate. The window is too small for them to get through, you could reach an arm out, or shove half your face through, but that's it.

I grind at the metal. I wear away at it. I don't let my thoughts wander, I concentrate.

Look at what you have done, she says.

Don't listen.

You wanted this. Remember?

Please stop.

Remember all those years ago. At the very beginning. There was a moment. Go back there.

No.

I will bring the moment to you here, then.

I was out of my mind.

Yes. And still. You thought it. You wished him dead, if it meant I could live.

It is so clear to me, suddenly. This isn't my wife. It is not Claire and it never has been. Claire is a woman so complex and so profoundly loving that she gave her life for her child's. This creature is my own monstrousness and nothing more.

Who should have to suffer the grief of losing their partner entangled with such confusion? Such guilt? I have never been able to grieve for her simply or purely because I have always had to contend with my own shame, my own responsibility, and the idea of the choice I made between the two of them. I never grieved properly because it felt like to do so meant wanting to trade my son for her, to make the other choice, but how is that fair? How is that a choice that is possible? Even the hypothetical of it is sickening, it is too much to ask of anyone, but it has been my constant companion.

There is a truth that needs to be spoken, if only within me.

I tell this thing—my ghost, my haunting—very clearly.

I will not be a prisoner of this choice any longer. I will love my son expansively, and I will feel no guilt for it. I will miss my wife, always. And I will be free of you.

⁓

I look through the hatch at my boy. He is gazing up at me, waiting. There is no fear in his eyes. He trusts me to save him.

Fen

The force of his lunge sends them both rolling into the water. She has the wherewithal to reach for a pylon. The waves are ferocious. They take Hank instantly, sweeping him into the churn, and she knows she won't see him again. Fen clings. She is calm. She has to hang on until the set of waves passes and she has a chance to climb back up into the boathouse. But they are so strong, they are battering her. She has the lung capacity and the calm to survive the time underwater, but she isn't sure she can withstand the waves, and if they take her, as they did Hank, she will be no match for them. Her hands are starting to slip.

And then a grip so strong upon her arms, reaching for her, pulling her free. They hold each other, she and her brother.

Rowan

The water has nearly reached us. I am appalled at how quickly the shaft has filled up. And if Dom hasn't got the hatch open yet, it means it's not as simple as grinding the rusted hinges off.

We are hanging on to the rungs, trying to rest our shoulders against the wall. It's tiring gripping on like this, hard on our frozen hands and feet. I tell Orly to sit on my shoulder, to rest awhile, but he says he's okay, he can stand.

"How come he hasn't got it open yet?" the boy asks me quietly.

"He will."

"What if he doesn't?"

I don't answer.

"Guess it's drowning, then. Of the three. Drowning, burning, or starving. Remember?"

"Yeah, I remember." I shake my head at the idiocy of those words. "I was talking shit," I tell him. "I was angry. It's not true."

"Seems like it will be."

"Hey. We're not dying in here."

We might be dying in here.

I feel it come upon me with eerie certainty. We might be dying in here. If so, then what? What is my choice? My path forward?

It is to protect him from fear. To help him feel only love.

"I forgot to tell you something," I say. I am looking up, and I see his eyes tilt from their vigil on his father to find me in the dark below.

"What?"

"You know how you were talking about the banksias? How they come to life after a fire, when everything else is burned?"

"Yeah."

"Well I didn't tell you the most important part of the story. Of my story, of the fire at my place. I said everything burned, but it didn't, Orly. Afterward, I was walking through the ash, looking for something, anything still living. And remember how I told you about the wombats and their square poos?"

"Yeah."

"Wombats have a thing they do in fires. They take their families underground, into their burrows. They have tunnels under the earth, and they go down there to take shelter, but they don't just take their families, they also take other animals down there. They save everyone they can. And then the mum and dad wombats stick their bums up into the entrances of the burrows to block the fire and the ash from coming down. And their bums get burned, and sometimes they die, but they protect the others."

Orly meets my eyes.

I smile. "They were down there. A whole group of them, huddled together. The wombats had saved a dozen little creatures, there were lizards and frogs and possums and a wallaby, and there was a koala, too, and they were all alive."

He is smiling now too.

"And those mum and dad wombats that stick their bums up to save their family, that's your mum and dad," I say, and we are both laughing, knowing it's true.

"So I wanted to ask if you guys would like to come and live there with me?" I say. "When we're out of here."

"To replant?"

I nod.

"Won't another fire just come?"

"Maybe. But we'll make sure the whole place is covered in bank-sias."

———

A person, a real, normal person, not some professional diver or whatever, can only hold their breath for a few seconds. Seriously, that's about it. *Maybe* a minute, if you can stay calm. A child, far less. I'll give him twenty seconds, tops, before he panics and draws a huge gasp of water into his lungs.

But. Maybe twenty seconds is all we will need. You never know. I start preparing him.

"Has your sister ever talked to you about holding your breath?"

"She taught me to swim."

"Did she talk about what happens when you're under?"

"She talked about calmness."

"Let's practice it," I say.

"I don't want to go underwater, Rowan," he says, terrified.

"There's nothing to be frightened of," I say, and I believe it, somehow, even though I have been petrified of water since I was thirteen years old. Maybe that's what being a parent is. Expanding to be more. Asking of yourself more, for them.

"We might have to go under, but only for a minute or two. So we'll need to be brave. Do you understand?"

He nods.

"We'll be brave, and we'll be calm. Just like Fen said. She was born for the water, right?"

Orly nods again. His teeth are chattering.

"I'm here with you," I tell him. "It's you and me, okay."

———

I think of River, in these last minutes. I let myself remember him, and for the first time in a long time I take pleasure in the memories. He was a gorgeous, smiling boy. He made the world richer for having been in it.

I look at the little boy above me. "Hey, Orly."

"Yeah?"

"I love you."

He puts his little hand on my head, like a pat. "Love you too, Row."

"Tell your dad . . ." I break off and swallow. The water is at my shoulders. I have already climbed as high as I can; both our heads are touching the top of the hatch. I can see how frantic Dom is up there.

This might come down to seconds so I won't delay him long enough to tell him anything. I will just have to hope Orly can pass something along. Because one of us will be able to press up through that window and breathe, even when the shaft is entirely submerged.

"Tell your brother and sister the same, okay? I'm not your mum, but I will always love you."

"Stop," he says. "Just stop. You can tell them."

"I think it carries on, even after." I breathe out slowly. Breathe in slowly. Stay calm. The water reaches my chin. "Press your face up now," I tell Orly.

"I don't want to. What about you."

"I'm right here. I won't leave you."

"Not ever?"

"Not ever," I promise.

I am so glad I came down here, that I could be here with him.

"Nearly there, hang on!" I hear Dom shout.

It lifts my heart. Orly might have a chance. He presses his face as far through the little window as he can. All light is blocked and I am in darkness. I tilt my face up. Soon I will take my last air and go under.

I have drowned once before. I thought of my mother, then. It was strange to me that I should think of her at the end, after years of trying to convince myself I hated her. Untrue of course, but armor against the way she blamed me, the way she couldn't stand to look at me. I have been so angry with her—even after she died I have held on to that anger and it has made me fearful—but being a parent is complex and it is altering and being the parent of a lost child is something no human should have to contend with. I forgive the distance she imposed between us to try to survive. I think instead of the love she had for us in the beginning, and of my sisters and our boat.

I think of Hank and how grateful I am that he taught me to appreciate the things that grow in the ground. He gave me access to wildness and that is no small thing in a human life. I think of this life, of my life, of the things I built and planted. I have been lucky to know such richness. But I also think of how my husband taught me something else, something so deeply wrong I am stunned that I ever believed it: that in the face of world's end love should shrink.

I think of Raff and Fen and Orly. I have spent my life loving other people's children. There is no safety in this. But what is the use of safety if it deprives you of everything else?

I feel immense grief, thinking of the time I spent resenting this little boy and wishing I could have been anywhere else. I should have been treasuring every precious second with him, with them all, instead of wishing those seconds away.

I realize I never told Orly what I wanted to say to you.

I am underwater now. There are little lights flashing, they look like sparks from the cut glass of your Fresnel lens.

I think of the whale, and her calf, and the sea embracing them.

I think I finally understand your words. *It's just a body. They hold on or they don't.* You're right, it's nothing to be frightened of. Mine will become the salt of this water. And every time you swim it will be me upon your skin.

⁓

Orly slips. He comes under. His body slides into mine and I catch him in the dark and his long pale hair is all around me. My survival instinct tells me to surge for the surface, to press my mouth to that small opening and draw breath—to do *anything* to end the agony in my chest—but I can feel Orly panicking, his eyes are wide, he is going to suck the water into his lungs and then he will be gone, and so instead of going for air, I cover his mouth with mine and I press into him the last of what I have in my lungs, in my body. Enough, maybe, for another second or two, and I feel him calm a little, and then I think I feel him pulled from my arms

and I am falling.

But there is someone here.

A woman.

Down here in the dark with me.

She catches me and holds me so tenderly, and I know her. She is his mother, and she died so he could live. I understand it so simply now, it is a love that lives in the body but unlike the body it never dissolves. It lasts forever.

Dominic

I drag him, coughing and spluttering, up onto the wet grass. I order him to breathe, and the second I can see that he's obeying, I dive.

She is sinking.

I catch her limp body and I pull it against mine, kicking for the surface. I use the ladder to carry her up and out of the hatch I took too long to open, unforgivably long, and I place her beside Orly.

But Orly is awake and breathing and Rowan is not.

I pump her chest and breathe into her mouth. I work on her body for a long time, I think I could keep going always, but Orly is crying and I can feel that she's gone. I can feel that she's gone.

I take my son in my arms and hold him. After a little while he moves us, or maybe I move us, so that we are lying with her, and we stay like this in the rain, while the earth crumbles away beneath us.

Raff

It is Raff who explains it all. The naval officers of the icebreaker RSV *Nuyina* are here to collect eight people and many tons of storage containers. Instead they find four people, far less cargo than they'd been told to expect, a boat wrecked among rocks, two missing people, and four dead bodies.

The last months, now that Raff can reflect on them, have been carnage.

He takes them south on their cargo barges. Shows them, from the sea, the caved-in seed vault. The crumbled cliff face. The absent beaches. Then he takes them to the graves on the hill, and while his arm means he can't help exhume them, he can witness it. Somebody needs to have seen it all, from start to finish, because there are going to be a lot of questions. Raff will try to spare his family as much of this as he can.

Back at the base, the materials and supplies are being dismantled and loaded. The island is being pillaged and it is happening quickly. Dozens of people have come off this icebreaker, and as Raff watches them work he is devastated that they did not come sooner. To help with the shattering burden of trying to save the world's seeds from a flooding underground cave. To help deal with a man who'd lost his mind, to refloat two humpback whales. The difference these sets of hands could have made to the last weeks of their lives . . .

The difference they might have made to a woman, who need not have drowned to save a boy.

But that kind of thinking will ruin you. And the reality is that they're immensely privileged to have anyone here at all, when there are islands all over the world sinking into the sea, and the people who live on those islands do not have naval ships arriving to rescue them.

He thinks about their future. Of where they will go. Orly is determined to take them to Rowan's land, and maybe there are crazier things to hope for, maybe the planets will align for them somehow and they will be able to stay there. It is possible he will never play the violin again, but if there is any choice in the matter, he won't rest until he does. He is a boy—a man now—who knows well what it means to lose the things he loves. There is such peril in loving things at all, and he feels sort of proud, in fact, that he just keeps on doing it. He's not going to take the punching bag with him when they leave.

His dad will struggle to survive a second time. It isn't fair. It is so terribly unfair. But Raff will carry him on his back for as many days or years as it takes. He will carry his whole family, if they need him to. It is a good thing his father has taught him to be strong.

Fen

It takes more than a week to get the ship packed. They watch from their lighthouse as helicopters lifting pallets of cargo fly back and forth. The long black hose of a pump sits on the surface of the water and reaches all the way from the ship to the fuel tanks, siphoning what remains of their precious diesel. The island is ransacked.

Fen stands with her dad. Mostly the four of them are together, but for a few moments this afternoon it is just Fen and Dom in the kitchen of their home. He leans on the table Rowan restored for them, the only thing they have claimed from the island for themselves, the only thing he has decided to take with them wherever they go. Fen has noticed Dom likes to have a hand touching it whenever he is near.

She takes her father's free hand. Feels him hold on tightly.

"We'll find another place," she tells him. "And we'll love it just as much."

He looks down at her, and she up at him. Grief has aged him a thousand years. But he says, "Tell me, darlin'."

"Tell you what?" she asks.

"Anything. Everything."

She leans into him.

Dom, Raff, Fen, and Orly walk together to the mountain behind their lighthouse. Fen is frightened of what they will find but they need to do this, they need to see, and so as they crawl up over the mound of earth and look, they are rewarded with the sight of a baby albatross in its nest, and both its parents picking tenderly at its fluffy feathers. The chick, against all odds, has hatched and survived the storm.

They sit and watch for hours.

"Rowan really wanted to see this," Orly says. It's the only thing any of them says.

⁓

When they go, when they sail away, the Salt family stand at the aft of the ship and watch Shearwater disappear into the horizon. The last thing they see is the tip of their lighthouse, rising into the sky. Fen feels a moment of panic, she runs to the railing and could almost fling herself over, she doesn't want to go, she hasn't said goodbye, not properly.

But they are here in the water, following the ship. Her seals, diving in and out of the waves, their fins lifted in farewell.

Dominic

The ship is being prepared, but instead of helping I take a few hours. I take these hours to walk back to the crystal lake I know you loved. I shed my clothes and I wade in. The albatross are still asleep: it's morning, they will come later. I sink beneath the cold surface. Somehow I can feel you here. I knew I would. Not a haunting, but something gentler.

I think of how you returned my children to me, each one of them.

I will go back to your body now. This beautiful body. This strong body that endured all it could. I will stay with it, I will wash it and wrap it and hold it as we leave this place. I will carry it across the sea, and I will return it to your land, to live among the snow gums. It is just a body but it was yours, and beloved.

Orly

You were frightened of the ocean but only because you thought it had taken something from you. It didn't. I wanted to tell you it didn't.

Should I tell you, too, that I think you gave something back to this place, a thing it had been longing for?

Shearwater has no trees, that's what you said, because you told me you missed them. But it's not exactly true. All around its shores are underwater forests. Like forests on land, these are ecosystems with canopies, understories, and forest floors. But the forests are not made of trees, they're made of kelp. You should know this—you washed up on our beach in a curtain of it. They're abundant, these forests! They can be home to thousands of species! Hundreds of types of fish make nurseries within them, and many feed on the kelp. There are worms, prawns, snails, crabs. Sharks are known to hunt within their corridors, while marine mammals like otters and sea lions—even sea birds, even whales!—use them for shelter. This is how Fen's seals survived, in the end. They swam, even the little ones, and they found refuge from the storm among the kelp forests. These wild and rich saltwater worlds.

I wondered if you might be a part of that now. If that's where you've gone. I hope so.

A Note on the Setting

It is important to note that while Shearwater Island is fictional, it is based closely on Macquarie Island, a subantarctic island halfway between Tasmania and Antarctica. At only thirty-four kilometers long and five wide, it is a World Heritage Site home to over four million seals, penguins, and seabirds—making it, as explorer Sir Douglas Mawson stated in 1919, "one of the wonder spots of the world."

Though I created several of the fictional elements on Shearwater for the purposes of my story—such as the seed vault to the south (based loosely on the Svalbard Global Seed Vault, the tunnel of which flooded in 2016 due to melting permafrost) and the lighthouse lived in by the Salt family—it was important to me to stay as true as I could to the features of Macquarie Island, one of which is its dark and bloody history. With its abundance of fauna, Macquarie was an easy target for oil exploitation in the late nineteenth and early twentieth centuries. Sealers hunted the fur seal population to extinction and then went on to nearly wipe out the elephant seals and the royal and king penguins. The remnants of this violent trade remain to this day—huge rusting penguin barrels sit on the coastlines among thousands of live penguins, a sight so haunting I will never forget it.

The research base on Shearwater was based loosely on the Australian subantarctic Macquarie Island Research Station, which sits on the isthmus between the north and south parts of Macquarie and usually houses between twenty and forty researchers at any one time. Thankfully, it is not yet being swallowed by the ocean.

At the heart of experiencing Macquarie were the colors and textures, the smells and sounds and sensations I wanted to capture in this book. How did it *feel* to set foot in this wild and astonishing place, both profoundly remote and bursting with life—a character of this story in its own right? The secret to that, for me, was in rendering the truth of the island's rich flora, its extraordinary wildlife, and its unique climate. For these details I drew on my own experience during a research trip with my partner and sixteen-month-old son, an adventure I will never forget, to a place that is surely one of the most precious in the world.

Acknowledgments

Thank you first to my agent, Sharon Pelletier, for your steady, unwavering support, and to my editor extraordinaire, Caroline Bleeke, for knowing how to find the true heart of my stories and, with kindness and so much cleverness, helping me to render them as best I can. I am so grateful to you both, and count myself incredibly lucky to be part of your teams.

Thank you to Sydney Jeon, Keith Hayes, Bria Strothers, Claire McLaughlin, Katherine Turro, Nancy Trypuc, Molly Bloom, Donna Noetzel, Megan Lynch, Bob Miller, Marta Fleming, Kerry Nordling, and the whole Flatiron team, as well as the team at Macmillan and Macmillan Audio. I treasure being part of the Flatiron/Macmillan family and am in awe of the wonderful work you all do.

Thank you to my brilliant film and television agent, Addison Duffy. I'm so excited about the amazing opportunities you have created for us within the world of adaptations, and can't wait to see where they all lead.

Thank you to my wonderful Australian publisher, Nikki Christer, and her team at Penguin Random House Australia; you are such a joy to work with, and I'm so very happy my Australian home is with you.

Thank you to my friend Kate Selway, for your knowledge and insight into science and the world of Macquarie Island, and for answering every one of my early questions so generously.

Thank you to the team at Heritage Expeditions—the trip you took my family on to Macquarie Island was life changing. Your expertise, your passion, and your willingness to cater to the mad people who brought a baby on a remote expedition halfway to Antarctica will never be forgotten.

Thank you to all the brave researchers on Macquarie Island, who do such important conservation work and who have brought Macquarie back from the brink of devastation.

Thank you to my dear friends Rhia Parker, Sarah Houlahan, Charlie Cox, Caitlin Collins, Raechel Whitty, Anita Jankovic, and all my book club ladies; you are each responsible for keeping me sane throughout the long, difficult process of writing this book and I'm very lucky to count you all as lifelong friends.

As I sit here writing these acknowledgements with a five-week-old baby strapped to my chest, I have never been more aware of the village it takes to bring a novel to life. I want to thank my family, who have all stepped forward in various different ways, from helping to care for my children, to listening to me rant and rave, from offering emotional support, to reading early drafts—you have made it possible for this book to exist. I am profoundly, endlessly grateful to you all, and love you very much. Thank you to Sue Walter. Thank you to Hughen McConaghy, Zoe Morgan, Nina McConaghy, Hamish McConaghy. Thank you to Liam McConaghy and Vivienne Rontziokos. Thank you to my dear grandmother Alex Taylor. And to my amazing mum, Cathryn McConaghy, who helps in every one of those ways, every single day.

Finally, I want to thank my partner, Morgan Walter. I don't know how to express my gratitude for your dedication to our family. I am in awe of how hard you work, and how much love and energy you bring to us. The support you've shown to me and my work is why this book exists. All the best parts of Dominic Salt are based on you. I love you, I love you, I love you.

And to my beautiful children, Finn and Hazel. This is a book about parents and children, and how deep that love goes. You are more than I ever could have hoped for; I have no words to express how completely I love you.

About the Author

Charlotte McConaghy is the *New York Times* best-selling author of *Once There Were Wolves* and *Migrations*, which are being translated into more than twenty languages. She is based in Sydney, Australia.

Recommend *Wild Dark Shore* for your next book club!

Reading Group Guide available at

www.flatironbooks.com/reading-group-guides